I0668233

The Enoch Probe

By Bob Little

First Kindle Original Edition, December
2013
Copyright 2013 by Robert L. Little
All rights reserved

ISBN 9780980027945

For more information contact
tersebob@gmail.com

Table of Contents

Introduction

A good way to get into the Scriptures and apply them to our lives is to imagine that we are in the time they describe. We can pretend that we are experiencing what the prophets depicted. What if we could actually be there?

Is it so fantastic? The prophets who have stood at the head of each period of time have seen our day. That begs two questions: How did these prophets see into the future? Is it possible that some of the wicked as well as the righteous have been able to see our day?

God knows all we do and have done before it happens. Everything is present before Him. Do we believe it? Perhaps we don't want to believe that He is watching us, but it must be so. Do others also watch us?

Just for fun, pretend that you can travel through time and see the era before the flood. Maybe there were people then who had progressed as far as we have.

Let's say you find yourself at a time when Adam was about 650 years old. You find people living in what seems to be a large modern city with sky scrapers and electric cars that roll along above your head. You meet the people and talk to them. You begin to realize that you're in the past and that man's progress in the ancient world was as great as ours.

You are told that this is the City of Enoch. At first you think you've found the city of Holiness where Enoch the Prophet lived. Then everything goes wrong. Your life is threatened. You meet men who are really evil and want to kill you. Fortunately you escape and return to your own time with a fuzzy impression of the age of Enoch the Prophet. Good luck. You're almost there.

Prologue

March 4, 1984

Professor Arthur J. Shalinski,

I believe I mentioned the Sedalia document some time ago. It has now been translated and the results will soon be ready for publication. I thought you might like to examine a bit of it and hear my opinion of the matter. It was found near Sedalia, Missouri, in January of 1946, encased in a cartridge about four inches long.

Very few of the academic community here have accepted it as authentic, but it does fit the conditions it describes. Only time will tell if it is valid. If it is a hoax, it is a very elaborate one. Someone has gone to a lot of trouble to scare us.

An analysis of the container, the material upon which the document is written, the ink used and the language of the document have done nothing more than tell us that they do not belong in the world of Sedalia of 1946. The container is of a very durable metal. It is plated on the outside with copper and lined on the inside with lead. When it was opened, it emitted a sharp hissing sound as if it had been filled with a gas of some kind that escaped.

The document was written on paper of an unusual composition. The wood pulp used was superior to any we know of. None of the major manufacturers could identify the product; yet it has a superbly refined surface which none of them felt able to produce. Specimens or samples of the paper left to the open air since 1947 have not deteriorated in the least or yellowed with age.

It was written by hand. The ink was intensely black, more suitable for brushing than for hard pen points. Since there were no scratch marks in the paper, it is assumed to have been applied with a brush.

The language gave us a challenge until we brought

in experts who were multi-lingual and also conversant in ancient texts. It has taken nearly forty years to decipher. It required the development of a phonetic system of its own and a great deal of patience with syntax. This of course proves nothing except that the document could be what it says it is.

I have enclosed a transcript of the first two pages for your examination. Please forward your opinion at your earliest convenience.

Sincerely,

Dr. Sean B. Lister
Managing Director
Dr. Kayd B. Myers Laboratories

Enclosure - Transcript of Sedalia Document

It is the year 640 of the ancient one.

To those who find this document greetings:

This is to warn you of an impending invasion of your world by an unscrupulous group of people from my world. They have developed a device for travel from one time period to another and for several years have been using it to probe the future where they might comfortably settle and dominate the people. They have determined that your time is best.

These spies (or watchers) took over this country and will take over yours. They come like saviors with great power but kill all who oppose them. They have a secret society. They will sacrifice you and your children. Their cause is wicked. They stole the white rock of Eden and made a device which empowers them to slip from one age to another. With it they can focus on the timelessness of eternity and reflect into any period of the future.

I am Madame Zanhope. My husband is one who has devoted his whole life to this project. He does not condone human sacrifice, but pays little attention to anything but his project. My daughter and I are in great peril as we are true followers of the promised Messiah. Their spies hunt us out and sacrifice the true followers to their false gods.

I pray that you do not have such wickedness in your day and that the spies never invade your time. This message is proof of their power. I have used their device to send it to your age. Perhaps the great flood prophesied by our fathers will wash us away before they use it on you.

We came out from the holy mountain in the year 502 of the ancient one. We settled among a fallen people. We brought much wisdom with us to teach them. Our men were good at first. They held the holy priesthood. Then, they became corrupted and began worshipping idols.

They have built a powerful and rich city. They

dominate the whole land of the exile. They are great in warfare and terrible in defense.

I have known much good in my day. I have clung to the teachings of the fathers. I have tried to rear my children in the truth, but my son has abandoned both me and the faith. He has become an assassin and does the bidding of the evil one. In our day the women and children suffer much.

Please defend yourselves against these men who can plant themselves in your midst without the possibility of defense. They will come in force.

Madame Zanhope

Part I - The Curious Ball

Chapter 1 Parachutes in the Sky

From his C119 cargo plane, Major Colin Bailey scanned the horizon. There was nothing in sight. The halo of a soft blue spring day blanketed the sky all around him. He was headed home.

The C119 was a far cry from the fighters Major Bailey had flown in Viet Nam, but it wasn't exactly your garden variety cargo plane either. It was known as the flying boxcar because of its freight car capacity. It made its debut a little too late for World War II, but was useful in Korea and Viet Nam.

The flying boxcar looked as if someone had taken two wing-mounted engines and stretched their housings back like pieces of child's modeling clay. These they hooked to the twin tails. Then they had disconnected the body from the tail section and pushed it forward to form a fat dumpy-looking fuselage.

Major Bailey thought the flying boxcar was a fantastic looking airplane. This one was in remarkable condition for its age. It was affectionately called "907". Those were the last three digits of its tail number.

The radio on 907 had sputtered out nearly a minute ago over Jefferson City, Missouri. No matter; flying was routine for Major Bailey. He could fly any ship blind; he'd done it many times before.

Major Bailey was a lot like his airplane. He was a short man with a big frame, just within the weight standards for a man his size. He was all muscle and all business. He had big hands and a square jaw. His eyes were steel blue. His mouth was wide and he had a pronounced cleft chin.

His pilot, Captain Devin King, was an average looking sort, slim and trim, a little taller than Bailey and always happy and social. At the moment he was in the cabin taking a break and chatting with the load-master, Sergeant Cory Thurston.

The cabin was configured for seats along the sides against the walls so passengers, if they had any, sat facing each other. There was space in the center of the cabin for equipment and some cargo. Sergeant Thurston's job was to oversee loading and to check on the engines during flight.

Thurston was an old timer, prematurely gray, tall, a little stooped in the shoulders and always telling jokes with a serious face. Everybody liked him.

Captain King was listening to one of Thurston's stories while checking on their top-secret cargo. Two other men made up the regular crew. They had been kept home to limit exposure to the cargo they were carrying.

Suddenly, Major Bailey's peace was shattered by a flash of blinding light and a thunder clap. The light was brighter and the thunder louder than he had ever seen or heard. A fire ball exploded in the cockpit and sizzled back through the cabin. He had never crashed before, but now he was sure it was imminent.

Then, without warning, Major Bailey was not alone. Some unknown object had interrupted his space - something right there inside the cockpit - something small and round like a softball but made of a shiny yellow metal. It blocked his view. It peered at him strangely through its one glass eye.

Next, it dropped down and wedged itself between the control yoke and the control panel. It was just below his field of vision. Out of sight as though hiding, it froze the controls and made it impossible to maneuver the plane. Sweat popped out on Colin's brow. The ship began to rise. He panicked. Without control, the plane would immediately stall.

He rose from his seat and shouted into the intercom: "Open a door. Get out now! The plane is out of control." Having given the order, he left the cockpit and went down into the cabin.

Captain King and Sergeant Thurston responded rapidly. A door at the side was soon open and all three men took their turns jumping out into the open air.

Major Bailey was the last to leave the ship. There was a quick jerk and he was drifting earthward beneath a silken white umbrella. By maneuvering his parachute around he caught a glimpse of his two companions first and then the end of 907.

The big ship continued to climb, then leveled out for some mysterious reason. It gradually lost altitude, skimmed the ground for a while, skidded along a plowed field and plunged into a grove of trees with explosive violence. There was a cloud of dust and smoke and then nothing.

He was still shaking. Who would believe that a shiny brass ball could do this to him? What was it that had taken over 907?

On the ground he could see two boys on a road near the field. They stared up at him as though they had something to do with his trouble. He felt sick inside. He had never lost a ship before. Then Major Bailey did something else he had never done in his life before. He fainted.

* * *

Moments before, those two boys had no idea what was happening with 907. Jim Holbrook nearly ran into his friend, Jaydee Ferris, as he spun around on his bicycle to find the direction of the sound they had just heard.

"What was that?"

"Look where you're going, you space-freak!"

"Space-what?"

"Space-freak! You nearly ran right over me!

Jim swung around to face his buddy, opened his mouth to say something sarcastic, but stopped short, letting his chin drop still further as he pointed into the gathering dusk. Jaydee followed his friend's arm and gave a little start.

"Look at the parachutes. That must have been a big airplane."

"There may have been other guys who didn't get out." Jim chimed in.

"It sounded like it crashed right over there by Uncle Jack's!"

The two teenagers peddled off together - away from the drifting parachutes. Just beyond a grove of trees they turned into a small road that ran beside a cottage. Smoke-like clouds were everywhere.

"I can't see through the dust!"

"Yeah, it must have crashed right behind the trees!"

They soon came to the end of the road and stopped at a barbed wire fence. Jaydee dropped his bike and ran to the gate. He quickly had the wire down and the two pushed on to the end of the grove. There lay a twisted mass of aluminum.

"Wow, let's see what's inside!"

"It doesn't look like there is an inside."

They clambered through another fence and into the midst of the dying cargo plane.

"Hey, it's still hot!" Jim croaked as he jerked his hand from the shell of the air ship.

"Here's the cockpit. Give me a boost, willya, Jim?"

"Maybe we shouldn't"

"Oh, don't be silly. Come on, give me a hand!"

Jim gave his friend a boost and he was soon out of sight. Suddenly, there was a sound like metal trays spilling over in the school cafeteria.

"Whadya do?"

"I fell through, you dumbbell." Jaydee's voice seemed to come from under the wreckage. "Go get a rope. I can't get out of here!"

"Where am I gonna find a rope?

"Look in the shed, the shed behind Uncle Jack's house!"

"But what if he comes out and finds me?"

"Don't be silly; he can't hear. Don't you think he'd be out here if he could?"

"Ok." Jim was back through the wire and into the shed in a hurry. It was dark in the shed and getting dark outside. Where would he find rope?

There was a little work bench beside the door, a few tools, and rolls of wire hanging here and there. Then he spied a rope, a little out of his reach. By moving a shaky wooden box up beside the bench, he might just reach it. The box was in place. He climbed up, teetering precariously just inches below the rope. Then he fell.

Suddenly, there was a sound like the cannon in the park going off. Below the place where the rope hung on the wall was a large hole. Jim knew that he had just been where that hole was now.

"What are you doing in my shed?" A man in a stubbly grey and white beard peered down at him in a heap of junk. Jim was scared to death. The man had a shotgun and wore a helmet on his head with a light on it. This was Jack, or as he was sometimes affectionately called: Uncle Jack.

"Dynamite!" Jack roared, "You're just a kid! I might have killed you, son. What're you looking for?" Too frightened to talk, Jim just pointed up at the rope.

"Now what do you want with that?"

"Jaydee can't get out of the hole."

"What did you say? You kids all mumble. Well, speak up!"

12

"Jaydee!" Jim yelled as loud as he could, half hoping that Jaydee would hear his desperation and rescue him somehow.

Jaydee had heard the gun go off. What had happened? What was taking so long? It was dark in the hole now.

In the shed, Jack continued to question Jim. "Jaydee? Jaydee who? Do you mean John Ferris' grandson?"

"Yeah!"

"Well, where is he?" The grizzly looking man took the rope down and pulled the boy to his feet. Jim took off through the door and around the shed toward the wreck. Jack followed along limping behind Jim.

"We're coming Jaydee; we're on our way!" Jim yelled.

Jaydee was looking over the size of the hole he had fallen into. He was not alone. There in one corner something was peering back at him. It was something small. It threw a strange light all around itself. It scared him. Where was his buddy?

Jim was atop the cockpit now.

Jack scratched his head. His mouth dropped open. "Where did that come from?"

"Come on," Jim screamed, "we've got to save Jaydee!"

Within minutes the old man was feeding Jim the rope and he was playing it down through the dark cockpit, past a large hole in its floor, into the faintly lighted space below.

"Where are you, Jaydee?"

Jaydee answered by showing his head in the hole beneath the cockpit. Jaydee yelled up with alarm in his voice. "There's something down here! It's glaring at me."

"It's probably a gopher, ya scaredy-cat."

"Don't be ridiculous. This thing has its own light

and it's round-like and shiny."

"You better get out of there!" Jim urged him.

Jaydee grabbed the rope and, with the help of Jim and Uncle Jack, quickly sprung from the hole and the cockpit of the vanquished metal bird.

Jack looked over the crash from stem to stern. He muttered something about the mess and the problems this would cause shook his head and turned toward the house.

Jaydee and Jim looked in at the open jump door checking for other crew members or passengers. There were none.

"Well, I'm going back up to my supper. You two better get home. Your Grandpa Ferris is going to be worried."

Jaydee looked at Jim and then back at Uncle Jack.

"Could we use your rope a little longer?" Jaydee pulled on the rope so Jack would be sure to get the meaning of his words.

"Oh, ok, but see that you hang it up in the shed when you're through." With that Jack started off toward the house.

Jim caught the rope and held it fast. "You're not going back down there, Jaydee, are you?"

Jaydee jerked the rope away from Jim. "Don't you see? That thing is probably a top secret flight recorder or something like that. We've got to safeguard it, Jim."

* * *

It was already quite dark when Jaydee and Jim left the lane and rode their bicycles into the yard at John Ferris' farm. John was sitting on the porch. Tabitha was curled up on his lap licking her paws.

Tabitha was really Eleanor's cat, but John had adopted her after Eleanor's death. He liked Tabitha and took good care of her. He combed her long golden fur

14

regularly and kept her hair free of burrs and snarls that she picked up as she roamed the farm.

When Eleanor had died six years ago, John had stayed with the farm in spite of his daughter's insistence to move to Kansas City where she could see that he was eating right. Now, it was fortunate that he was in position to have her son Jaydee and his friend for Easter vacation. He laughed when he thought how an "old man" who supposedly couldn't cook for himself was able to look after and cook for a couple of sassy youth.

"Sorry we're late, Grandpa."

"Never mind that," he said in his kindly way. "Your supper's getting cold. I missed you both at milk time. The cows missed you too."

"We saw a plane crash, Mr. Ferris."

"Jim!" Jaydee was angry that his friend had revealed their secret.

"I saw it. I suspected that's where you'd be. You'd better stay away from it." Then John said as an afterthought, "Where's your shirt, Jaydee?"

"Oh, it's here." Jaydee answered grabbing something off his bike rack as he dropped the bike on the grass. In his hands was a wadded up shirt which seemed to have a bigger shape than it ought to.

"That's good. Your mother would pester me to death if I didn't return you with all your clothes." John opened the door of the house and the cat, Jaydee, Jim and Grandfather entered the gloomy front hall. Hurriedly excusing themselves, the teenagers made a beeline for the kitchen, and John and Tabitha retired to the living room where he contemplated the surprising events of the day.

He had been in the barn feeding his four milk cows when the plane crashed. As he watched through the window of the barn, he saw one of the men go limp in his parachute. Shortly after the aircraft commander touched ground, John had the Air Force on the phone. The

15

emergency crew promised to be there within an hour.

As he left the house, Alex Goodrich drove up. Together he and Alex carried the unconscious commander out of the field to the house. The pilot and load-master had found their way to the farm house on their own. John made them comfortable and checked on them several times while he finished his chores. The Air Force medics took them away within an hour. The unconscious man had revived, but seemed to be incoherent. He kept babbling something about a metal ball. John hoped the man would be alright.

John was also worried about Jack. Uncle Jack, the kids called him. He and Jack were old friends. Actually, they had worked together for many years. Then, because of a tragic event, they both quit. They changed their names and came to this quiet part of the United States to disappear.

What if they were recognized? John mused. Uncle Jack would worry. He would be more worried than John. Jack was that way.

The TV went on in the study. That would be Jim. Jaydee sometimes joined him, but tonight John guessed he would have lots of questions.

It was no surprise when Jaydee came into the living room and sat down on the arm of his grandfather's big easy chair. "Grandpa, what will the Air Force do with the airplane?"

"Oh, they'll gather up all the debris, take them back to their air base and try to find out how they all came apart and what caused the crash."

"What if something is missing?"

"There will probably be some missing parts. The Air Force will still be able to find the answers they need."

"When Jim and I were coming up the road, an Air Force sedan pulled out of your driveway and passed us. What were they here for?"

"A couple of investigators wanted to look around.

16

The pilot and crew landed here you know and a few of their things were left in my room. They picked up the parachutes and looked for anything that might have dropped from the airplane in our fields."

"Did they see your pistol on the shelf in your closet?"

"How did you know about that?

"Oh, Mom told me. She said I wasn't to get it down under any circumstance."

"I see."

"Mom doesn't think you should have it. She says nobody should have guns except the police."

"I know; she's mentioned that before."

"If you had to hide your gun from the Air Force or somebody, where would you put it?

"I'd have to think about that one. You're getting into pretty heavy stuff. Are you concerned about my gun or something you want to hide?"

"Just wondering. A friend I know was talking about hiding something real good so his sister couldn't get into it."

"How big is this something he wants to hide?"

Jaydee shrugged his shoulders. "Oh, about the size of a baseball."

"Maybe he could put it inside his baseball mitt and stash it in his sports bag."

"My friend thought that he could mess up his closet and hide it there. What do you think, Grandpa?"

"It would have to be something special to go to that kind of trouble," he said good naturedly.

"Do you think Uncle Jack has anything to hide?"

"Maybe, why do you ask?"

"Cause those Air Force guys are going to be all over his place."

* * *

17

What did Jaydee have to hide? Grandfather Ferris ran it over and over in his mind. Something was in that plane that his grandson brought away with him. He would talk to him about it tomorrow.

He wondered. Would an investigation prove hazardous for Uncle Jack? Should he confront Jaydee about the "something" he brought away from the crash? He decided to accept the possibility that nothing serious would happen tonight.

He remembered taking things from a crash that he visited in his youth. It wasn't just wrong - it was dangerous, but he didn't understand that at the time.

The boys must have gone to their room. The television was off and there was no light coming from the study.

In the quiet of their room, Jaydee and Jim were beginning a ceremony which would have shocked Jaydee's grandfather. Jaydee took the wadded up shirt off his dresser and the two teenagers knelt on the floor. The shirt and its contents were laid between them.

Slowly and dramatically, Jaydee unwrapped the object. Jim had never seen it before. It was marvelous without the theatrics, but Jaydee wanted to savor the moment.

"Hurry up!"

"I don't want to spoil my shirt."

"Your shirt! Come on, Jaydee, you don't care that much about your shirt! Let me see!"

"Ok, ok."

The final covering of the shirt fell away and the mysterious ball rolled out on the floor - or should I say: drifted out on the floor. It moved a few inches in the air just above the floor and then settled between the two young men. As they watched in awe, it turned its eye on first one and then rotated to examine the other.

"Wow! Jim breathed, reaching hesitantly for the globe.

"Don't touch it!" Jaydee threatened.

A light shone out of the eye like a ray gun, illuminating the whole room. The boys sat enchanted while it clicked and whirred at them, seemingly recording every inch of their attire and physical makeup.

The brass ball recorded the following: "Noted: two boys about fourteen years of age, both about the same height - one a leader, named JAYDEE, the other a follower, named JIM. JIM is husky and has dark hair and dark eyes. JAYDEE is taller, has blonde hair and blue eyes. He is toe headed and thin of face."

The boys were examining the ball in turn. They lay on their stomachs with their elbows supporting their heads.

"What is it?" Jim asked excitedly.

"I don't know. It looks like one of those Russian satellites."

"Sputniks?"

"You know - one of the early space probes."

"Oh. You're always talking about space stuff."

"Look how it's sizing us up, Jim. Maybe it's some experimental spy machine that the Air Force was carrying on that airplane."

"We'd better get it back to them super fast." Jim sputtered.

"We can't do that. I just said maybe it belongs to them. If it did and we told them we'd seen it, they'd lock us up for knowing their secrets."

"What'll we do?"

"I'll think of something."

"Maybe you're right, Jaydee. It probably doesn't even belong to the Air Force. "

Jaydee squinted at the hovering object. "Could be it's something from outer space."

"There you go again - space, space, space!"

"Why not? Maybe it was sent here by some alien race."

"More than likely it's a robot probe designed by the Russians. Look at all these strange symbols and designs all over it!"

"Yeah, that's neat." Jaydee said. For a moment, he slid away from the mysterious ball, pulling himself up into a crouched position - always looking back and just guiding himself with quick glances, hastily groping behind him. He pulled a book off the night stand and began thumbing through it, turning pages as fast as he could. As he did so he settled down beside Jim on the floor again.

"Do you think you're going to find this thing in your science fiction book, Jaydee?"

"Here it is; listen! 'It was a round ball about the size of a baseball made of something like aluminum. On one side was an aperture through which the monster could see its prey from a distance.' Well, doesn't it fit the description?"

"It does a little, but that's just a story."

"A story? My chemistry teacher says science fiction often shows us things before they are invented."

"I don't believe that. Your teacher is a nut. Everybody says so."

"Well, I don't think so!" Jaydee burst out.

Jim clenched his jaw, but he couldn't very well argue with a friend whose grandfather is letting you visit for Easter vacation.

It seemed like forever that Jaydee didn't speak while he looked long and hard at the shiny round ball on the floor in front of him. Finally he sat back as though to get a different perspective. "That's heavy!"

The teenagers gazed at the mysterious ball for a long time. First it shone directly into Jaydee's eyes and then Jim's. It wasn't a harsh light. It was as though it was reading their minds. It was a long while before Jaydee felt good about wrapping up the curious object and the two slipped into their beds.

Meanwhile, in the living room, John Ferris was still thinking about Uncle Jack when the phone rang.

"Hello, Alex. . . Yes, the Air Force medics felt there was nothing wrong. . . I haven't been over to the crash site, but the boys have. . . No, I'm sure Jack's fine; Jaydee is just worried that the Air Force might bother him. . . Yes, I intend to keep the boys away from there. . . Well, tomorrow they go home to Kansas City for the weekend. . . I don't see any reason to worry. . . Ok, Alex. Goodbye.

Alex Goodrich was a good friend, but John felt that he didn't know and probably would never know the secrets of his two neighbors. That was because he talked too much. He prided himself on being the eyes and ears of the community.

Alex asked a lot of questions about Uncle Jack. He wanted to know why he didn't see more of him and why Jack was satisfied with just a small garden and why he didn't come to the local farm meetings.

How could John tell Alex without betraying a confidence that Jack wasn't really a farmer at heart and had another hobby that kept him busy? Now there were two other people that were interested in Jack - two little fellows that probably could find out just about anything. Besides them there was the whole United States Air Force. Although not so persistent as two nosey young men, the Air Force was an organization to be reckoned with.

While he was thinking about it, John went to his closet, took down his .357 Magnum, flipped out the cylinder, and examined the barrel. He carried the revolver into the living room. Placing the hand gun in his belt, he felt along the back wall until he came to a slight depression in the middle of it. He slid his hand up as high as he could and tapped gently. A hole opened in the wall at eye level and he slipped the revolver inside. This wasn't an easy place to find in an emergency, but he guessed it would do until the boys and the Air Force had gone away.

* * *

Early in the morning, Tabitha went padding into the room where the Jaydee and Jim were sleeping and jumped up on the bed beside Jaydee. A light came on in a wad of clothes beside her. She snatched at it, playing with it repeatedly like a cat would with a ball of yarn.

Suddenly, something moved within the mass. Now, motivated by a protective instinct, Tabitha swung a paw into the wad at full force. The light veered around to meet the cat full in the face.

There was a scream of terror and Tabitha leaped several feet in the air. She landed on all fours in the middle of Jaydee's back. There was fire in her eyes. Jaydee looked up in drowsy wonder.

Up from the mess of shirt sprang a bright brass ball. It did a 180 turn and then came towards the cat moving rapidly. Tabitha let out a second screeching howl and made a beeline for the safety of John's room. It was enemies at first sight.

Chapter 2 Old Jack's Secret

Air Force helicopters were in the field behind Uncle Jack's and military trucks and sedans were all over the road and drive leading up beside his place. Security guards with rifles were all around the yard and out into the field near the crash site. Swarms of men and equipment spread out behind the house combing the area for bits and pieces of C119, USAF #208907. Each particle was identified where it lay, numbered and given a coordinate in relation to the position of the dead air ship.

Uncle Jack fumed up and down - a bright color in the midst of a sea of men clad in drab blue uniforms and white coveralls. His little garden was trampled into mush, the fences were down and "Everywhere," Jack thought, "people were poking their noses where they had no business."

"A body has no privacy." Jack's protests were met with kindly reassurances of repair and a speedy withdrawal.

"Don't worry, Jake, we'll be away from here in no time at all."

"My name isn't Jake; it's Jack and I'm not worried. I'm mad. The sooner you poachers get off my property, the better."

Colonel Glenn Jones winced. Jack's sharp tongue had found its mark. Dealing with civilians wasn't the Colonel's usual job. What he needed was a good Air Force spokesman.

Adding to his irritation was Major Bailey's condition. The man had no visible injury. He would be most useful here on the site, but the veteran aircraft commander was having a nice rest in the psychiatric ward at the base hospital. His pilot and load-master were equally unhelpful. They knew nothing. They had only obeyed orders by leaving the airplane without questioning the situation.

Bailey maintained that a small brass ball with a big eye had taken over his plane and he wouldn't change his story.

A man in civilian attire approached the Colonel. "No brass ball, Glenn, and nothing that might have resembled one!" The technician knew his job. His reputation would be on the line if he hadn't checked all possibilities.

Uncle Jack's eye twitched a little. Was it noticed? He didn't think so. He wasn't about to help find anything. If he thought for a minute it would have saved his fences or garden, all hope vanished before he was consulted. The damage was done. Let them find their brass ball if they could. Just the same he'd feel his own secrets were safer if the Air Force was on its way.

Down the lane, two teenage boys were doing some soul searching over their own secret.

"You said we'd take it to keep it safe, Jaydee!"

"How can we be sure these guys are supposed to know about this thing? Maybe the ball was part of an ultra secret mission."

"You read too much science fiction."

"Well, why don't you walk right up to them and tell them we have it? What will you say when they ask why?"

"I could say we found it out in the field."

"That's clever, Jim, but we didn't. That gadget probably copied all our moves and we'd catch it for lying to the Air Force."

Seeing the boys arguing in the lane, Tyler Houston, the Air Force technician, acted on a hunch. He stepped through the cordon of security guards and approached the two young men.

"Did you two see a metal ball around this wreckage?"

Jaydee's "Nah," seemed convincing enough, but

Jim backed his bike up and gulped. The technician gave him a long look starting at his hands and up to his eyes. Jim gulped again.

"Where do you two live?"

"We live in Kansas City. We're staying with my grandpa for Easter vacation."

"And where might that be?"

"Oh, it might be up the road two houses." Jim tried to match Jaydee's calm. Somehow he had a feeling that the technician wasn't fooled. "We got to go now."

Jaydee and Jim turned their bikes and cycled out of the lane and up the road. The technician walked down to the road and watched them until they turned in at the Ferris place. Rather than tell the Colonel now he decided to follow up on his idea later.

On the way back to the crash site, he glanced through the window of Uncle Jack's shed. On the wall opposite, a hole about three inches in diameter gave him a clear shot at the wreckage. He walked around the shed. The hole was fresh. The old wood had shattered like particle board. He guessed something hard had hit it at tremendous speed. Maybe the Major wasn't crazy.

"Colonel Jones, come take a look at this!" The Colonel who was standing not more than ten feet away spun and nearly stumbled over himself getting to the technician's side.

"What have you found?"

"Do you suppose we could get the old man to unlock this shed?" Fingering the hole so the Colonel could get his point, he added: "We may find what we are looking for inside."

The Colonel's jaw dropped. Then a broad smile spread over his face. "I don't see why not!"

Ten minutes later they found Uncle Jack just sitting down to enjoy a plate of fried potatoes and weenies.

"You've snooped all over my place already. Your

25

people would scatter my tools everywhere. I likely wouldn't find them when you got through."

"We're not interested in your tools," the Colonel smiled, "We think the round ball might have crashed into your shed."

"There's a hole in the side opposite the window." The technician added by way of explanation.

At that Jack looked the man square in the eye. "That's just an old hole!"

"It looks new," the technician ventured. "It has some fresh splinters all around it."

"That's likely where those fool kids down the lane have been pickin' at it. They're just like you folks - want to see what others keep covered up.

"You've got to admit that locked sheds make puzzling conversation. I don't believe it was locked when we first got here." The Colonel's voice went from humor to firmness.

Uncle Jack got out of his chair. "Now you see here," he said with his finger under the Colonel's nose, "I always keep it locked, and even if it wasn't, us little folks have rights."

"We can get a warrant." His Colonel was still firm.

"Well, I suppose . . ."

"Colonel, there's no need for anyone but us to see inside the shed. Jack could stand right there while we look around." The technician turned to Jack to finish. "Would that be all right?"

Jack looked off into the corner of his small house. Maybe he was being too protective. It was very unlikely that they would learn anything at all about his secret - especially if it was a little darker and they were in a hurry.

"Ok, just give me a little time to finish my supper."

"Thanks; we'll be waiting outside." The Colonel followed the technician out. "Whatever you think, Tyler. You're the expert. If you think one quick look will serve the purpose, let's do it."

It was dark when Uncle Jack left the house. He had on his miner's hat with the light in it. If they went by the light in his hat, he could point it where he wanted. They'd never know a thing.

But the two Air Force leaders knew their job. Each had obtained a high powered lamp and each looked determined.

Jack decided to make the best of the situation. "The light is broken in the shed, so I guess it's just as well you brought your own."

Jack undid the lock and stood in the doorway while the two men pierced the gloom with their light sticks. The Colonel stumbled over something. Both lights came together on a crack in the plank floor. One board was a little higher than the others, but didn't seem unusual.

"Here's the hole, Colonel." From the inside, the wood around the area was white. There was no doubt; it was a new hole, but it seemed to come from inside the shed and looked like the result of a shotgun blast.

Tyler fingered the wood, and then looked out at the wreckage and back at the opposite side of the shed. Running his light over that wall and the junk leaning against it, he could find no evidence of a ball or anything else that might have impacted on it.

"Have you moved anything on this side of the shed within the last three days, Jack?

"Of course not. I couldn't have got near this shed without you seein'!"

The technician looked at the Colonel. "I guess it's a blind lead, Colonel. It looks to me like Jack tried to shoot our bird after it was down. It's my guess it scared the heck out of him."

"Were you scared, Jack?" The Colonel asked.

"Well, maybe I was a bit." Jack agreed. He thought it wouldn't hurt to use their idea.

The technician and his boss turned around quickly and started for the door, but as they did so, the Colonel tripped again. This time, the crack in the floor boards moved and in the sudden flash of lights that followed the outline of a trap door was revealed.

Both men looked at Uncle Jack.

The Colonel never left anything alone. "What's down there?"

"Nothin' to do with your airplane." Jack was unusually edgy.

Reading Jack's face the technician took interest. "Show us!"

"Just hang on there a minute. This here is my private cellar. You got no business down there without a warrant."

"We can get one very shortly." The Colonel was adamant. "It's just a matter of time. The sooner we finish our investigation the sooner we'll be off your property. We aren't interested in your still or other paraphernalia. We just want to finish this investigation.

"Your secrets will be kept," the technician added.

"Not while all your boys are lookin' on. Do you think I want everyone to know where I hide my valuables?"

"We can shut the door while we make sure our brass ball did not get into your private belongings."

Jack couldn't see a way out.

"Here, I'll shut the door myself," the Colonel added.

Jack reluctantly took a small crow-bar from the wall. If they got too nosey down there he could just let them have it. He pried up a section of the floor. Beneath it was a hole about the size of a man's shoulders.

Immediately the Colonel's flashlight fell on the opening.

"What's this? It goes way down."

Jack scratched his head. "That's a mine shaft"

"A mine shaft?" the Colonel gasped.

The technician edged forward peering into the hole. "Colonel, I think we ought to have a look."

"You're right."

"I can't guarantee you won't get bit by black widow spiders," Jack whined, clenching his fist tightly around the iron bar in his hand.

"We'll take that chance," the Colonel retorted. "You lead the way."

"It's your funeral," Jack countered, as he edged through the hole.

Within a few minutes all three men were standing in a chamber right below the shed. The room was about the same size as the shed. The Colonel and his technician ran their lights over the walls; a variety of strange objects caught their eyes. Bits and pieces of pottery, bones and skulls, pieces of jewelry and other precious objects came into view.

"This is a treasury of artifacts, Colonel," the technician sputtered. Then turning to Jack he asked: "Did you find all these things here?"

"They turned up as I been digging this hole." Jack forgot himself in a moment of pride.

The Colonel peered further into the hole that tapered down from the center of the room. "This looks like a good job of shoring up. All of these timbers are strong." Railroad ties were laid, one below the other forming steps along the sides of the shaft. The Colonel started down, occasionally stroking the dirt walls to see how loose they might be. He was apprehensive of what might happen if the walls caved in around them.

Once they were well below ground, Jack led the two men wherever he chose. He avoided revealing the secrets of his dig by always shining his light away from any tell-tale works. The minute he shifted his light the Colonel and the investigator shifted their attention also. It was a clever ploy and Jack was proud of his deception.

His tour seemed to cover the whole excavation, but in reality there were many nooks and corners that his audience never saw. Just as they entered one tunnel, the Colonel paused.

"What's down this way?" he asked.

"Oh, we've been down there, Colonel. You remember the baskets that we saw."

The Colonel remembered some baskets, but he was not sure where. He did not want to show his ignorance so he pretended to remember. When Jack finished his tour, the two men agreed that Jack had no curious ball to hide.

Tyler was anxious to get out; he was not used to being underground. The longer they stayed the more the walls seemed to push in against them.

* * *

In the base hospital, Major Bailey was also concerned with walls. He was having a hard time sleeping. He just couldn't relax. All day long people had been questioning him about the curious ball that had interrupted his flight.

There were a lot of other questions too. They asked questions about his father and his mother and how he felt about them. All these questions were designed to see if he was crazy. He knew he wasn't and what's more he knew they knew.

He had seen the ball. He knew he had seen it. Now, every time he closed his eyes he could see a round shiny ball floating in the air over his head leering down at him. He knew this was fantasy, but still he didn't like to close his eyes.

Sleeping pills did no good. He wanted some information from the crash site. On the one hand he wished he had gone with Colonel Jones, but on the other hand, he was afraid to go.

He had never been frightened like this before in his life. He began counting the specks in the ceiling. Before long the specks were tiny brass balls. Finally, they grew eyes. Then he was in a room of shiny brass balls floating all around him. Each ball had an eye and all eyes were upon him.

Then someone was shouting in his ear. He wanted to stop up his ears, but he couldn't. The voice was saying: "Major Bailey, Major Bailey, can you hear me?"

He was asleep, but Colonel Jones was very anxious to talk to him.

Major Bailey felt miles away. He knew that Colonel Jones was out there somewhere. He wanted to talk to him. He wanted to ask him about 907. His words wouldn't come out. He looked at Colonel Jones. He tried to raise his arm. It was very heavy.

Colonel Jones turned to Tyler, the technician. Tyler had come with him hoping to get some more clues from the grounded pilot. "Well, he's not going to help us tonight. They've drugged him up so much that he won't come to until noon tomorrow." The Colonel started for the door.

"That's ok, Colonel. I think I have some idea where his mysterious ball might be. I would have told you earlier but I didn't want to disappoint you again."

"I'm all ears, Tyler. What do you have?"

"Remember the boys on bicycles that were hanging around Jack's?"

"Yes, what do they have to do with it?"

"Colonel, I suppose you have forgotten how inquisitive you were at that age."

"I see. You think they might have gotten there before us and picked up this thing?"

"It's a good chance they took it home. One of them seemed awfully nervous when I asked about it."

"That sounds like a good possibility. Meanwhile,

let's close down the crash site. Is there any reason to stay longer?"

The technician thought for a moment. "No, we have all the parts that could be found. We've searched the whole area several times."

"You try their house tomorrow and I'll go after a search warrant just in case. Don't they live where we picked up Major Bailey?"

"Yes, if you run into resistance, the name you need for the warrant is John Ferris and the address is in the medical report." The two men left the room leaving the sleeping Major Bailey alone. Mustering all his strength, he raised his head up on his pillow and uttered some words that were unintelligible and then fell back into a deep sleep.

Chapter 3 Grounded

It was the beginning of Easter vacation. Jaydee and Jim got together in Kansas City their first day home. It was Saturday. The late bus ride and their separate homes couldn't keep the two friends apart on normal occasions, but they were especially drawn together now.

They got their Saturday jobs done early, passed up invitations to the matinee, shopping for computer games and afternoon baseball which had always held their interest before.

They brought the mysterious ball to Jaydee's house in a suit case. It was a bright spot among Jaydee's valuable possessions in his closet.

The two teenagers talked up charging admission to every boy in the neighborhood to see the shiny round marvel. In the meanwhile, Tabitha, who had also come to visit as an honored guest, sat on the window sill washing up and soaking in the sun. She was content to keep her distance from the ball.

Jaydee and Jim discussed issue from different perspectives. Jaydee was ready to pull out all the stops. On the other hand, Jim was always the cautious team member. "But, what if they tell their parents?"

"We'll just have to make them promise not to tell anyone."

Jim looked over their list of friends. "What about Steffan Howe?"

"Oh, he's out of it. He'd tell his whole family."

"Don't you think $5 is too much to charge?"

Jaydee crossed Steffan off their list. "If they can't afford $5, they don't deserve to see it and we'll make them pay up front."

"They may not believe we have such a great thing until they see it." Jim pointed out.

"Yeah but once they've seen it they won't need to

33

pay."

"So?"

"No problem. We'll give them a money back guarantee."

"Yeah, that should work with everyone but Trevor Lake. He'd take his money back and say it wasn't worth it just to be mean."

"He's out of it too." Jaydee said.

"Ok!"

Jaydee looked at the closet door. "Maybe we can get the curious ball to perform."

"How do we do that?"

"You got me."

"That sounds like something your mom would say."

"Yeah, it does. You call the guys and I'll see if I can tease the curious ball into action."

Jim went out to use the phone and Jaydee opened the closet door and looked inside. As he did so the barrel of his air gun leveled off at him. Behind it was the brass ball. It had grown arms and hands and was holding the gun.

"Jim, Jim, come here quick!" At Jaydee's shout, Tabitha came to attention on the window sill and Jim came rushing into the room. "Oh, wow! That's good, Jaydee, how did you get it to do that?"

"I didn't."

"You didn't," Jim was amazed. "Can it shoot that thing?"

"I don't know." As if in answer, the air gun discharged. The window across the room cracked in all directions, Tabitha hit the rug on a run and the two boys dropped to the floor. Jaydee slid under the bed. It was too tight a squeeze for Jim. Then, the little ball floated back into the closet and hid itself in the heap of junk.

Jaydee's mother came in just as the window disintegrated before her eyes. "What happened?"

34

"Oh, no!" Jaydee moaned as he slithered out from under the bed.

"'Oh, no' is right! You're grounded for the rest of the weekend, young man! You are not to leave this house and you cannot have anyone over to visit."

"Mom, you're going to pop a blood vessel."

Jaydee's mother continued without noting his comment. "If I can't get that window replaced today, young man, you're not going back to your grandfather's period." Spying the gun, she added, "Where did that come from?" She started to pick it up but was afraid to touch it. "Get that out of the house this minute!"

"How can I do that if I'm grounded?"

"Jim can take it home with him."

"But Mom!" Jaydee was frustrated, but not angry. There went the chance to make a fortune on the brass ball.

Jim walked around to the closet and picked up the gun before leaving. "Thanks for the neat gun, Mrs. Ferris."

Jaydee gave Jim a slug in the arm as he came by just to let him know how he felt.

* * *

After lunch Jaydee played some games on his mother's computer. He could hear her talking to his dad at work on the telephone about the incident.

"The whole window is out. We should have let him stay with my father for the weekend too. I just can't handle it."

The more she talked the more Jaydee felt like hiding. He went into his room and into the closet and pulled the door shut behind him.

It was dark for a few minute and then the ball lit up, making things bright in the small, gloomy space. Jaydee picked it up and looked into its one eye. It made a happy sound as though it was trying to cheer him up.

35

He pulled a blanket down from the shelf above him, spread it across the toys and lay down, putting the ball on the floor of the closet in front of him. They looked back and forth at each other for a wonderfully long time.

He felt warm and secure. After ages, the light dimmed and Jaydee went to sleep. When he woke up the ball was sitting on his head. As he took it off, he noticed that there was something wet where it had been sitting. He wiped it off with his hand. It was bright red; it was his blood. He didn't feel anything.

"Vampire!" He mumbled under his breath and opened the closet door. The air was fresh and cool outside. He stumbled out into his room and looked out his bedroom door.

The house was quiet.

"Mom!" Jaydee went from room to room. No one seemed to be home except Tabitha. She had stayed in hiding all afternoon. When she heard Jaydee shout she came running into the kitchen in search of food and companionship.

On the table was a note. "Fred, Jaydee has run away. I can't find him. If you get home before I come back, look for me at the Carter's. Love, Jessica."

"Maybe I should have run away," Jaydee thought. He was probably in big trouble now. He poured himself a glass of milk and got out a package of chocolate chip cookies. This called for an energy infusion and deep deliberation.

He sat at the kitchen table trying to think of a solution. "What should I do next?"

"Wait," he thought, "I haven't done anything wrong. I can convince Dad of that." But how would he explain the window? He couldn't tell about the ball.

Just then the door bell rang. It was the glass man.

"Is this the Ferris house?"

"Yeah."

"Where's the broken window?"

"In my room."

"It figures. Mrs. Ferris - is that your mother?

"Yeah."

"Well, she wanted it replaced today. Is she home?"

"No."

"That's a problem. How do you feel about letting me see it?"

"I don't know."

"Well, I don't usually trust teenagers but your mother said this was an emergency.

"I know; it gets cold sometimes at night."

"Well, if she wants that window replaced this afternoon, you better let me see it."

Just then Stanley Conover drove up. He looked at the glass repair truck and then yelled: "What's the problem, Jaydee?"

"I'm in trouble, Stanley, and this guy needs to come in to fix my window."

"I see. Well, if you're already in trouble, I'll take the rap. Will that do the job?"

"Great!" Jaydee liked his cousin Stanley. He was a slim young man with dark hair and the look of success about him. Besides that, he always kidded around.

Jaydee liked him for another reason. Stanley listened. He was a real friend. Jaydee could talk to him and feel as an equal. He made Jaydee feel grown up.

"How did it happen, Jaydee?" Stanley asked as the three of them entered the house.

"It just happened." Jaydee said leading the two men into his bedroom.

"Yeah, it looks to me like you flew through it," Stanley said as the glass man measured the size of the window and picked the glass out of the corners.

"It was a pellet." Jaydee volunteered.

"Like in a gun-type pellet?"

"It was in the gun."

"And you shot it out?"

"No."

"One of your friends did?"

Jaydee looked down into the closet at the ball. "Yeah - I guess you could say he's a friend."

"I have to go get the glass. I'll be back in about twenty minutes." The man slipped by Stanley and Jaydee and made his way to his truck.

Neither Jaydee or Stanley seemed aware that the repair man left the house. "How are you doing with your Grandfather Ferris?" Stanley asked.

"Ok, I guess."

"Has he complained?" Stanley was looking at Jaydee's dresser.

"No."

"You're all right then." Stanley picked up a framed photograph.

"Is this a picture of your grandfather?"

"Yes, it is."

Stanley handed him the picture. "His name is John Ferris isn't it?"

"Yeah."

"I always wondered how your mother happened to marry a man with the same name as her father."

"Oh, that's not Grandpa's real name. He changed it when Mom and Dad got married."

"Really. I've never heard of that happening before. He must have a special reason to do that."

"Maybe."

"Are you having a good time on the farm?"

"Yeah, I saw a plane crash."

"I guess that was the one I read about. The pilot's in the hospital. They think he may be crazy. He claims a round ball with an eye in it made him crash the plane."

"Oh." Jaydee tried to sound disinterested, but his

38

heart rate was climbing at high velocity.

"Yeah, the Air Force has been looking all over for that ball. They want to believe the pilot, but haven't found anything to back him up. He's some kind of ace from Viet Nam, I guess."

Jaydee swallowed deeply.

"You all right, kid?"

"Oh, yeah. It's just something got caught in my throat."

"I see." Stanley looked annoyed. He seemed very interested in Jaydee's grandfather. He kept asking questions and Jaydee tried to answer them.

The glass man came back and returned to his work while Stanley and Jaydee stood watching. He brought in the window and carefully fitted it to the frame while Stanley continued to ply Jaydee with questions.

Oblivious to the discussion behind him, the glass man stepped back to admire his work. "Well, that about takes care of the window." The workman picked up his tools and handed the bill to Stanley.

Stanley signed it, received a copy and followed the glass man out. Turning to Jaydee, he said, "Tell your folks hello for me. I'll leave the bill on the table."

The glass man had done a good job. All the glass was cleaned up so that you wouldn't even know that the window had been broken. Jaydee looked at the bill. It was a big window - two hundred dollars! Mom would be most unhappy.

He got the ball out of the closet and showed it the window. Then he took it into the living room and showed it the bill. Discouraged, he went into his mother's room and sat the ball down beside the computer to play a game.

"See what you did," he said picking up the ball again and shaking it. "If you hadn't broken the window, I'd be showing you off to all my friends instead of playing a dumb old game on the computer."

He put the ball down and started flipping through the different menus in the computer. His mother was a teacher and liked to have all kinds of information programs. There was geography, history, maps and even an encyclopedia. Jaydee noticed it rise and shift back and forth to see around his head. The mysterious ball focused on the computer screen. He wondered what the ball was doing this for or what it could be thinking.

Bored, Jaydee threw himself on his mother's bed and was soon asleep. A light went on in the curious ball. It floated up to the key board. Its little arms extended from its side and it pushed a few keys with its tiny hands. Rapidly, it scanned the material in the menus.

Finding this procedure too slow, it floated up and down, scanning the computer setup. Then producing a short skinny cord, it plugged itself into an extra port on the back of the computer, and commanded the computer to download everything it had.

The little brass ball hovered above and hummed along as the computer dropped its whole memory into the ball's mysterious system. When the job was done the shiny brass ball unplugged itself and floated out into the hall and off to Jaydee's closet.

Tabitha the cat had been watching from a safe vantage point. When she was sure the troublesome ball would not return, she jumped on the bed and curled up beside Jaydee. At first she kept an eye on the bedroom door so as not to be taken by surprise. Finally, she fell asleep too.

* * *

Sunday was another matter. Jaydee was still grounded, but he was allowed to attend church. That was a miracle.

His mother had been glad to see him curled up on

40

her bed with Tabitha. Magically, he found himself in his own bed on Sunday morning and he didn't have to explain until she'd cooled off over night.

Jaydee managed to explain away the window. He just told his dad it was his fault and said he was sorry without going into details. He steered away from any mention of the ball. Thank goodness Jim wasn't there with his super honesty.

"There is one thing you should know, Jaydee."

"What's that, Dad?"

"Stanley isn't your real cousin. It's not a good idea to let him in when we're not home."

"Why is that, Dad?"

"Well," he hesitated, "he's a good friend, but not family."

"You mean I did wrong?"

"Let's say it was ok this time."

"Thanks, Dad." That was that. There was no problem.

Jaydee got to see Jim before Sunday school and told him about the vampire habits of the brass ball. He also filled him in on the situation with the pilot. Jim was all for a full confession. Jaydee was about to concede this point when Sunday school class started.

"Let's see, Carlie's here, John, James, Kelsey . . ."

"That's Jaydee and Jim, Brother Sloan. Why do you always call them John and James?" Sidnie asked.

"Well, those are their real names, Sidnie. Besides, I rather like the names, James and John. Remember, Jesus had two apostles by those names. They were brothers and he called them Sons of Thunder. Jim and Jaydee are very enthusiastic young men who have definite opinions. I like to think of them as my Sons of Thunder." Brother Sloan continued on with the roll while Jim and Jaydee made faces at Sidnie. Neither one of them liked James and John for names but they were pleased over their new found importance.

If Brother Sloan wanted their attention, he had made big strides in that direction. It also helped that he was teaching one of Jaydee's favorite subjects. The lesson was on Enoch the prophet.

Brother Sloan drew seven circles on the board and wrote a name in each. Each circle represented a patriarch. Adam was the first and Enoch was the seventh. He said that patriarchs were righteous leaders of mankind and that after Adam left the garden, he and mother Eve had Cain and Abel. After Cain killed Abel, they had another son named Seth and he and his family obeyed God but Cain and his family did not.

He told how Enoch was born to Jared when Adam was 625 years old. Enoch was so righteous that he walked and talked with God. He was a prophet who founded a city which he called "City of Holiness". His people were called Zion and when he was 430 years old he and his people were taken up into heaven. Jaydee was the first to ask a question:

"Were Enoch and his people taken up in a space ship?"

Jim cut in before the teacher could answer. "There weren't any space ships in those days."

"That is an interesting question, Jaydee, but Jim is most likely right. God doesn't need space ships to take people up into heaven."

"What about Elijah? He used a chariot for him."

"Right, but if God had used a space ship, he would have told us in the scriptures."

Jaydee was getting a little discouraged when a marvelous thing happened right there in class.

Rylie Petersen asked if Sodom and Gomorrah could have been destroyed by a chariot.

Brother Sloan shrugged "That's the same, Rylie. God doesn't need space ships or chariots to make things

42

happen. Maybe God caused a volcano to erupt and destroy Sodom and Gomorrah." Rylie's question took Jaydee and Jim by surprise. It was all they could do to contain themselves. Jim and Jaydee waved their hands in the air wanting to be the first to ask the next question. Jim, who was somewhat less animated, was called first.

"Did the chariot that took Elijah fly by itself, Brother Sloan?"

"I really don't know; maybe the men who wrote the Bible couldn't understand how God took Elijah so they invented a chariot to do the job."

"If it really was some kind of chariot do you think God had used it more than once and might use it again?" Jaydee asked.

"I have no idea."

There was a knowing look between Jaydee and Jim. They could hardly wait until after class to discuss the possibilities.

"You don't suppose one of your space ships came and got Enoch and Elijah do you, Jaydee?"

"Could be. You heard Brother Sloan."

"He didn't seem to know."

"Well, maybe we know more than he does."

"Yeah, maybe Enoch had something to do with the brass ball too."

"It wouldn't surprise me."

"You think a lot about Enoch don't you, Jaydee?"

"Yeah, I guess I do."

"I do too."

"You do?"

"Yeah, I hope someday to meet him." Jim noticed that Jaydee looked away. Jim knew that Jaydee didn't like to talk about life after death. "Do you really think he had a space ship?"

"Could be"

"Maybe God will guide us to a space ship through

43

our brass ball."

Jaydee looked off into the distance, hoping not to show how preposterous he thought Jim's ideas were. "Maybe he will."

Chapter 4 A Mind of Its Own

Jaydee was determined not to have anymore incidents with the curious ball before school let out in June. He and Jim watched the ball tirelessly day and night. Well, almost day and night.

At first they believed that a closed closet door was all that it took to detain their little brass friend. On Monday, however, they were surprised to find it waiting for them at recess.

The funny thing is that no one saw the ball but Jaydee and Jim. It hovered high overhead dipping down when no one was looking to make itself know to the boys. The only time the other boys might have seen it is when someone hit a fly ball to the field. But the few times that happened the brass ball was hovering over home plate. There was not much chance of its discovery that way.

That would have been fine with Jaydee and Jim. It was kind of reassuring to have it up there looking down on them, but, just when they were getting used to their bright brass shining angel, everything changed.

It was Jaydee's turn at bat. The pitcher wound up and threw, but the baseball never reached the batter. The curious ball plucked the baseball right out of the air and disappeared into the blue. It was as if the baseball had vanished in thin air.

Then, suddenly, out of nowhere the baseball reappeared just in front of Jaydee's bat. He swung. The bat connected and the ball flew and flew. It was far out in left field beyond the reach of the left fielder - beyond the view of the team. It was gone.

No one remembers seeing the baseball from the time it disappeared until the time it reappeared in front of Jaydee's bat just waiting to be struck. It was like magic.

Jim looked at Jaydee and Jaydee looked at Jim. It was a moment of truth. Jaydee ran the bases and walked from third to home. The baseball was never found.

"That was some hit!" yelled Bob, the yard monitor. Everyone was too excited to finish the game even after Bob returned with another ball.

Somewhere Jaydee and Jim's curious friend was examining the baseball. Its little arms stroked the surface of its leather cousin. It loosened the threads and peered inside. "ONLY RUBBER STRINGS." It recorded.

* * *

"We'll have to think of some other way of locking up the curious ball." Jim mused as he and Jaydee were returning home.

"Maybe it won't come back." Jaydee said. "It must know we don't want it to be roaming about."

Jim pursed his lips. "I hope it never comes back."

But there it was, zipping along in back of the boys. As they turned the corner, Jim could see it just behind them.

"Don't look back, Jaydee, but it's there."

Jaydee turned. There it was. Apparently, it liked being with them.

For hours after school, Jaydee and Jim sat mulling over the antics of the curious ball, wondering how they could curtail its activities. They rethought their idea to charge their friends to see it. Now, they would auction it off to the highest bidder after the showing. They were sure some of their friends would want the ball after seeing it's amazing powers. Jim and Jaydee would allow absolutely no returns.

They worked up a flyer on Jaydee's word processor. While they worked the curious ball hovered over their shoulders and watched as the boys designed the blueprint for what they were to call a science project. That was Jim's idea.

46

During early evening they canvassed the neighborhood. They even took the bus to the homes of boys that lived beyond their area.

The plan was set in motion. After school the next day, their customers began to arrive. Even a few girls had picked up the flyer and came to see the brass ball.

One by one they were admitted to Jaydee's room to experience the wiles of the mysterious visitor from the other side of nowhere. Each waited his or her turn patiently in the living room. Jaydee's mother was curious and a bit worried about her son's "science" project. When she saw five dollar bills pass from each child to her son's hands, she became suspicious.

"What is going on here?" She asked. "I see you taking money and I don't understand it."

"Mom," Jaydee whined as he closed the door to his bedroom behind Brendon Hardy. "It's part of the experiment. Part of the project is to see if science can be profitable."

"I want to see this science project right now!"

Jim stepped between the bedroom door and Jaydee's mother. "Do you have $5, Mrs. Ferris?"

Since Jim was holding his mother off, Jaydee slipped back into his room leaving Jim to defend the cause. Mrs. Ferris was exasperated. "You'd charge me in my own home?" She pounded on the door. "Let me in there!"

"Okay, okay." Jim backed away. "You're next. Just as soon as Brendon comes out."

Just then the door swung open and Brendon emerged from the room. His smile demonstrated the pleasure he was feeling. "That's the greatest thing I ever saw! Have you seen it Mrs. Ferris?"

"No, but I intend to see it now."

There was a moment of anticipation as Mrs. Ferris opened the door, but she didn't even get a glimpse of the curious ball. It swept by her and out into the living room. It

47

raced around the room in the air several time and then, as Brendon left the house, it followed immediately upon his heels and out into the sunshine.

Mrs. Ferris was petrified by the action, Jim sprang to the front door, but was too late and Jaydee flew into a rage. "Now look what you did, Mom!"

The whole thing was too much for Mrs. Ferris who drifted into the kitchen in a hail of tears. "What have I done to deserve this?" She cried.

Jaydee reviewed the situation with Jim and they decided that there was no reason to complain. They'd collected a few bucks and got rid of the troublesome brass ball. Best of all Mom would never know what their "science project" was.

* * *

At Brendon Hardy's home that night there was great excitement as Brendon showed his folks the amazing little ball. True, it had followed him home and into the house, but after that it played dead. It was amazing only because it was so interesting to look at. Brendon couldn't make it do a thing.

The senior Hardy, master mechanic, and father of four, was intrigued by the intricate little device. He rolled it over and over in his hands, got out his magnifying glass and tapped it repeatedly to see if it was hollow or if anything would shake loose or drop out of the shiny ball. He looked into the eye of the ball and wondered what it saw.

Meanwhile the little ball was conducting its own examination. It added the following information to its data files: "MAN ABOUT 45 WITH HAPPY WIFE AND CHILDREN, GREASE STAINED HANDS, HOMELY LOOKS AND TIRED FACE."

Mr. Hardy was about to lose interest when the amazing little ball shot up from his grasp and circumnavigated the room. It continued to record: "NO

COMPUTER, NO TV, LOTS OF TOYS, DINNER ON
THE TABLE, MAGAZINES, BOOKS, HEALTHY
FAMILY."

Suddenly the ball came to rest on a table in a dark
corner. Two little arms extended from its body and it began
to sift through some books. It selected one particular book
and started to scan its pages. The family was too startled to
make a move. Startled was probably not the right word.

"That's the most bizarre thing I've ever seen!"
Brendon's mother gasped.

No one else uttered a word. They were too stunned.
Still the question on their minds was: "What book is that?"

Over a thousand pages were recorded in less than
ten minutes. Recovering from their initial shyness, the
family members crept closer and closer hoping not to
disturb the little creature.

Then, after turning the last page, the brass ball
folded its arms and headed for the door. It hovered there for
a few minutes like a dog wanting to go out. Automatically,
Mr. Hardy stepped forward and opened the door to a clear
evening sky. The ball sped out.

Brendon was the first to the stack of books. The
family crowded around. "It was the Bible," Brendon said
with wonder. "Why would it want to look at the Bible?"

* * *

At school the next day, Brendon related the events
of the previous evening. Jaydee and Jim marveled at the
weird antics of the curious ball.

While they delighted in hearing of the adventures
Brendon described they wanted no more of the little brass
ball. They were glad that it had flown off into never-never
land.

Jim and Jaydee were discussing their good fortune
when the teacher caught them. She called them up to her

desk and assigned them an hour after school in detention.

Jim didn't mind. Detention was always in the school library and he loved to read books. Jaydee, on the other hand, hated the library. He opened the outside door and looked longingly at the ball diamond. Some of the boys whose parents came home late were starting a game.

"Come on, Jaydee." Jim tugged at Jaydee's arm. "I don't want to get in more trouble."

"What could it matter, Jim. You go on and I'll come along soon."

As Jim let go of Jaydee's arm, a burst of light on shiny metal flashed by them through the door and into the hall behind them.

"Oh, my gosh!" Jaydee said. "It's that ball again!"

They walked to the Library. The little ball followed them. They opened the door carefully just wide enough for each of them to slip through. The ball followed.

The detention teacher glared at the boys. She did not notice the ball as it sped into the room.

Jim headed for his favorite books and Jaydee strolled over to the computer. There were no restrictions on the use of the computers. The teacher in charge of detention was just to see that they stayed in the library for the allotted time.

The ball followed Jaydee. Jaydee wondered what sinister brain could be driving the curious ball.

He brought up chariots and then space ships and then Enoch. It was surprising what one could find on the computer. After bit, he noticed that the little ball had plugged into the main Library computer. This computer had just been donated to the library and was connected with the Library of Congress collection of digital books.

No one noticed the ball snatching file after file from the computer. It was so fast that the power began to dip a few times as it worked away. This attracted the librarian and she came over to where Jaydee was working.

"What did you do?"

"Nothing."

"The lights flickered."

"I know, but it wasn't me."

"Well, see that you don't wreck anything." Jaydee looked at the curious ball sapping the other computer, but said nothing. He was happy that the librarian hadn't noticed the intruder.

When the hour was up, Jaydee and Jim left the library along with the brass ball. As they opened the outside door and watched the ball slip out ahead of them, they took a deep breath and let it out slowly. They hoped the curious ball would disappear forever.

"Did you see what it did?" Jaydee asked.

"Yeah, I sure did." Jim responded. "If it's controlled by aliens, it sure is stealing all our secrets."

"I guess it could be spying on us," Jaydee said. "but what can it hurt? I just hope it stays away from us. I don't want it interfering with our fun."

The little ball did not bother the boys for some time. That night it floated away on a villainous mission. Just five miles away from Jaydee's house was a strategic power plant. The brass ball found a roosting place among the towers surrounding this structure and began methodically cutting cables and wires. Sparks showered the compound below and the city became dark.

In the dark people panicked, traffic was delayed and evening fun came to a sudden close. Emergency generators ginned up and police and security officers popped into action.

Repairmen scurried to the scene of the power disconnect. Within hours the failure was found and wires were carefully spliced together. However, the systematic cutting of wires puzzled the work crews. What could have canceled the cities power supply and why? They kept the problem to themselves lest a cry of sabotage should cause alarm.

Meanwhile the little ball was still at work. Next it destroyed telephone relays and after that radio transmitters throughout the area.

Airline flights were canceled as landing lights were dashed to pieces. Pilots were rerouted to other cities. The little ball was taking over. Kansas City was becoming isolated and so was its citizenry.

However, the breakdown was not confined to Jaydee's home town. Computer systems running into the Pentagon and major cities throughout the nation were blacked out. All over the United States people were concerned as power, telephone and radio service failed.

At first some thought it was some kind of test being conducted by Homeland Security, but as damage spread leading authorities realized that it was not a planned shutdown. The nation was under attack. With no radio, power or telephone, there was no way of telling how widespread the disaster had become. Enough was relayed by ham radio to disclose that all was not well. Although it was not a planned test, it served to alert the nation to its vulnerability. As to the source of the damage, everyone was literally and figuratively in the dark. What could have been the purpose of this outage?

After a night of fear and worry, Jaydee and his parents awoke to a new day. In the light of dawn, things didn't look so bad. Power was on, radio reports disclosed the extent of the problems and anxious family and friends reported their whereabouts and welfare. Jaydee's parent went to work and Jim and Jaydee went to school.

"That was really something!" Jim reported.

"Yeah, my parents nearly blew a fuse." Jaydee said. "At first they thought I did it."

As they reached the corner, Brendon Hardy joined them. "I'll bet your little ball was behind that mess."

Jaydee grabbed Brendon by the collar. "My little

ball. It went home with you. Don't you remember?"

"Let go!"

Jim turned on Jaydee. "Well, what do you think, Jaydee? Could it have done all that damage?"

"That little ball? No way!"

Just then the brass ball appeared above their heads. It floated innocently overhead as though to confirm Jaydee's declaration. If it was a spy or a saboteur, no one could tell by its antics.

Chapter 5 To Hide a Friend

The little ball continued to haunt Jim and Jaydee until the end of school in June when they went off to visit Grandpa Ferris again. This time they managed to escape without their brass friend. Grandpa picked them up at the bus station.

"You know those Air Force investigators are still looking for you. You'd better steer clear of them as long as you're here."

"They've got nothing on us." Jaydee said. "We've done a lot of talking about this thing they think we have and decided that if we had it we would just give it to them."

"That's right Mr. Ferris. Jaydee and I don't want any brass ball around."

Ferris looked at the boys with approval. "I think you've made a good decision."

With that settled the boys set out to explore the fields behind the farm looking for anything that might have been missed from the airplane crash...

"I wonder if that Major who parachuted from the crash is still in the hospital." Jim said as they were examining Uncle Jack's new garden.

Jaydee bent down and sifted some of the soil from the garden in his hand. He looked off into space for a while and then back at Jim. "Probably. I think he went bonkers."

"It's been over a month. Don't you think we ought to go and see him? It might help."

"Naw, let's go swimming."

There was a good swimming hole on a canal just a few yards away. The weather was hot. The two were soon out of their clothes and into the water. The water was cold and deep.

"Help!" Jim cried as he cramped up and started to go under.

"No! Jim, Jim!" Jaydee shouted and swam towards

him. He dove under the water but couldn't find Jim. Jaydee became frantic as he ducked under the water again and again.

Suddenly, out of nowhere came a swooshing sound and a splash. Water churned and in an instant Jim's head broke the surface. He gasped and it was then that Jaydee saw the brass ball pull Jim from the water and dump him on the bank. Where had it come from? Neither boy had seen the little ball before at the farm.

Jaydee quickly climbed out of the canal and rushed to Jim's side. Jim's eyes rolled around in his sockets like he was searching for something.

"Did you see it?" Jaydee asked.

Jim rose up on one elbow. "Did I see what?"

"Did you see what rescued you? It was the ball."

"The ball?"

"Yes. The ball." Jaydee leaned over Jim. "Are you all right?"

"Sure. I'm fine. What's wrong with you? How could it be the ball?"

"I saw it. It dove down into the water and brought you up. When I tried, I couldn't even find you. How can that little machine do it?"

Jim got up and looked around. "Well, where is it now?"

They both surveyed their surroundings. The brass ball seemed to have disappeared as quickly as it had splashed into their swimming hole.

The boys lay down in the shade of a nearby peach tree and gazed up into the sky. It had been an exciting experience, but neither expected what happened next. Without warning, the tree began to pelt them with peaches. Luckily the peaches were ripe and soft. Before they could move they were surrounded with fresh ripe peaches. Some were smashed but just as many were just right for eating and so they ate a few. Jim held one at arm's length.

"Where do you suppose these peaches came from?"

"Out of the tree, dummy."

"No, I mean how did they happen to all fall out of the tree at once?"

Just then one more peach hit Jim square in the jaw. Above him in the tree was a shiny round object. The ball had reappeared. It swooped down and landed on Jim chest peering at his face.

"Look at him! You'd think he really cares about us."

"Oh, come on! He's been nothing but trouble ever since we found him. We need to turn him over to the Air Force. Then, he won't bother us anymore."

Jim frowned. "Can't you see, Jaydee? He's our friend."

"You think he's our friend?"

"Yeah, I do!"

Jaydee got up and looked at Jim. "Well, in that case, I think we need to hide this thing from the Air Force because they're sure to find out we have it."

* * *

Uncle Jack pulled the shades down on all his windows. He sensed that there was something outside that he could not understand. Someone was lurking around out there in the dark. He took his shot gun down, loaded it and laid it across his legs as he sat in the kitchen.

There was only a faint patch of moonlight. The Air Force had hauled the remains of 907 away. The hole had been filled in. All the fences had been repaired and a new garden of nursery plants stood watch where technicians and airmen had tromped before.

Jack wasn't totally happy with the prospect of taking vegetables from hot house transplants, but it did meet the requirements he had made. There were even a few

56

exotic specimens to compensate for the delay he would experience until the new crop came in.

Now there was a definite sound of footsteps in the yard. Someone wasn't creeping around quietly, but didn't care if Jack heard. Two teenage boys strode out of the darkness and leaped up the steps to the door. They looked quickly both ways as though expecting an unknown assailant, then pounded on the door.

Jack had dozed a little and gave a start at the commotion. "Who's there?" he barked.

"It's us," came the reply.

The boys were no cause for alarm. Jack unbolted the door and stood his gun in the corner by the stove as he let Jim and Jaydee into the house.

"What brings you two out so late?" Jack mused as he peered down at the teenagers.

"We got to find a place to hide the brass ball before those Air Force guys come back to Grandpa's to look for it!" Jaydee thrust himself on into the kitchen. He had the mouth of a burlap bag in one hand and the bulk of the bag cradled in the other.

"That's the thing you found in the plane?"

"Under the plane!" Jim retorted as he followed Jaydee into the room.

The two stood for a moment blinking away the darkness from their eyes. Then, "You gotta help us!" Jaydee said.

"I suppose I could," Jack countered, "since those folks aren't my friends."

"It isn't theirs anyway!" Jim argued. "Grandpa Ferris says we should put it back, but it isn't theirs!"

"Well, I'll see what I can do!"

"Can we hide it now?"

"Yeah, yeah, I guess so if you aren't afraid of the dark."

Uncle Jack took down his lantern hat and followed

the boys out into the yard. There was little moonlight.

"Where do we go?" Jaydee asked.

"Into the shed."

The three quickly crossed the yard. Jack was unusually swift for a change. If their secret is safe, he thought, mine is too.

Jack led the boys down into the trap door as he had the Colonel and his technician. Jaydee and Jim were full of oh's and awe's. Jack had locked the shed from the inside and pulled the trap door closed behind them.

Except for the light in Jack's helmet, they were in the dark. They were repelled by the skulls in the closed room.

"What is this?" Jim sputtered.

"Shut up!" Jaydee chided. "It's a mine shaft!"

"Can we just leave the ball here and go back out, Uncle Jack? I'm cold!" Jim reluctantly followed Jaydee and Jack as they descended into the hole. Jaydee, who was almost as chilled by the grim aspect of the upper chamber, was determined to stick close to Uncle Jack.

They went down for a long while. As they rested on a landing, Jack shined his light onto a hoist that stood over another shaft. As Jaydee and Jim looked over the edge, they saw that it seemed to fall off into eternity.

"Climb on!" Jack's voice had just the shadow of pride in it as he invited them to join him. Reluctantly the boys got on. Jack pulled a few ropes and worked some magic on the gears and the hoist began to settle down into the hole.

The air got mustier as they went down. Finally, they came to a stop. From here, passages took off in three different directions. There may have been no gold or silver in Uncle Jack's mine, but there were a lot of artifacts lining the walls like those above.

They had walked along one passage for about a city block when Jack stopped, leaned against a pillar and pushed it to one side. Behind it a narrow door opened up. By turning sideways each of the three slipped through and came out into a wide chamber. Here, Uncle Jack opened up a metal door which looked like a door from an old submarine, and the two young men followed him into a perfectly clean metal-lined room with a beautifully tiled floor. Around the room were tables fastened to the walls. In the center of the room were other tables. All these tables were lined with mechanical devices of every description, or perhaps devices one could not describe.

"This is my laboratory. You may leave your curious ball here."

"What do all these things do, Uncle Jack?" Jim was bewildered

"Yeah, what's this do?" Jaydee fingered a machine on the table next to him.

"Well, let's see. That's a machine for cutting metal."

"I don't see anything that would cut metal here, Uncle Jack. Are you sure?"

"Of course, this is my laboratory, isn't it?"

"Show us how it works."

"Well, I can't right now. I don't have any spare metal."

Jim, who had moved about from machine to machine, came back to Jack and Jaydee with a short piece of metal. "Would this do?"

Jack hesitated.

Jaydee moved forward and took the scrap. "Of course it will!" Confident, he handed it to Jack.

Jack cautiously fastened the piece of metal in the machine without saying a word, moved a few knobs and stood back. Nothing happened. "I don't understand." he said, "It doesn't seem to be working."

"Yeah," Jaydee quipped. "It must be unplugged."

"I guess so," Jack said.

"So, plug it in." Jaydee challenged him.

"I can't; I don't know how."

"You mean this isn't really your laboratory." Jaydee was very sure of himself.

"You're right. I just found that door one day when I was digging and came in and here it was."

The boys marveled more than ever. This was definitely a wonderful find. They both checked out the room from one end to the other.

On one wall was a meter of some sort that glowed in the dark when Uncle Jack's light was flashing elsewhere. Its red markings formed a pattern that changed ever so slightly as they watched it. It had many rows of little marks. Some went off and others came on, creating a different shape. It was like a digital clock, forming numbers out of short oblong patches of light, but there was no understanding this meter. It made no sense to them.

Finally, Jaydee took a deep breath and looked up at Uncle Jack. "Nobody knows about this place but you - not even the Air Force?

"No, nobody but me."

"Ok, we'll leave the ball here." Jaydee brought the bag up on one of the tables and, slipping the ball out of the bag, placed it upright on the table top.

The sphere seemed to rise gently from the table - no, it really did rise, it lit up, spun around, tilted up and down and began flying around the room wildly on its own power.

Jack and the boys were paralyzed - rooted to the spot. After a few minutes of looking around the room the little ball rested again on the table, chirped a few times, turned off its light and went to sleep.

"Well, I'll be." Uncle Jack exclaimed. "That's the strangest thing I've seen in all my days."

"It does things like that," Jim volunteered.

"It's no big!" Jaydee scowled at Jim.

Jim shrugged his shoulders and the three left the laboratory.

The room was dark now. The brass ball lay silent, but the meter on the wall began to change rapidly, its light flashing wildly in the dark.

Chapter 6 The Rift in Time

Major Bailey was awake. Today Colonel Jones was coming to discuss the crash. Bailey was beginning to feel that the mysterious ball was a nightmare. Maybe he should tell the Colonel that he had temporary insanity when he gave the order to bail out.

He had just shoved his food tray aside, when two little round heads appeared above his table. He was relieved to see two sets of eyes in each head and each head attached to a body. The two beings came around his tray and stood by his bed so he could see that they were two teenage boys.

"Hello. What are you doing here?"

"We came to visit you," Jim said hesitantly.

"That's nice, but who are you? How did you get in here?" Bailey asked in rapid succession.

Jaydee formed his words carefully. "We told the nurse we were your sons."

"My sons? I don't have any sons. Weren't there any guards outside?"

Jaydee courageously moved closer. "We told him we were Sons of Thunder and he just laughed and let us in."

"Sons of Thunder? What does that mean?"

"You know, James and John." Jim said confidently, as if everyone knew their Bible.

"I see." It was refreshing to listen to kid things. "I don't understand."

"That's ok." Jaydee quipped.

"What brought you here?"

"We saw you parachute," Jim answered.

"We saw your airplane right after the crash too," Jaydee continued.

"You did? Did anything unusual happen to you?"

"Yeah, we found a round ball that has an eye in it that follows you all over." Jim felt good about confessing.

The Major gasped. For a moment he lost his cool. His eyes rolled back, sweat broke out on the back of his neck and he clenched his fists. Then, realizing that the young men were talking calmly and straight forward about the very thing he knew was true, he relaxed.

"Have you got this round ball with you?"

Jaydee gulped. "No, but we know where it is. We feel awfully bad about people not believing you so we came to let you know."

"You've done a bad thing you know - taking this ball."

Jim looked nervously at the pilot. "We're real sorry."

"You need to bring this ball-thing to me."

"Is it yours?"

"Well, no, but it made me crash. I need to show it to my boss."

Jaydee looked at Jim and took a deep breath. "I don't think it's yours. It was sent to us."

"What are you saying? This thing made me crash and you say it's yours! Is it a toy of yours?

"No."

"Can you pay for my airplane?"

Jaydee and Jim were silent for the longest time.

Finally Jim tried to reason. "Maybe we could let you see it."

Major Bailey thought about that a while. If they brought it in, he might talk them out of it. Once they brought in the ball anything could happen. He could be absolved of the blame.

"Yeah," Bailey said, hiding his impatience, "that would be all right. Bring it in."

"We got to go now." Jim shuffled away toward the door, tugging all the time at Jaydee.

Jaydee would not budge. "Are you some kind of war hero or flying ace?"

63

"Yeah, I guess. I've shot down lots of enemy airplanes. "

"How many?" Jaydee persisted.

"Oh, six or seven."

"Have you been in a space ship?"

"Only to look at one."

"Can you show us a space ship some time?'

"I suppose I could after I get out of here. Where do you live?"

"In Kansas City."

"What's your address?"

Jaydee hesitated. "I'll tell you next time I come." Jaydee started to follow Jim.

"Wait, kid." The big man leaned over and stretched out his hand to Jaydee.

"Let's be friends. Ok?"

Jaydee took his hand. "Ok."

The Major produced a pad and pen. "Why don't you write your address on this pad?"

Jaydee took the pad and the pen like he was going to write his address and then, changing his mind, handed it back. "I don't know. I'd better wait till next time."

"When will that be? I'm not used to waiting."

"Maybe tomorrow."

"You do that!"

Major Bailey lay back. Kids were hard to figure, but here was the key to his future.

"So long, Mr."

"So long."

* * *

John Ferris was standing in the yard when Tyler Houston drove up in a blue Air Force sedan. Tyler was a tall slim muscular looking man with glasses. He was wearing cool blue slacks and a white shirt and tie. He looked more like an engineer than an Air Force expert.

"Hello, are you John Ferris?"

"Yes, I am."

"I'm Tyler Houston. I work as an investigator for the Air Force."

"Yeah, I guessed as much. Your people have already been here."

"Well, I've run into a problem and I need your help."

"I don't see how I could help you."

"We've finished our investigation at your neighbor's, but it seems that two teenagers have been visiting the crash site and we think they've carried off something of importance. I understand they are staying here with you."

"You must mean my grandson and his friend."

"I suppose. Have you noticed if they have brought home anything unusual?"

"Kids are always bringing home unusual things, Mr. Houston. You'll have to be more specific."

"It's been described as a round brass ball about the size of a soft ball."

"Is this a part of your airplane?"

"I'm not at liberty to say."

"It sounds to me as though this object you describe may not belong to the US Air Force."

"We believe it might have been the cause of the crash."

"I see. Well, I haven't seen such a thing. I'm not at all sure that my grandson has either. What leads you to believe that he took it?"

"Just that kids gravitate to things like this."

"Oh, really. Well, I hope you find it."

"Couldn't you just let me look through the boy's room?"

"No, I won't violate the boy's confidence in that

way. Have you asked him about it?"

"Not exactly. I agree with your line of reasoning, Mr. Ferris, but we would like to complete our investigation soon. The career of one of our finest pilots may be at stake. If you could just let me see the boy's room, he need never know."

"No, Mr. Houston. Even if the boy was here I wouldn't let you in the house without a search warrant because of the circumstances."

"What is that?"

"What if you found this piece of hardware? Would you let the boy keep it?"

"Oh, we couldn't do that. We'd need to examine it. Maybe after . . ."

"After it was dissected and determined to be perfectly harmless, you might give it back."

"Yes."

"As far as I can see, Mr. Houston, this thing doesn't belong to the US Government and if my grandson has adopted it, he probably values it highly. Whatever it is, I'm going to do everything I can to protect my grandson's interests."

"You may not want to do that, Mr. Ferris. You may find yourself in a lot of hot water."

"I'll chance that, Mr. Houston." John Ferris had marched up his steps and closed the door in the face of the technician who was following him. He watched through the screen door as the blue Air Force sedan drove away. He wondered at his own foolhardy defense of his grandson's rights. He may very well be in serious trouble. This could result in his past closing in on him. His friend Jack would probably suffer more than he.

* * *

The two boys sat on Uncle Jack's porch suffering

with their consciences. Their friend didn't answer the door and they needed to make sure that he didn't disclose their hiding place.

"How could we be so stupid?" Jaydee lamented.

"I'm sorry, Jaydee. It seemed like the right thing to do."

"Well, at least the pilot knows he isn't crazy."

"Yeah, I feel good about that, Jaydee, but it really isn't their ball. They don't really know that much about it." Jim made a gesture indicating a very small space between his finger and thumb.

As they looked out into the darkness, they saw a light come on in the old shop behind the house. It hadn't occurred to them that Uncle Jack had been down in his mine. Before long the door opened and the old miner came out into the yard. He was dusty and looked very tired.

"What're you two here for?"

"We just wanted to be sure that you wouldn't tell anyone about the brass ball."

"What makes you think I would tell anyone?"

"Well . . . er we told the pilot." Jim blurted out.

"You did what?"

"It's true, Uncle Jack. We told him so he wouldn't think he was crazy."

"That's real dumb. You didn't tell him where it was did you? You didn't tell about the laboratory?"

"No, Uncle Jack, we didn't even give him our address." Jim was almost in tears.

"Thank goodness!" Jack was very relieved. "I guess my secret isn't safe as long as that brass ball of yours is down there. You might get to feeling like telling everyone."

"Oh, no, Uncle Jack. We won't tell," Jim pleaded.

"Well, I'd feel a bit easier if it weren't there."

"We'll move it, Uncle Jack." Jaydee offered. "We'll move it right now."

"Suits me fine."

"Will you take us down, Uncle Jack?" Jaydee asked.

"Ok. I'm awfully tired, but if it's got to be done, it's got to be done."

The three hurried off as fast as Jack could walk. It was a long scary trip until they arrived at the door to the laboratory. When they opened the door the room was flooded with light. The mysterious ball was glowing more brightly than ever before.

Jaydee and Jim reached for the ball at the same time. Suddenly, there was a flash of intense light. A sound like thunder caused the miner to fall back and then the boys and the ball disappeared into thin air. In their place was a dark chasm like a deep mine shaft. A huge rift seemed to be cut in the room as though it was a hole in the wall, but it wasn't in the wall. It was in the middle of the room.

Jack didn't just hear the thunder, but he had felt it and had seen the light and he knew that Jaydee and Jim were gone. The ball was gone and he was alone. As he looked at the rift more closely, it appeared as though someone had taken a photograph of the room and pasted it up and then tore it apart from the center out leaving the edges and the rest of the photo intact. Sparks fired away from its edges.

Jack turned away and hurried out of the room and down the long tunnel as fast as he could go. He ran the lift up so speedily that the gears smoked. He climbed up to the shed and closed the trap door behind him. For a long time he sat in the dark shed, his light out and his head in his hands. What had he done? Where were the boys?

* * *

John Ferris had no idea where his grandson was. It was dark and Jaydee had seldom been away this long at night. Jim was gone too. What would Jaydee's mother say if she knew her son was out this late?

He paced up and down the lane thinking he probably should go over to Jack's house to see if they were there. Perhaps his lecture had been too harsh. Undoubtedly they would come home soon.

Just as he was turning into the house, a dark green sedan drove up. Other cars followed. They pulled up on the lawn, in the drive way and beside the house. Several men climbed out and surrounded him. There were no guns in their hands but he was sure there would be if he tried to move away.

"John Ferris, or is it Jason Cabot?" The question took him completely by surprise. He never should have talked back to the Air Force technician.

"Yes." He could think of no other answer. They had him.

"We have a warrant for your arrest."

"What are the charges?" John smiled cautiously.

"You are wanted for destruction of government property."

"What am I suppose to have destroyed?"

"I think you know what it was." The thin young man took him by the arm and started to lead him away.

"I'm not sure that I do."

The man sneered. "A government PT boat!"

"A PT boat - What was it worth?"

The young man looked John full in the face as if to get a better look. "Almost two million dollars with interest and all."

"Interest?"

"Yeah, it's been stacking up all these years since the Bay of Pigs." John knew he was referring to the failed invasion of Cuba under President Kennedy.

"Wait, you can't take me away like this, I have a grandson and his friend staying with me. I can't leave them alone. I've just been expecting them to come home.

69

"That's all right, I know your grandson. He thinks I'm his cousin, Stanley. I've notified his parents and I'll ship the boys home when they turn up."

"You what?"

"Come now, Jason. For a former CIA agent you must think we're pretty dumb."

"Aren't you with the CIA?"

"The CIA gave up on you years ago. I'm with the FBI. Documents will soon be made available to the public which implicate you and your CIA buddies. You grossly overstepped your authority." Stanley slipped a handcuff on John's wrist. The other was attached to his own wrist.

"But we were under orders."

"That's your story."

"You can't do this to me. I was doing my duty!"

"You were insubordinate and you know it. You and all the others who went in to help out their Latin friends were ordered to stay out of it. The only difference is that you and Jack will live to regret it. "

"Jack, my friend Jack didn't have anything to do with it."

"Well, maybe the two of you can alibi for each other." The agent was just pushing John into the car when an Air Force sedan pulled up.

Colonel Jones had rolled down his window as the car came to a halt in the middle of the road. "What's going on?"

"Nothing to trouble you, Colonel. We've just apprehended a long time fugitive." Stanley said flashing a badge across the car roof.

"Not so fast. We have a warrant to search this house." The Colonel said pointing to Tyler Houston, his driver.

"Search it all you want, Colonel. We won't stop you."

"Perhaps I should accompany them." John

70

suggested. "They may have a hard time getting into some of the things they want to see without a key."

"Well, ok. They could break the locks, but I guess that we should cooperate with the Air Force." Stanley pulled John back out of the car and accompanied the Colonel and the Air Force technician into the house. Another agent followed close behind.

Alex Goodrich pulled up in his truck just then and parked behind the Colonel's car. Now there was no way any of the FBI men could drive away without a lot of trouble.

"What's happening?" Alex asked some of the agents who were out doors.

"Who are you?" was the reply.

"Oh, I'm a friend and neighbor."

The agent moved up to Alex and took him by the arm. "Is your name Jack?" He got right up in Alex's face.

"No, it's Alex, and you can take your hands off me."

"You best get in your car and get out of here if you know what's good for you." One of the other agents came up out of the dark.

"I don't believe I saw your credentials," Alex said. "Would you mind showing me who you are and what kind of authority you have?"

The two agents looked around and found themselves alone. The other agents were spread out around the house. Some were laughing and joking, some were leaning against the house.

The one got in Alex's face again and the other grabbed both his arms from behind and bent him forward. Alex moved so swiftly that neither agent knew what hit him. Both doubled up without a sound. Then, Alex gave a low whistle. The other agents turned to face him. As they did this, several shapes came out of the darkness. There was one man for each agent and two more came up beside Alex.

"It looks like you did it again, Alex. You never wait till we catch up with you."

"Thank goodness you got here, Freeman. Where did you park?"

"Oh, just down the road out of sight like you said."

"You made a good approach and your timing was excellent. Let's see what we can do for the folks inside."

Freeman and Alex entered the house cautiously. Alex assumed the status of a nosey neighbor again and Freeman followed like a disinterested friend. The Colonel recognized Alex. That helped the scheme of things.

"I'm Alex Goodrich - one of the neighbors. Is there anything I can do to vouch for my friend, John Ferris?" Alex eased up beside Stanley and a little behind him while Freeman "accidentally" bumped into the other man knocking a heavy object from the agent's belt and onto the floor. The embarrassed man bent to pick up his gun. As he did so, Freeman bumped him again casually, knocking him sprawling on the floor.

"Oh, I'm sorry." Freeman announced and quickly retrieved the weapon before the agent could get to it. At the same time, Alex took Stanley by his free hand in a paralyzing grip.

"If you'll give me your key I'll get the two of you out of these cuffs."

"I don't understand, Alex." John was happily surprised to be freed. "How did you get involved in this?"

"Let's just say I'm an old friend who has been watching over you for a long time, John."

"My superiors will be very unhappy with you, Mr. Goodrich."

"You mean Comrade Castro's friends, Stanley?" Alex jammed the empty handcuffs into Stanley's pocket. "Maybe you better round up your make-believe FBI and move out quietly."

Stanley and his partner slipped out the back door

and soon one could hear them jockeying for road space out front.

Colonel Jones had observed quietly to this point and Tyler Houston had just come back into the room. "You mean these men weren't government agents?"

"Did you see their ID, Colonel? They were phony as can be," Alex said, turning to the Air Force officer.

"Come to think of it I didn't even see the Colonel's warrant," John added.

"I've heard you can get careless after retirement, John. You need to join our Missouri Clod Busters. We'll keep you on your toes."

Tyler waited patiently for Alex to finish and then tapped the Colonel on the shoulder. "I think we need look no further. Nothing in this house resembles our brass ball".

"Yes, I apologize for the inconvenience, Mr. Ferris." The Colonel shook John and Alex's hands and Tyler and the Colonel stepped out the door of the kitchen. The exodus of Stanley's 'FBI agents' had left plenty of room for Mr. Houston to turn the blue Air Force sedan around and to drive away.

John, Alex and Freeman followed the Colonel and his companion as far as the yard.

"How did you know what was happening?" John asked.

"Your son-in-law called when that imitation agent told him to come get your grandson."

"How did he happen to call you?"

"Oh, I gave him my number when he was here last year. He couldn't reach you so he called me. Of course, my boys have been watching your house more lately because of the crash."

"Your men? What've you got out here, a private army?" John asked, indicating the men who came with Alex.

"No, just a large association of retired peace

officers. Some of us are retired military. Freeman and I are Deputy Sheriffs." Alex patted his companion on the shoulder. "If we need to, we can deputize the rest of the association."

"I'm impressed. I thought you were just a local dirt farmer."

One of the men who had been watching the road approached with another man - one who had a grizzly beard.

"Alex, I can't make a thing out of what this fellow is telling me."

Alex stepped out into the darkness. "Jack, what brings you down here?"

Jack didn't say a word until he saw John. "Your grandson and that other boy disappeared right before my eyes!"

"You mean you were looking after them for me and they got away from you? I wasn't expecting you to watch them, Jack."

"No, I mean I was looking right at them and they were zapped by something and then I couldn't see them anymore." Jack was noticeably distressed.

"Where were you when this happened?" John was looking for a way to calm his friend. Jack didn't make any sense.

"We were down in my mine shaft with that ball of theirs."

"You mean there is a brass ball?"

"Yeah, the one the Air Force thinks caused the crash. That ball zapped them and left a big hole in the tunnel."

"That sounds like there was an explosion! Was it an explosion, Jack?"

"I don't know. Maybe you'd better see for yourself."

"Oh, no!" Now John was excited and began to

move in the direction of Jack's house.

"Maybe we better drive over there," Alex suggested.

Alex's truck had been driven up on the lawn. Jack, John and Alex got in.

"I'll round up the boys, Alex, and meet you over there," Freeman said.

Alex agreed and quickly drove the half mile or so between the two farm houses. Then Freeman went from one to the other of the Clod Busters as he found them surrounding the house. When all the Clod Busters had heard from Freeman, they started down the road too.

Ahead at Jack's place, the miner led his friend, John, and Alex into the old shed.

"You and Jack go down. I'll keep my men up here in case you need them," Alex said.

"You knew about my mine shaft all along," Jack said with surprise.

"Yes, Jack. My men and I know a lot about you. You're a real hero to us."

While Alex's men arrived and gathered around the shed a small fluffy animal scampered past them unnoticed, examined the view into the open trap door and leaped into the dark hole going from step to step until it reached the bottom.

Shortly after, Jack and John climbed down into the room beneath the shed. As they reached the landing, Jack looked into John's face. "Who are these people, John?"

"Young guys who took up the slack when we left the CIA, Jack. Alex says he's retired and has an association for retired police officers. They've been looking after us."

"What for; can't we take care of ourselves?"

"I guess not, Jack. A bunch of Castro's friends showed up tonight wanting to arrest me." John said absently as the two men descended into the darkness. Neither man noticed Tabitha perched on the edge of the lift as though she were going to a cat show at the County Fair.

Jack ran the hoist down as fast as he dared. "They don't have any authority over here."

"They pretended to be from the FBI."

"You fell for that?"

"Yes." John was anxious to get down to the bottom. "This sure is a deep cave."

"We'll be there directly."

Tabitha was the first one off when they reached the bottom. She set out on her own, exploring passages at random, unnoticed by Jack and John,

The two men were soon slipping behind the pillar and into the door to the laboratory. Jack had left the door open in his haste to get up the shaft. Inside they could hear the crackle of electrical sparks. John was deeply concerned as he looked at the 'hole' Jack had described. He now had a better appreciation for the seriousness of the situation.

"What happens if we step into this hole of yours?"

"I don't know, John."

Just then, Tabitha shot through the door of the laboratory. Something in the dark passages outside had given her the scare of her life. With a scream of terror, she whipped through the room and into the hole. Perhaps no one could have persuaded her to make that decision had she been her calm collected self, but something had driven her into an extreme state of frenzy - something in the dark passage.

"What was that?"

"It looked like Tabitha!" John said with apprehension. He looked at Jack for a long moment, waiting for added explanation to his question about the hole. What was beyond the dark hole? It was a mystery. What would happen to them if they stepped through the rift?

Jack didn't have the answer. Perhaps a more important question was: "What should they do?" Jack knew

John was worried about his grandson and now he must also be worried about the cat.

The way ahead was mysterious, but Jack was always fascinated by the unknown. He had nothing to lose. He had no family and few friends.

Jack knew what they had to do. He would do anything for John. "Let's go after the cat!" he said. Maybe they could find Jim and Jaydee and the cat at the end of that dark hole.

"Ok," John said and stepped into the hole. Within seconds, Jack followed.

Meanwhile, in the shadows of the mine outside the room, a dark hairy figure of a man searched for a way out. He was tall and appeared to be very old.

Up above, Alex assured himself that Stanley and his bunch had left the area and weren't stalking Jack and John. He took Freeman with him and climbed down into the room below the shed. They climbed down to the landing and found the second shaft. They pulled up the lift and let themselves down into the mine. From the lift they could hear the sparks down the long tunnel.

The door to the laboratory was still open so they were led by the sputtering sound coming from the hole in the room.

"This must be the hole that Jack described."

"No sign of Jack and John," Freeman ventured. "They must have gone into the hole."

"Freeman, you go up and tell the men to go home. I'm going to follow John and Jack into the hole."

"That looks pretty dangerous to me."

"I've seen worse. Don't worry about us. Everything will come out all right. Goodbye for now, my friend." Alex paused and examined the hole for a moment and then waved to Freeman as he stepped into the unknown.

After he disappeared, there was no reason for Freeman to stay. He hoisted himself to the top and then let the platform down again for Alex and the others to use later - he hoped that same night.

He was sure that the teenagers and the three men would return safely. He just had no idea when. Freeman left the trap door open as well as the door of the shed, thinking that this might make it easier for them to find their way.

The mysterious figure in the mine saw the platform descend. He had watched Freeman go up and he saw how to use the lift now. Slowly he brought the lift to the room above. He found his way into the shed and out into the moon light. Everything was quiet in the country side.

Part II - Kidnapped

Chapter 1 The City of Enoch

When the mysterious ball released its hold on Jaydee and Jim they found themselves sprawled on the floor looking up at two men dressed in white smocks. The men looked like doctors in a hospital. As the boys struggled to their feet the "doctors" helped them up and brushed them off.

"Welcome to the City of Enoch."

Recovering from his shock, Jim was the first to speak: "What happened?" he said.

Jaydee couldn't believe it. "Enoch! The City of Enoch? You can't be serious!

One of the "doctors", a very tall dark haired man, with a close cropped black beard, offered his hand to Jaydee. "I'm Dr. Zanhope and this is Dr. Canaan," he said, pointing to the other man. Dr. Canaan was much shorter, fat, and had grey hair and a mustache.

"You have made a splendid trip into your past. You really are in the City of Enoch nearly thirty-five hundred years before what you call common time." Dr. Canaan added with a big smile. "We have been observing you through the time probe for many days."

"You mean the mysterious ball?" Jim asked.

"Yes, young man, our time probe," said Canaan with obvious pride.

"That's too weird to be true!" Jaydee fairly bubbled. "Wait till Brother Sloan hears about this!"

"Not too soon, young man. We hope to show you around first and also show you off to our colleagues," Dr. Zanhope said releasing Jaydee's hand.

"Oh yes." Dr. Canaan smiled broadly.

Jaydee had no idea of returning very soon. He

wanted to see everything he could. Thinking of Jim's ambition, he asked: "Can we meet Enoch?"

The two doctors looked at each other for a moment. "I think that might be arranged," Dr. Canaan said.

"Oh, look, Jaydee." Jim pointed out the instruments on the tables, "This is the same laboratory as Jack has." Looking around, Jaydee had to admit, "It's the same!" There was one difference. Everything seemed new and shiny like the brass ball.

One by one the doctors explained the purpose and demonstrated the use of each apparatus. The machine that Jack had said was for cutting metal was really for implanting micro chips by laser in very delicate operations.

"Implanting in what?" Jaydee asked.

"We can implant different kinds of micro chips and processing devices in machines like our time probe or in plants or animals or even humans."

"Why would you do that with animals or humans?" Jaydee asked.

Dr. Zanhope smiled. "Mostly for tracking information,"

Jim was drawn to the meter on the wall with the bright red lights in different patterns. "What does that thing do?"

"That is our time and space clock, young man. It tallies the time and place where our time probe is traveling."

Behind Jaydee and Jim was a sparking hole. Neither of the boys turned to look where they had come from until now. On the table beside them, the mysterious ball sat quietly.

"Will this hole go away? Jim asked.

"We think so, but it will take time to heal."

Jaydee looked down the deep tunnel. "Heal?"

"Yes, we have ruptured time. It will take a while to come together again," said Dr. Zanhope.

It was Dr. Canaan's turn. "Speaking of healing, one of the first things we must do is see just how your bodies survived the trip. Would you mind coming into our examination room and we'll look you over?"

As the boys followed the doctors into the next room, technicians came in and began working over the tiny ball. Wires were attached to it and it was hooked up to other machines in the laboratory.

The technicians were concerned with the dark hole in the middle of the room. None of them would approach it and some seemed to be very agitated by its presence. They finished their work promptly and left the little ball to rest from its journey.

* * *

Jim and Jaydee passed their examination with ease. From there they were escorted around the building. It was late when they finished their tour.

"Why can't we understand the other people in your laboratory, doctor?" Jim asked as the two doctors and the two boys entered what looked like a waiting room. Here, the doctors removed their smocks.

"Let us show you to your quarters and we will explain further." Dr. Zanhope opened a side door and showed the boys into a spacious and comfortable living room. He also showed them a kitchen, a bedroom and a bathroom. The rooms weren't much different from their own homes. The table was set with fine china and was filled with foods of every kind.

"These will be your rooms while you visit us," said Dr. Zanhope.

"Through our study we have been able to learn your language," said Dr. Canaan motioning for the two teenagers to sit down. "I'm afraid it will be a long time before anyone else here can do that."

"Maybe we can learn your language." Jaydee stopped in front of the doctor and looked up at him with his hands on his hips.

Dr. Canaan rubbed his chin and looked down at the boy. He sat and Dr. Zanhope did also. The two boys followed their example. "That might take you many years. You see our language includes every language spoken in your time."

"You mean you can understand Chinese, Russian and Arabic also?" Jaydee leaned forward in his seat.

Dr. Zanhope was very willing to explain. "Yes, these are all branches of our language so to speak but of course they are purer in our day. In their purest forms these dialects and branches of our language are complicated to you."

"Aren't they complicated to everyone?" Jim was interested to know.

"No, we understand them because our brains are multi-tracking."

"You mean like a tape player?" Jaydee suggested.

"Yes, perhaps." The doctor was struggling to find an image that Jaydee would understand. "It means we are able to follow two or more interpretations at once."

"Does that mean like when they're translating talks from several different languages that you could understand them all without translation?"

"Yes, that is precisely it."

"Wow, I wish I could do that." Jaydee was excited.

"We have been thinking about your being able to understand us. Of course it wasn't a problem until our probe . . . er 'Lea', was sent into the future."

"You think you might be able to make us multi-tracked?" Jaydee asked.

"Perhaps. Your brain was once multi-tracking but shortly after your birth all other tracks were re-zoned to two tracks."

"Re-zoned! That sounds scary," Jim said.

"I'm sure this is too complicated for you to understand," Dr. Canaan said abruptly.

"It's very interesting even if we don't understand. What started you probing into the future in the first place?"

"What makes you study history?" Dr. Zanhope came back.

"Teachers and parents!" Jaydee growled.

"I like history!" Jim thundered.

"Well, some of us are just as interested in the future. We understand that great things will happen in your time. But we have explored many ages with our little friend. She has been to visit several great empires."

"I thought I heard you use a name for your time probe. Do you have a name for it?"

"As a matter of fact we do. We call her 'Lea'," Dr. Canaan said.

Dr. Zanhope continued. "Through our time probe we have visited Egypt in the time of the Pharaohs, Greece at the time of Socrates, Jerusalem at the time of Christ and just recently we probed Central America at the time of the early Mayans.

"What are you looking for?"

"We are trying to find a place to colonize and people we can convert to our way of life. When we do we will move the entire City of Enoch ahead in time."

This puzzled Jaydee. "Why would you do that?"

"To escape the flood."

"I see," Jim beamed. "By any chance are you thinking seriously of our time?"

"Why yes, we are."

Jaydee was worried that the doctors might not like what they found in the twentieth century. "How much information can you gather with your time probe?"

Dr. Canaan glowed with pride. "A surprising amount."

"Yes, we not only learn about languages, but cultural history and government," Dr. Zanhope explained. "We can observe dress, customs, and various procedures and even read the minds of the people. Our probe can, if we desire, attach itself to a person and do a direct transfer of information from the brain to its memory."

"Yeah, I guess that's what you did to me."

"Yes, you had an expression for it. I think you called 'Lea' a vampire. Later we even tapped your mother's computer and down loaded everything it had of value. The last two days we have been playing computer games. It has been quite an education."

"That is pretty sneaky, Dr. Zanhope. You know a lot about us, but we don't know anything about you."

"Well, we have just the cure for that. We have planned to show you around and introduce you to some of the marvels of our great city."

"It sounds like a lot of fun. When do we start?"

"I see no reason for us to delay, but it is late for you now and I suggest we start first thing in the morning."

"I would like that," Jim laughed.

"For now, eat your dinner and relax. We will see you after you've had a night's sleep."

The two doctors said good night and left Jaydee and Jim on their own.

"Wow, what an adventure," Jim said as he sat down at the table to eat. "I'm so excited, Jaydee. I'll get to meet Enoch!"

Jaydee joined him at the table. "Yeah. We'll have a lot to tell Brother Sloan. Won't he be surprised to know how advanced and professional these people are? They may even have space ships."

"It looks like they don't need a space ship to bring the City of Enoch to our time," Jim said.

"What do you mean?" Jaydee retorted.

"Well, right now they are planning to send the

people forward in time. You heard the doctors. They want to find a people who they can convert to their ways. That's got to be us!" Jim said excitedly.

"I never thought of that possibility." Jaydee was a little discouraged to think that they wouldn't use space ships. "Maybe they'll use both."

"Don't be silly. Why would they need both?" For once Jim felt he had scooped Jaydee.

Jaydee thought for a moment. "Doesn't it say something about them coming down? How can they come down if they haven't gone up?"

"Yeah." Jim was just a little deflated. "That could be just to throw us off. Maybe it's figurative."

* * *

Even as the boys spoke, John and Jack stepped through the rift in time and appeared in the laboratory of Doctors Canaan and Zanhope. They recognized the laboratory at once. The brass ball on the table indicated that Jaydee and Jim had been this way.

Jack surveyed the room. "The boys must be somewhere in the neighborhood."

"How much of a head start do you think they have on us?" John asked his partner.

"Not more'n an hour," Jack answered. That's my guess, reckonin' from the time they disappeared."

"It looks like we stepped from one side of this room to the other, but we've come through some sort of hole. What has really happened?"

"I don't know, John. It's all a muddle to me."

The two men looked around the room. There were papers on the laboratory tables that weren't there before they came through the hole.

"This writing has many familiar symbols," John said.

Jack picked up a paper and examined it closely. "It looks like different writin' all mixed up."

Although the two men were language experts and each could speak several languages, they had no clue at first as to the meaning of the papers.

"Maybe it's a code. You're good at that, Jack. What do you make of it?"

"These symbols look familiar. I can't . . . well I'll be, it makes sense, John. Look, here's a symbol for brass and here's a ball. These are notes on the brass ball. I'd stake my life on it."

"Can you make anything else out?"

"Well, it's not in code, John, so your guess is as good as mine."

The two grew silent. After examining the writing for a long while they both looked up. "These are notes on time travel," John ventured.

"Just what I was gonna say!" Jack countered.

"If I'm guessing correctly, Jack, we may be in another time period."

"Oh, nobody would believe a thing like that, John. We've just been tricked. This is all some kind of hoax."

"Could be, but it's very convincing."

"Maybe we should look around before we jump to conclusions, John."

The two were just about to leave the room when Alex stepped through the rift in time. "Where are we?" He was very confused.

"It looks like we've stepped into another time period."

"What makes you think so?" Alex asked.

"That's just what John thinks because these notes talk about the brass ball and time travel. That's why!" Jack steadied Alex as he staggered across the room.

"We had just decided to look around more when you showed up. Now that you are here, do you wanna come along?"

"No, if it's all the same to you, I think I need a rest."

"Suit yourself," Jack said guiding Alex to a chair beside the brass ball. As the two men left the room the sputtering from the hole slowed and the chasm began to grow smaller.

* * *

In another part of the same building, Jaydee and Jim had just finished their dinner and were about to begin their own exploration. They decided to start with their quarters.

The first thing they noticed was the absence of windows. Next they saw that there seemed to be nothing to entertain them. There was no radio, no television, no computers and no comic books.

Additionally, their dinner had given them a feeling of well being and seemed to have refreshed them. Their energy was boundless.

Jaydee tried the door, but it was locked. The teenagers looked at each other puzzled.

"Did we do something wrong?" Jaydee asked.

Jim had a similar thought. "Maybe they don't trust us?"

Jaydee banged on the door, but it sounded very solid. "I think they are just trying to keep us from getting out of here. I think we're like laboratory animals."

"That's not good. I thought we were guests." Jim went over and cleared the table for want of something better to do. It was a habit that he had learned at home. Perhaps he believed that some reward would follow.

"Jim, I feel trapped."

"Me too!"

They sat at the table looking back and forth at each

other for a few minutes. Suddenly, holographic images of dogs and cats chasing each other appeared right before their eyes. These computer created three dimensional images of domestic animals were followed by wild animals from the forest. Sometimes the animals were at a distance, but just as often they were right there on the table roaring at them. This was exciting.

Then followed scenes their parents would never have approved for them to see. Jim turned away and soon Jaydee did also. As soon as they did the images and their sounds disappeared.

Jaydee turned back and looked at Jim. "Did they expect us to watch that?"

"I don't think they have entertainment for children here."

"My dad wouldn't watch things like that." Jaydee heard himself say.

"Maybe we'd better try to sleep, Jaydee."

"Yeah, that looks like the only thing left to do." The two boys wandered into the bedroom and sat on the two beds.

"Do you think we ought to have a prayer, Jaydee?"

Jaydee agreed, and they knelt beside their beds. Jim prayed that they wouldn't be afraid, that he would really get to meet Enoch and that they would be allowed to return home.

As the boys climbed into bed, the lights dimmed automatically as though someone was controlling them.

"Do you think we are prisoners, Jaydee?"

"I guess," came Jaydee's reply. Outside they could hear the sound of thunder.

There was silence for a few minutes. Then, out of the darkness, Jaydee could hear Jim crying softly.

"Don't cry, Jim. We'll get out of this somehow." Jaydee's pillow grew a little wet but he refused to cry out loud. "I have to be a brave boy scout," he thought.

* * *

The quarters that Jaydee and Jim shared were not accessible to John and Uncle Jack. By now, they had gone through the entire laboratory and its adjacent rooms. It was all empty, yet well lit. There were three doors that were closed and locked, but no boys.

Jack recognized the door that led out of the laboratory. It was the same door through which he had first entered from the mine.

There was one difference. Now, it could only be opened from the inside. Once they stepped outside, there would be no way back unless they propped the door open or someone stayed behind to open it for them.

To determine this for sure, Jack had gone out into the vestibule for a moment and tried the door, but John had to open it for him. In spite of this, Jack and John decided to leave the building to explore beyond the door and see if the boys had gone back the way they had come.

Alex opted to stay in the laboratory in case the kids showed up or John and Jack had to get back in.

"I'm too tired to be roaming around." Alex said. He didn't know how safe he would be, but thought he might duck back into the rift in the laboratory or still leave by the door if necessary.

After his two friends had left, Alex strolled back into the laboratory to examine the rift and to look at the brass ball. The rift had closed up.

Beside the brass ball was an instrument that looked like a TV wand. He picked it up and examined the buttons on it. One had an arrow that pointed up and one left and one right.

In addition, there was a button that had a fuzzy circle around it. He guessed that this was the control for time travel if that really was the use of the little ball.

89

A dial on the side was set on a symbol that he recognized as 600. A second dial was set at figures that he guessed were 49. If this was the case, they might be in the 649th year of the world's history.

He wished he could remember what happened at that time. He guessed it was recorded in the Bible. If they had really traveled back in time, he'd like to see how things compared with the Scriptures.

Alex decided there was nothing to worry about for the rest of the evening, so he wandered into the examining room, climbed up on one of the tables and slept fitfully.

He dreamed a beautiful girl was touching his face. Somewhere in the night, Tabitha had jumped up on the table and amused herself by gently tapping his face as he snored.

Later, Alex dreamed several times that he had fallen off a cliff. Early in the morning he awoke perspiring, climbed off the table and managed to go to sleep soundly on the floor. At this point Tabitha abandoned him to his own devices.

* * *

Meanwhile, Jack and John settled on obtaining food and as much information as they could in the surrounding neighborhood. As they emerged from the building, they saw immediately that they were not in the tunnel. It was dark yet they could see that they were in a very modern city. The ground was wet. It had been raining.

The air was clear and crisp compared to all the big cities they had visited in their careers. It was cleaner even than the countryside where they lived.

John took a deep breath. The air was invigorating. He felt ten or twenty years younger. Maybe he could leap over a tall building like Superman. Jack spoke of similar feelings.

Where the buildings were tallest they could see a lot of light. There were what looked like elevated walkways and small vessels that darted in and out of the buildings.

All of this greatly surprised them. They had thought they were deep within the earth and expected at least tunnels and a lift of some kind to take them to the surface.

"That's spooky, John," Jack said, looking around. "I thought we were under ground."

"We should be," said John. We came down on your lift. I think we must have come back in time lots of years to have ended up at ground level." They were on a hill overlooking a great valley full of flat topped houses of an unusual design.

"Maybe you're right about the time travel."

John began walking rather carelessly down the middle of the street gawking at the houses. "Look at these buildings?"

Suddenly, a shadowy figure sprang out of the dark at John. John instinctively took a defensive position.

Jack fell in behind him. "There's two of 'em," Jack yelled.

Instantly their attackers were upon them. Both assailants were dressed in black sweats. Their faces were partially covered with a black scarf and both had a big knife.

As the first plunged forward, John side stepped, directing the force of the man's charge around him. Jack tripped the assassin and he went sprawling on the ground. The second man fell in the same place and it looked like one ended up on the other's knife. Only the first got up and he ran away.

"Look at this pig sticker, John!" Jack had picked up the knife of the attacker. It was very wicked looking and had the head of a dragon on it.

"That thing was made to kill people," John said,

taking it from Jack, examining it and handing it back. "We'd better be more careful and keep to the shadows."

"Maybe it would help if we looked like them," Jack added, holding up the black scarf he had taken from the dead man.

"You can put that on if you like, but I'd just as soon look respectable."

Jack dressed himself in the outfit of the assassin and the two slipped on down the street to a building that looked like it might be a store. It was lit up and people were inside laughing and talking.

John was the first to approach the building. As he came into the light, people broke their tight circle and let him enter. They weren't disturbed by his manner of dress. His simple farmer's attire was similar to theirs. In contrast, when Jack followed, they sprang back. Two of them quickly disappeared and the rest stood their distance.

The proprietor spoke to Jack. His words seemed a mixture of four different languages. His meaning was clear.

"No trouble please. What do you want?"

Jack assumed a harsh manner, picked the best words in the four languages he had identified and said: "I want something to eat!"

The man understood perfectly. He brought out bread, meat and something to drink.

"What is this?" Jack demanded, pointing to the drink.

"Our best wine," said the proprietor.

"Give me good plain water!" Jack said gruffly.

It was clear that black robed men were to be feared as Jack was immediately furnished with the water. The proprietor then turned to John. Politely, he asked, "Is there something I can do for you?"

John assumed the same polite manner, but in somewhat the same mixture of languages asked for the same food.

"Why do you offend me by asking for the same as this assassin?" he whispered, drawing John aside.

Noting the slight, Jack glared at the proprietor. There was silence. Another customer slipped away.

John took advantage of the proprietor's concern to question: "I am fine - but where is this place?"

"You are in the City of Enoch, Friend. How is it you come here not knowing where you are?"

"This assassin took me from my country and brought me here in the dark."

"I see. Then you are his prisoner?"

"No, I have just this hour convinced him that I am not the man he wants."

"That is good. God is with you."

John leaned forward and asked, "Can you tell me of some place I can stay tonight?"

The proprietor scanned Jack and took a writing stick of some kind and drew a hasty map on the counter. "You are here. Be sure that the assassin does not follow you. Go to the door here," he said indicating a building he had drawn on his crude map, "and say that Shuwa has sent you. These are good people. The father's name is Greuban. They won't ask anything in return and I won't either. They will keep you tonight."

John thanked him, ate his food and left in silence. Shortly Jack caught up. The black robes were soon discarded and the two found themselves in front of the door of Greuban's house.

"Shuwa has sent us, John said. We need a place to stay."

"You speak strangely, but we know Shuwa. Come in."

Apparently, Shuwa was well known and respected, for their landlord treated them with kindness.

"What country is this?" Jack asked as they were escorted to a room.

"Everyone knows this is the Land of the Exile."
Greuban said. "How is it you don't know?"

"We were taken from our country and moved at
night. We are confused. We have also suffered much
torture. We have lost track of time. Can you tell us what
year this is?"

John heard children's laughter from the room next
to them. Noting John's surprise, Greuban excused himself
and left John and Jack standing in the hall for a moment.
John thought he heard Greuban say something about
keeping the children hidden and not to let them laugh
anymore.

Returning, Greuban apologized. "My wife thought
it funny that you had lost track of time." Shifting their
attention he unlocked a room a little farther down the hall.
"This room will be quieter and more comfortable."

"How sad to have been so mistreated," he
continued as though nothing had happened. "Many tragic
tales have come to us of late. I am truly sorry for you.
Verily it is the year 649 of the Ancient One."

"I see. Then, we haven't lost many years."

"That is good." Greuban showed them a bathroom
nearby not unlike a modern convenience. "Sleep well. I
shall have something for you to eat in the morning."

John and Jack talked long into the night.

"What's this 'year of the Ancient One,' John?"

"I think it refers to the ancient of days mentioned in
Daniel. Some say it means Adam.

"Then the year 649 of the Ancient One could mean
the 649th year of Adam's life?"

"That is what I think."

"That's impossible - back to the year 649? How did
we get here?"

Jack continued to think of more and more questions
that John couldn't answer. What had caused John's
grandson and his friend to travel through time? How would

94

they find the two teenagers? How would they return to their own time? What if they were killed by assassins? Finally, they slept.

The lights of the great City of Enoch had twinkled out all over the valley. The sky was beginning to streak with a faint glow.

In his dream, a dark figure stood over John. The figure held a long, wicked knife. John suddenly came awake to find that someone was standing over him.

"Who is there?"

"It is I, Greuban!" came a reply. "You must leave at once."

John's feet were on the floor. He sensed a great danger. "What is it?"

"The assassins are upon us. They have tortured and killed our friend, Shuwa. A family member just warned us. The assassins know where you are. I and my family must flee for our lives."

With that he disappeared. John shook Jack awake and the two were soon dressed and slipped from the room into the dawn. It was cold on the street. It would be colder still if they met the assassins. They hid in a byway. It was none too soon. Over the roof tops they saw shadows moving toward the home of Greuban. There were three, maybe four of them.

The dark specters slipped over the edge of the roof and down into the doorway. They disappeared into the house.

Doors slammed and glass broke. There were harsh words shouted and spoken and then the figures reappeared in the door. They deftly swung up to the rooftops again and disappeared.

John and Jack shivered from their hiding place and joined a throng of men who were headed down the avenue in the first light of day.

In the dawn's light they could see the mountains

that surrounded the valley clearly in the distance. The mountains sloped up in the west to some tall peaks. On the east were only gentle hills.

From their vantage point, John and Jack could see the high outer walls of the City. Mounds or mountains of uniform dimensions were evenly spaced around the perimeter wall. These were obviously man-made. They were shaped like pyramids, but were so covered with trees that it was hard to tell this at first.

Below them, in the City's center, was a mountainous area surrounded by tall buildings and elevated walkways. The avenue they were following ran straight toward this part of the City.

Chapter 2 The Song of Rachel

The outside door to the laboratory opened and closed. A girl dressed in a white smock entered the examining room and approached Alex as he lay sleeping on the floor.

The girl was tall and slender. Her dark hair was done up in a braided knot with a few strands hanging loose here and there. Her eyes were large and blue. Her features were delicate. Her skin was pale. She looked to be about thirty.

In spite of many years of training, Alex didn't stir. He was sleeping soundly.

The girl knelt and touched his face to assure herself that he was living. Only a snort of breath issued from the quiet sleeper. She quickly withdrew her hand. The man's face was cold. As she looked more closely, she noticed that his flesh was very wet. The man began to shake slightly.

She rose and sang quietly, trying to calm herself. Her song was a manifestation of her sweet and loving personality. As she sang, she went over lists of instructions. Her song was short. She bowed her head in prayer. Her lips moved but her voice was silent.

Looking up, she scanned the room. She opened a closet and took from it a covering of heavy white material and laid it over Alex. She took a pillow from the closet and propped his feet up.

At that moment, Dr. Zanhope came in. "Good morning, Rachel," he said.

"Good morning, Father," she said with concern. "This man is terribly sick."

Noticing the stranger for the first time, the doctor knelt down beside Alex. "Where did he come from?" he asked.

"Isn't he one of the time travelers?" Rachel suggested.

"There were only two young men yesterday when I left," he said, examining Alex carefully. He noted the gasping breath and the cold clammy skin. He looked into his eyes and listened to his heart.

"He is in shock!"

"What can we do?" The girl was rubbing Alex's hands.

"Get me a flask of Tocolaine!"

Rachel measured out a very small quantity of a liquid into a tiny vial from a bottle in a cabinet nearby. She handed it to Dr. Zanhope. He gently tipped Alex's head to one side and poured the Tocolaine into his ear. The breathing changed markedly. Alex opened his eyes and looked into the faces of the two medics. They were blurry.

"What's happened?" Alex was frightened by what he saw. His mind was full of shadows. It seemed to him that he was paralyzed.

"You have come through a rift in time just before it closed. You have what I call 'time phase anemia'." Dr. Zanhope spoke calmly.

"I am Rachel and this is my father, Dr. Zanhope," the girl continued, indicating the doctor. "He will help you if anyone can."

"Give me a hand, Rachel!" The doctor spoke as he prepared to lift the patient onto the examining table. Alex didn't understand, but was powerless to interfere. That "if anyone can" settled in his mind, causing fear.

"Why is it that sometimes I cannot understand you?" Alex asked weakly.

"You have come into a time when all languages are one," said the doctor.

"You can only understand when we confine our speech to the words you know," Rachel added.

"But, where am I?" Alex's tongue grew heavy in his mouth and the room became blurry.

Dr. Zanhope pulled back Alex's eyelids and looked

at his pupils. "He's unconscious again!" Listening to his chest again, he said: "He's no longer in shock; he is breathing more normally."

"But he isn't normal!" Rachel retorted. "He may die. You yourself have said that time phase anemia can be fatal."

The doctor dropped his hands to his sides and regarded his daughter with patient steady calm. "You are right, Rachel. He's in a serious condition. Do you have a suggestion?"

"No, I don't. I'm sorry. All this experimenting . . ." She broke off, realizing that it was a useless argument they had addressed many times before.

"I see. It is the experiments." The doctor turned to the time traveler again. He motioned for Rachel to bring up an apparatus in the corner, which she quickly wheeled over to the table.

"It's more than that." She stripped away the man's shirt and attached straps and wires to Alex's body. "This whole idea Enoch has to rescue his people from the flood to come is insane. He's tampering with God's plan for man. He's an evil old man!"

"Hush, daughter. Do you know what you say?" Dr. Zanhope set the apparatus in motion and began to monitor Alex's vital signs. "He's our patriarch. He's the leader of our people."

"Not our people!" Rachel brought her father a set of instruments on a small tray.

"We have made them our people and it is enough." There was a final tone in Zanhope's voice.

The lights on the console of the apparatus began to blink bright orange. Rachel became more agitated, but she was afraid to speak her feelings.

"Quick! More Tocolaine!" the doctor shouted.

The girl rushed to the cabinet looking back at her father. "How much?"

"A dram, a dram. Quickly! We could lose him."

As Rachel returned with the Tocolaine she noticed that Alex's body began to twitch. "Here!" She put her hand to her mouth to stop a scream. Just then Tabitha brushed her dress. The girl looked down, picked her up, and began to stroke her lovely silken hair. Dr. Zanhope had not noticed, but Rachel became very calm.

"There!" Almost instantly Alex's body relaxed as the doctor poured the precious liquid into his ear.

The two medics stood back observing their patient. "He's a strong man," said Dr. Zanhope.

"He's so handsome," Rachel added.

For the first time the doctor knew the reason for his daughter's devotion to the patient.

"Oh, my daughter. You cannot become attached to this man. He may die and you know nothing about him."

"He came bravely after the two boys."

"We don't know that. Besides, how can that possibly determine his character?" The doctor motioned to remove the straps and wires.

"He was calm when he woke up." Rachel dropped Tabitha and removed the attachments as she looked up at her father.

"So was your brother and he was a bully." Looking at Rachel for the first time in several minutes, Dr. Zanhope noticed the cat out of the corner of his eye.

"Was that a cat?"

"Yes, Father. It's the strangest thing. She came in just as I gave you the Tocolaine."

"How is it possible? All of the cats for miles around were sacrificed years ago. How did you come by her?"

"I don't know where she came from. Is it possible that she came from the future?"

"You mean you've never seen her before?"

"No."

100

"We should do everything we can to protect her."

"I will make her my personal project, Father."

"Good."

The two worked silently over the man for several minutes. Finally the doctor looked up. "There's nothing else I can do. He needs rest. If we are fortunate, you and I, his body will mend by itself."

The girl looked earnestly and pleadingly into her father's eyes. "We must hide him from our coworkers. They mustn't learn that anyone else has come through the time rift."

"For once you are right. Where do you suggest we put him?"

"We can put him in the guest room with the boys."

"With the boys! How will they react? What will we tell them?"

"The truth."

"It is well." The doctor motioned for the girl to lead out rolling the table into the boy's room. They moved silently through the waiting room and down the hall.

Rachel took a metal object from her pocket and touched the door with it. The door opened. Tabitha, who had been walking discreetly a few paces behind them and who had sniffed at the door while Rachel was getting ready to open it, dashed in.

At the same time, two very wild teenage boys sprang out the door and ran into the girl and the man behind her. When they saw the body on the table between their visitors they came to a halt.

"It's Alex," Jim shouted.

Jaydee peered down at the table. "What happened to him?"

"He came through the rift just before it closed," said Dr. Zanhope. "He is seriously ill. He has time-phase anemia."

"What is that?" Jaydee became quietly serious.

"It means that some of his blood cells are missing - enough so that he is very weak."

"We have done everything possible to help him," Rachel added. "All we can do now is let him rest."

"Who are you?" Jaydee was surprised Rachel spoke so they could understand.

"This is my daughter, Rachel. Can we bring him in here with you now?"

"Yes, of course, doctor but don't you have a hospital?" Jaydee asked.

The doctor pushed the table on into the room. "We do but we are the only ones that would understand this disease."

"That's right," Jim chimed in. "No one else would be doing time travel."

"Did you give him a blood transfusion?" Jaydee ran his hand down Alex's arm and then touched his face.

"Blood transfusion?" The doctor was thoughtful. "Oh, yes. That is something you do for your people when they have lost a lot of blood."

"Maybe it would help," Rachel suggested.

"Perhaps it would." Dr. Zanhope puzzled over the idea for a bit. His thoughts were interrupted by a sound outside.

They could hear someone enter the main door to the laboratory and Rachel motioned all into the apartment. She shut the door behind them.

"Quickly! Somebody has come in the front door. They mustn't know that your friend is here."

Dr. Zanhope suggested that they go down the hall and into the bedroom. As they did so there was a click at the apartment door and it opened.

"Good morning boys!" They could hear the voice of Dr. Canaan in the living room.

Dr. Zanhope and the girl pushed Jim and Jaydee back out into the hall and pulled the table with Alex on it behind the door of the bedroom. The boys continued down the hall. There was no time to explain further.

Tabitha had followed them all into the bedroom and would have followed Jaydee and Jim into the hall, but Rachel caught her and carried her back into the bedroom. She silenced Tabitha by cuddling her and petting her under the chin.

Dr. Zanhope cowered in the bedroom. He did not trust his associate, Dr. Canaan. For years he had lived in secret fear of him, ever since his wife was betrayed as a True Follower. From that time on Zanhope had begun to reexamine his beliefs. The guilt he felt over the death of his wife at the hands of his comrades haunted him day and night.

Apparently, Canaan did not suspect what was going on in the bedroom when the boys emerged from the hall. "We were in the bedroom," Jaydee confessed."

"Good, I hope you slept well. We will bring you some breakfast as soon as it is ready."

"Why were we locked up like laboratory rats?" Jaydee asked.

The doctor tried to look puzzled. "I didn't know. Perhaps Dr. Zanhope didn't want you wandering around the laboratory or out into the street. I should have explained that there are evil men in the streets at night. We take this for granted in the City."

"Oh, that's all right," Jim chirped.

"But if this is the City of Enoch, the streets should be safe!" Jaydee charged.

"Little by little, my boy. People do not change overnight. That will come with time." Dr. Canaan was friendly in his manner. "I will be back in a few minutes with your schedule for the day." The doctor left and the boys dashed into the bedroom to see what they could do to make Alex comfortable.

As they entered the room, they noticed Tabitha for

the first time. Jim was dumbfounded. "Where did she come from?"

"Is she your cat?" Rachel asked.

"She belongs to my grandfather. Her name is Tabitha," Jaydee said.

"My father has asked me to be her protector while she is with us, but no one must know she is here. Understood?"

Dr. Zanhope was impatient and broke in with many questions. "How do you give someone a blood transfusion? Does it matter if their blood is different?" Jaydee and Jim tried to answer his questions one by one.

Rachel left and came back with tubes and needles and a small microscope as well as other fixtures. Her father stopped her with this question as she returned: "Did Dr. Canaan see you?"

"Yes," she said. "But I just told him we were working on a project in the other wing."

"Good girl! No need to involve him." The doctor began to examine the equipment his daughter had brought. "Cutters, we need cutters."

Rachel drew an object from her pocket that resembled a pair of scissors and handed them calmly to her father. After a few tests, they determined that Alex and Rachel had the same blood type and that she would be the donor. She and her father laid Alex on one of the beds and she climbed onto the table.

"Aren't you scared?" Jim asked.

"A little."

"You sure are brave, Rachel," Jaydee said.

Dr. Zanhope asked Jim to keep a look out to see when Dr. Canaan came back.

"Why do we have to keep Mr. Goodrich a secret? This would all go better if we had some help, wouldn't it?" Jaydee looked first at the doctor and then at his daughter.

"I can't spell it out for you now, young man.

Perhaps I should say that we must be very careful that we don't embarrass our leaders." The doctor completed his work and stood watching the first blood trickle down the tube and into Alex's arm.

Rachel held Tabitha close and looked down at her arm as the blood pulsed down the tube and added: "Many people are anxious concerning our project. Some are jealous"

Just then they heard the outer door open again. Jaydee and Jim emerged from the bedroom in time to see a young man in a smock roll in a tray of fancy foods for their breakfast. The two teenagers sat down at the table and had a prayer and then ate the breakfast. Once the waiter had left, they joked back and forth with Rachel in the bedroom about the great breakfast they were having.

"Save something sweet and yummy for Tabitha and me," Rachel quipped.

They were nearly finished when Dr. Canaan returned and announced the schedule for the day. They would see the City, attend a banquet with the ten kings of the City and end up at the palace. Dr. Canaan hoped to arrange an interview with Enoch. The boys were delighted.

After they departed with Dr. Canaan, Dr. Zanhope wandered out into the living room and pressed a metal object to the door to establish a security lock. Then he examined what was left of breakfast to see what was there. The boys had eaten well, but there was enough left for many more young men their size.

"Father, Father!"

"What is it, my daughter?" Dr. Zanhope rushed into the bedroom. Alex had come to and was trying to raise up.

"Lay back, my friend. You are much too sick to get up."

"What are you doing to me?" Alex pointed to the somewhat unorthodox equipment.

"We are giving you a blood transfusion." As Dr.

105

Zanhope spoke Alex looked up at the girl. The girl looked like an angel.

"Who is she?" Alex had forgotten the introduction earlier.

"This is my daughter," Dr. Zanhope explained.

"How long have I been out?" Alex asked.

"Perhaps thirty of your minutes," the girl said softly.

"You said I had anemia of some kind by coming through the rift?"

"Yes. You are concerned about that?" Dr. Zanhope asked.

"My friends came just before me. Could they be suffering from the same sickness?"

"You must mean the two young men? They are fine. I examined them myself."

"No, you don't understand. There were two men who came through just ahead of me."

"Where are they?" Rachel asked weakly.

"They went out through the main door to look for the boys."

"Then they are out in the City!" The doctor was frantic. "Without an escort they will be in grave danger!"

Chapter 3 The True Followers

John and Uncle Jack had followed the crowd of "workers" for some time. Looking back at the end of the avenue from which they had come they could now recognize a large stepped pyramid.

On every level around it were flowers and trees. The high city wall was attached to it and ran from the pyramid for as far as they could see. They supposed it connected to the next pyramid they saw along the city wall.

They came to another high wall. In it was an immense gate. Each person was inspected as he passed through the gate. The guard stopped Jack for a minute and then let him go on.

They had just passed through the gate when it was swung open wide. Those in the middle of the road were pushed roughly to the sides.

An army of black cloaked soldiers marched through the gate . They had baggy black trousers and red turbans, spears and bright blue shields. Behind them followed many men and women chained together and prodded on by more black cloaked soldiers.

"What's this?" Jack asked without thinking.

"You must be a visitor here not to know," a man next to him volunteered.

"We are." John joined in hoping to gain some knowledge from the man.

"Our soldiers round up these fanatics every day or so. They call themselves 'True Followers'. They trouble the people constantly." The man continued as the soldiers passed and they were allowed to fill the road again.

"What happens to them?"

"They used to just put them out of the City, but now that there have been many attempts on the lives of the Kings, they must put them to death."

"That seems drastic!"

"It's not. We must protect our citizens."

Jack and John's attention was drawn to their surroundings as the man spoke. The wall they had just passed marked the beginning of a wide agricultural band in the City. Below the avenue on the right and left were fields of corn. "Your city is self contained." John indicated the fields on either side.

"Oh, the farms? Yes. The City is made up of mile wide circular bands. Every other band is dedicated to farm land. Nevertheless, we are not self contained. Here, we grow no staples other than corn. Wheat rice and dairy are brought from the surrounding farms."

"There are farms outside the City too?"

"Yes, but it is very dangerous to live outside. There are armies of ruffians who burn and pillage."

"You mentioned kings. Is your city so large that it needs several kings to govern it?"

"Yes, our city is the largest in the world, but the Kings are only figure heads. There are ten kings and twelve judges. The judges hold the real power."

"Are you going to some kind of work?" Jack asked.

"Yes, I am a clerk for one of the judges. I work in the city center. I have gotten my exercise for the day. I will take the sub level the rest of the way."

"What is the sub level?" John asked as they began to descend a stairway.

"You are on your way now. Come and see."

They had that minute descended a stairway and entered a "tube train" as Jack called it later. No fee was charged and no one seemed to operate the monster. After the passengers had entered, the doors closed automatically and the "tube" went on. It moved very fast until it came to another stop, loaded, closed and continued on its way until it came to a huge cavern, where everyone disembarked.

"Well, what do you think?" the stranger asked.

"That was the most interesting ride I've ever had."

John looked the coach over one more time and started walking along in the direction of the rest of the crowd, hoping to appear a part of it.

Jack was reluctant to go on. He examined the "tube" some more and had this to say: "Well, that beats all the extra crewmen on the railroads back home."

Their friend bid them a good day and entered a door which was carved into a supporting wall. Several others joined him. Another man who had been walking along with Jack and John and listening to their questions took up where the law clerk had left off.

"We have just entered the city center or the Old City. Would you like me to explain the things you see as we continue?"

"Please do."

"This part of the City is built into the island from which the original City sprang. Here are the office buildings and palaces that make up the civic center. We are beneath them right now."

The sound of rushing waters came from the direction in which the rest of the crowd was moving. As they came closer they could see what looked like a waterfall cascading down the wall of the cavern in the distance.

"This is jim dandy," John said, "but what do you do with all this water running under the City?"

"This is where the electricity for the City is generated. The water turns large turbines." Jack and John could now see the first generator. Beyond this was another turbine and another as far as the eye could see.

A wet spray like fog was in the air. It was hard to see their 'guide' in the mist.

"From here the water is pumped throughout the City for irrigation and home use. What is left is pumped into the peripheral canal."

"Peripheral canal?" Jack asked.

"Yes, there is a canal that runs all around the City."

While Jack was surprised at the canal, John was surprised to see many beggars sitting in the shelter of the tunnel along the way. "Are there many like these?"

"Yes, but they will never starve. The City provides a bowl of rice for each one each day."

"A bowl of rice?"

"Yes, just one bowl. It is sufficient to keep them alive. If they want more they can beg for it."

"I must leave you now. If you continue on with the crowd, you will come to lifting platforms which will take you up to the surface. Have a good time in the City." With that, the man disappeared into a dark tunnel.

Jack and John walked on as more and more people left the main thoroughfare. Out of the mist a little old man with a white beard and white hair met them. He took John by the arm as though to steady himself and then followed along beside him still clinging to his arm.

"I am Mahai. You are being watched," he said. "When you come to an archway, turn to your left. Do just as I say and you will be safe."

At first John thought that the man was crazy, but as he gazed into his eyes he could see a very rational and serious look. The old man released John and continued a little ahead.

John nudged Jack to attract his attention. "He says to stay with him."

Jack was skeptical. "Where are we going?"

"I don't know." The look in John's eye warned Jack to humor the man.

They came to the Alex and turned left. Here the cavern became narrower. They had passed all the turbines, but the air was still damp and the walls were green with moss. Mahai continued ahead and slipped through a passage which appeared out of nowhere.

"Another rift?" John laughed.

"Who knows?" Jack responded good naturedly.

After going for some time in the passage they came into a larger place. Here the old man motioned for them to wait. Shortly another man - a very young man - came out of the dark and touched them both on the shoulder.

"I am Daniel." Daniel was slender and tall. He had no beard and his hair was close cropped and dark. John noticed his unusually long fingers.

"Your lives are in danger. We have brought you here to save you from certain death. The assassins are everywhere. If you don't hide, you will be dead before the day ends."

"How do we know that you're our friends?" Jack asked.

"We have watched you since you entered the City from the laboratory of Dr. Canaan."

Two other men joined them in the cavern. In the dark John recognized their landlord of the night before and a man who might have been his son. The two men smiled.

"These are Greuban and Hawthorn. I trust you remember them as friends."

"We had to take refuge here with our families," Greuban said. "We are happy to see you are safe too."

"You seek two boys. Isn't that so?" Daniel asked.

John was puzzled. "Yes, of course, but how does that make you our friends and how did you know?"

"For the time being try to believe us. The boys are safe. They are seeing the City and will most likely end up in the audience chamber of Enoch. We will show you that chamber when the boys are there."

"Meanwhile, we will show you the City center from a secret place. Follow me." Greuban and Hawthorn disappeared into another chamber and Daniel led Jack and John up a dark stairway.

Their eyes were becoming accustomed to the dark, but as John turned to follow the young man, he stumbled on the stairway. It was treacherously steep and there didn't seem to be any but natural hand holds or railings.

As they ascended, the way got drier so they didn't slip so much. They climbed endlessly, leaning on the wall when they could and taking care not to fall where there were no walls.

Ahead they could see light. They emerged in a garden with rocks and grass and large trees. Suddenly, from out of nowhere, they saw a huge black bear barring their way. They were astonished!

"Don't be frightened. We are the bear's caretakers. He won't harm you."

Mahai, the white haired man, had followed them. He gave John and Jack each a strange pot to carry and instruments like a small trowel and a hand rake. "We are employed as gardeners and zoo keepers. These will make you appear as one of us. We will be able to go where we want and not be noticed."

Daniel tapped a metal card on the barred enclosure and a gate opened for them to go out. Here the garden continued, but they found themselves walking among people who were watching the bear and other animals in caged enclosures like the one they had just left. Among the animals they were surprised to see saber toothed tigers, mastodons and real dinosaurs.

"The City of Enoch was originally founded on a large island in the middle of a lake," the old man began. He led them to the edge of the plaza and pointed out across the City. "This was once the edge of the island and the City."

"What became of the lake?" Jack asked.

"It was drained," responded the younger man as he dropped to his knees and pulled a few weeds from the flowers that lined the path.

"While the City was confined to the island it was pretty safe from the warring bands of Genun," the old man continued, "but as it began to expand, walls were built to

112

enclose the lake and a perfectly circular canal was dug around the wall to divert the river. This carried the water from the river Dabadan, which used to empty into the lake, to the river, Oban, which ran out of the lake on the other side."

"This project was one of many which was started by the Watchers," Daniel added as he drifted off down the path. "They have made a lot of changes in our city."

"Who are the Watchers?" John asked.

Mahai pointed off in the distance to a high mountain with twin peaks so clouded over that it could barely be seen. "They came from the holy mountain. They were once True Followers.

"True Followers - aren't they a bunch of fanatics that are trying to kill your kings?" Jack asked.

"That's a lie trumped up by the Watchers to make it seem all right when they kill the True Followers," Daniel said.

John scratched his chin pensively. "I see. How did the Watchers come to have such influence here?"

"The Watchers came flying down the mountain in their gliders. The people thought they were gods or at least angels."

The time travelers and their hosts were now approaching a large stately building. The old man pulled aside some low hanging branches so the three could follow Daniel on an obscure maintenance path.

"The people were superstitious," the young man went on, as they caught up to him on the path. "They believed in witchcraft and black arts."

"Yes, my son is quite right." This was the first time that any relationship was mentioned between the two strangers. "Because of their superstitions, the people readily believed all that these men told them."

"What did the Watchers tell them?" John asked.

"At first they taught them many good things about

God, the purpose of life and the promised Messiah. They taught the people how to improve their fortifications, make armor and swords. They revealed the secrets of the stars, higher math, and how to grow better crops. Finally, they showed them how to generate electricity and what to do to improve their health, but then the power they had over the people began to corrupt their minds."

"About this time they conspired with Enoch." The youth knelt again, took up a few weeds and placed them in the pots John and Jack were carrying.

"Conspired? I don't understand," John said. "Our impression of Enoch was that he was so righteous that he walked and talked with God,"

"Oh my young friend, it isn't so." The old man paused, taking John by the arm and looking up into his eyes. "There is a prophecy of an Enoch to come who will lead this people back to God, but this is not the one."

"You don't believe that the ruler of this City is the one?"

"No, this Enoch is a worldly man, full of schemes and desires for power and riches. He pretends to be good, but has an evil black heart. He has corrupted the Watchers beyond your wildest dreams. He has made almost all of their leader's kings over the people and has given them many wives and concubines."

Mahai noticed John was distracted by a ornate building just before them. "You see this great building beside us?"

"Yes, I was about to ask what it was," Jack said, craning his neck to catch a view of its heights.

"This is the palace of Enoch. While he lives in comfort supported by his high taxes, most of his people go hungry." Mahai knelt beside the building and spat upon it.

"They seem prosperous enough," John said, indicating the bands of agriculture that circled the valley below.

"All of this belongs to the Kings and their friends. Those who won't accept them and the ways of Enoch are left to their own devices." The young man motioned for them to follow him as he climbed down around the foundation of the palace.

From the path below they had a marvelous view of the City. Alternate bands of farmland and houses circled around the City's "island" center. Wide avenues radiated from this point to its gates and bridges in the distance.

Downhill from them horses and their riders were racing along an open track that must have run clear around the island. Crowds of people sat on bleachers on the edge of the hill, cheering them on. The track was bridged by the tube trains and the avenues that ran above the trains.

Far in the distance, at the end of each avenue, was a pyramid shaped mound covered with trees and flowers and capped with what looked like a temple. Clustered around each pyramid were other stately buildings.

"Can you see the temples on the pyramids?" Daniel asked.

"Yes, I was admiring their beauty when I could see them closer," John said.

"Don't!" said the old man who had cautiously made his way to their position on the path. "They are temples of an abominable cult and of debauchery."

Silently the foursome returned to the cage of the bear. They entered, passed through and ducked behind the wall of rock into a slender passageway. This time they ascended still further and emerged on the side of a hill. Here were other surprises.

"Do you know where you are?" Mahai asked.

"No, I suppose we are above the City," John ventured.

"This mountain is called Armon. It rises above the palace and looks out over the whole city. The top which you see in the clouds is call Ardis. This is where the

115

Watchers made their evil covenant with Enoch."

"What is this beautiful place called?" Jack asked indicating the high place beside the mountain.

"This plateau to the side is called Paradise after the Garden of Eden. It is covered with flowers, trees, waterfalls and walkways. It houses the temple of Enoch. Here hourly sacrifices are performed - human sacrifices!"

Daniel picked up the narrative here: "True Followers who are discovered in the City are put to death here. Most have been driven into the country for fear of being discovered."

The time travelers and their hosts climbed to a position overlooking the temple. The temple was built of large white stone. Before the temple were altars decorated with gold and marble. Flowers lined the walk ways that led to the altars.

Directly below them fires burned in a large brass statue fashioned in the shape of a great and marvelous dragon with a mouth as big as the body of an ox. A stairway led to the mouth of the dragon and immediately before it was another altar. It appeared to be high noon by the sun dial in the center of the complex.

A priest in dark blue robes mounted the steps to the image. The image glowed red with a fire from within. In the priest's arms a tiny form was thrashing about. Its screams couldn't be heard by the four men on the side of the mountain.

"There's just not enough small animals to satiate their false gods." Daniel's words revealed a hatred that John couldn't miss. Just as the priest reached the top of the steps they noticed a crowd had gathered below. The crowd was chanting something that the men couldn't hear.

Suddenly a woman broke away from the crowd and rushed up the steps. She grabbed at the priest. He kicked her and she fell down the steps. She didn't move. He lifted the small form in his arms above his head and plunged it down into the mouth of the image. There was a flash of light and a whiff of smoke.

Daniel turned his head away. "This is evil," he said. Not used to animal sacrifice, John and Jack were disturbed too.

"Let's return to the cave before we are seen," Mahai counseled.

"This could happen to the boys," Daniel said as they entered the security of the darkness.

"Unless we move quickly, it most assuredly will," the older man added.

"How do you know this?" Jack asked.

Mahai's voice echoed out of the dark behind them. "It will happen because of a new law. There haven't been enough small animals to sacrifice for years. Because of this, the definition of animal has been given new meaning by the judges of the City. Anything foreign or any undesirable person has been redefined as subhuman. It's just a matter of time before the boys will be delivered to the priests of the dragon."

John was shocked. "That would cover us and any unwanted person. It would include anyone less than perfect?"

"Yes and every child before it could talk."

"That's impossible!" Jack protested.

"Children!" John said. "Why?"

"Because they can't talk they are less than perfect."

"If that is true, Jim and Jaydee are in grave danger," John said.

"It is true."

Chapter 4 Noni's Lament

Dr. Canaan showed the boys the City with much charm and gusto. They rode the skyway from the laboratory. It went everywhere. Giant cables were networked across the valley and held aloft by tall metal towers.

From their car in the sky the teenagers could see the great size of the City. Dr. Canaan said the City was about twenty-four miles across.

It was shaped like a large saucer. In its center they could see a tall mountain with a very high peak that reached into the clouds. On this high place were many gardens and stately buildings. Against this mountain they could see a magnificent pyramid like the Mayans had built. Flowers and trees grew up its sides and a temple was built on top.

Around the City were other pyramid temples. Next to each was a palace complex. Dr. Canaan showed them each site and introduced them to the royal families that were home.

He knew each of the Kings personally. They were old friends who had come down from the holy mountain together.

Nine out of the ten kings were invited to gather at the palace of King Samyaza for a sumptuous feast. There were over a hundred others who would celebrate with them. Dr. Canaan and the boys were also invited.

King Samyaza was a portly person, well spoken and dignified. He showed them his horses and the gardens and baths before his guests arrived. There were royal musicians and entertainers and cooks and bakers standing in waiting. The King showed his young visitors the kitchens and the royal winery. Dr. Canaan was obliged to translate what was said to Jaydee and Jim, but everyone understood what the two aliens from the future were saying.

"Wine isn't good for you," Jaydee said as they emerged from the dark storage chamber where the wine was kept.

"Oh, that is definitely not so," Canaan responded. "Wine aids the digestion and is good for cholesterol. It is only in your time that wine isn't good for you. Even your Jesus drank wine."

"That was pure grape juice," Jim retorted.

"Well, let's not argue," said King Samyaza.

When Dr. Canaan explained what the King had said, Jaydee joined in. "Jim isn't arguing. He is just stating what we have learned. You've learned a lot, but that doesn't mean you know everything."

"No, I suppose not. You feel that wine isn't good for people?" asked the King addressing young Jim.

"Yes, there are many people who ruin their lives drinking wine and other beverages like them," Jim answered.

"Perhaps you have a point, young man," the King said, giving Dr. Canaan a wink. The wink needed no translation.

As the guests began to arrive, the boys were introduced to Kings Amzarak, Armers, Barkayal, Akibeel, Tamiel and Asaredel. Later Kings Arazyal, Batraal, and Zavebe arrived. Among the guests were many of the chief judges of the City. They received places of honor beside King Samyaza. Dr. Canaan and the boys sat beside the lesser kings and other guests.

"So, you are visiting us from the future?" King Arazyal asked, leaning over and addressed the two teenagers. He was very handsome and smelled of a lot of perfume. King Arazyal was apparently vain because his hair was done in ringlets and his mustache was curled up on the ends.

"We come from the twentieth century," Jim said

119

proudly when he was told what the King had said.

"You know this is very hard to believe," King Zavebe commented from beside Dr. Canaan. He was very dark. Even his beard was dark black.

"It's true." Dr. Canaan was ill at ease defending his project with his fellow emissaries from the holy mountain. The boys could see how uneasy he was, so they looked around for a new topic of discussion.

Beside King Arazyal was a very beautiful woman. Indicating this woman, King Arazyal said: "This is my wife."

"She is very beautiful," Jaydee said, but his attention was drawn to a young lady who sat opposite them at the table. She was truly beautiful.

"Do you have many children?" Jim asked.

"No," the King answered simply. "We don't keep children. Women who have babies look abominable. My wife drinks a potion to prevent babies." As Dr. Canaan translated, he noticed Jaydee wasn't interested in the discussion. He followed his gaze to the young woman. He smiled broadly.

"Besides," King Arazyal continued, "we are too busy to trouble ourselves with the little animals."

"Excuse me for interrupting," Dr. Canaan interjected. "I see that you have noticed King Samyaza's daughter, Jaydee. May I introduce you?"

Embarrassed, Jaydee came out of a daze. "I'm sorry, what did you say?"

"May I introduce you to Noni? She is the daughter of King Samyaza. If she were a son she would sit with him, but girls hold a lower station among our people."

Jaydee was glad that custom brought Noni to their table. "Pleased to meet you, Noni." Jaydee said her name carefully hoping to remember it better.

Noni only waved. Jaydee was disappointed.

"It isn't right to prevent babies just to keep your

120

figure," Jim continued. Music began and food was passed to the guests. Jaydee felt a tug at his elbow. Noni was standing there. Did she want to dance with him? She looked very lovely and inviting.

"I think Noni wants to show you something, Jaydee." Dr. Canaan suggested. Jaydee saw that a rather plain woman was standing beside Noni. She motioned for Jaydee to follow. Jim noticed his partner's departure, but said nothing. He was listening intently to King Arazyal.

"Do you have a law which says it is wrong to prevent babies?" The King asked.

"No, it is wrong because God says so." Jim felt a little deserted in Jaydee's absence. He was also feeling a small pang of jealousy.

"How do you know that? Does your Bible tell you that?" The King seemed genuinely interested.

"No, our Sunday School teacher tells us so." Jim shifted in his chair.

"Your Sunday School teacher may claim many rules for your day, young man," said Dr. Canaan. "but they don't apply to us."

"But you have a prophet!" Jim countered, thinking that Enoch would certainly agree.

"Yes, we have Enoch. He is our prophet and he has said nothing about our families. Besides if it were a sin, doesn't your Jesus grant us all salvation if we but confess him?" the King asked with a twinkle in his eye. Jim was stunned. Why had Enoch said nothing about families?

* * *

The young lady and her older escort led Jaydee down a long stairway and into a dimly lit passage. They walked for a long way. They made several turns and entered a spacious and comfortable apartment. A comely woman was seated in the apartment. She rose and came over. Taking Jaydee by the hand she looked into his eyes and said something he did not understand.

Noni put her finger to her mouth and beckoned him to follow her to the other side of the room. Here a large screen appeared on the wall. Below it was a keyboard with symbols Jaydee didn't recognize. Noni sat down and touched the keys with her delicate finger and the screen came to life.

Across the face of the screen Jaydee read: "I AM SORRY I CANNOT TALK TO YOU WITH A VOICE. I HAVE NONE. I HAVE BEEN THIS WAY SINCE BIRTH."

"I am sorry too," Jaydee said.

The message continued: "I HAVE BEEN WANTING TO MEET YOU AND YOUR FRIEND SINCE MY FATHER TOLD ME OF YOUR ARRIVAL. SO YOU WON'T MISS YOUR MEAL I HAVE ASKED MY MOTHER TO BRING REFRESHMENTS FROM OUR KITCHEN." Noni indicated the rather portly woman who had addressed Jaydee as he entered the apartment. "WOULD YOU PLEASE SIT DOWN?"

"Oh, of course," Jaydee said taking the seat beside Noni. He felt something special sitting by Noni.

"DO YOU HAVE A GIRL FRIEND?"

"No," Jaydee answered. "I am too young for a girl friend."

"DO I MAKE YOU NERVOUS?" The mother set a tray beside Jaydee.

Jaydee said no, he didn't think he was nervous. Noni and her mother bowed their heads momentarily. Not wanting to appear ungrateful, Jaydee did also and said a little prayer under his breath.

When he looked up, he noticed that both Noni and her mother were smiling.

Noni typed the next message on the screen. "DO YOU BLESS YOUR FOOD?"

"Yes, when we remember." Noni's mother laughed delightfully.

Jaydee was anything but nervous. He felt very much at home for the first time in the City of Enoch.

"My mother and I live here with my mother's sister, Ruth."

Jaydee took some tidbits off the tray. They proved to be some kind of cheese. "Where does your father live?"

"He lives with his other wife by himself. He does not even provide for my mother."

Jaydee stopped eating and put down the piece of bread in his hand. "How do you make a living?"

"This is really my apartment. My father sees that I have everything I want. He keeps my disabilities a secret. Otherwise, I would be sacrificed."

Jaydee resumed eating. "Why is that?"

"People, even babies, who are imperfect are to be eliminated. He does not like to be seen in public with my mother, but he likes to see me. Her large body is obvious, but my deficiencies are not. That is our custom. Is it not the same with your people?"

Jaydee gulped. "I suppose some do not want to be seen with their wives, but I do not think that we get rid of imperfect people."

"How do you feel about that?"

"Not good." Jaydee realized that he hadn't thought much about it but he felt bad that Noni's parents were not like his. "It must be hard for you?"

"It is a sacrifice that we make to have children."

Jaydee was suddenly aware of being very close to Noni. "I see."

"May I touch your face? I want to know what you look like."

Jaydee didn't realize that Noni couldn't see well enough with her eyes to distinguish his features. "Yeah, sure."

123

"Does that mean yes?"

"Yes," Jaydee answered.

Noni's touch was warm and vibrant. She turned sideways and held his head between her hands. She felt along his cheeks and nose and chin. She ran her fingers around his mouth and eyes. Jaydee was sorry she couldn't see. He felt a great sympathy for Noni.

"May I hold your hand?"

"I guess so." Jaydee put down the food he was eating and gave Noni his hand.

She ran her fingers along the lines in his hand and felt each finger. She noticed his palms were a little moist, but didn't say anything. Jaydee began to feel a little strange. He pulled his hand away.

Noni returned to the keyboard. "Would you like to see my room?"

Jaydee felt attracted to Noni. He thought for a moment about being alone with her in her room. "No, I don't think I should."

"I am glad. You are a nice boy. I like you very much."

"Was this some kind of test?

"Yes."

"What would you have done if I had said yes . . . that I wanted to see your room?"

"I would have asked my mother to come with us."

"You're pretty shrewd."

"I try to be."

"Do you have friends?" Jaydee asked drinking some white liquid in the glass on the tray. It was milk.

"No."

Jaydee wiped his mouth. "That's strange. You mean to say that you don't visit with other girls or boys your age?"

"It is a safeguard. They might tell others

124

ABOUT ME."

"Does Enoch say anything about all this?"

"I DON'T KNOW. HAVE YOU MET HIM?"

"No, but we may."

"HE PRETENDS TO BE A HARMLESS OLD MAN, BUT BE CAREFUL OF HIS SECRETARY. HE IS AN AMBITIOUS, EVIL PERSON."

"How can that be?"

"HE ASPIRES TO REPLACE ENOCH. HE COMES FROM OUR PEOPLE, THE WATCHERS," came the reply on the screen.

"Are all your people wicked?"

"MOST ARE. A FEW ARE STILL TRUE FOLLOWERS."

"What are True Followers?"

"THEY ARE THE ONLY ONES WHO FOLLOW THE TEACHINGS OF ADAM."

"Are you a True Follower?"

"CAN I TRUST YOU TO KEEP IT A SECRET?"

"Yes. I will keep it a secret just as I will never tell anyone of your disabilities." Jaydee was sure of that. He cared a lot about Noni.

"I, MY MOTHER AND HER SISTER ARE. DO NOT TELL DR. CANAAN. HE IS NOT ONE OF US. YOU SHOULD NOT TELL DR. ZANHOPE EITHER. THERE IS PROMISE FOR HIM THOUGH. HE MAY SOMEDAY COME BACK. HIS DAUGHTER IS A FOLLOWER BUT SHE IS NOT BAPTIZED."

"You believe in baptism?"

"YES, DO YOU?"

"Yes."

"ARE YOU BAPTIZED?"

"Yes." Jaydee felt comfortable to say so.

"DO YOU RELY UPON THE MESSIAH TO CLEANSE YOU FROM YOUR SINS?"

"Yes we do. He has paid the price, but we must repent and follow his example. We know him as Jesus Christ."

"THEN YOU ARE A TRUE FOLLOWER ALSO, NOT JUST A BELIEVER." Noni turned to Jaydee after she typed the message. He looked into her eyes. He could see that there were tears there.

Jaydee smiled through his own moist eyes. "I hope so."

Noni looked down for a minute. "WE MUST GO BACK TO THE DINNER," she typed.

Jaydee was devastated. "Will I see you again?"

"I HOPE SO!" That was her last message.

* * *

The coming together of the many Kings of the City of Enoch gave opportunity for a celebration. It was the 40th anniversary of their arrival among the people. The dinner was soon over and the music stopped. King Samyaza arose to address his guests.

"My fellow believers," he began. "We have had many successes since we came down from the holy mountain to this forgotten people. They have accepted us and made us feel at home among them. They have not only accepted us but have accepted our beliefs in the promised Messiah."

"This day celebrates not only their spiritual deliverance, but also their physical salvation from the impending flood that has been prophesied. These two lads (here he indicated Jaydee and Jim) represent the proof of that deliverance."

"Dr. Canaan and his staff have successfully brought these two young men from beyond the flood. Within the very near future, we hope to transport the whole city of Enoch into their time. There, we will build another great city. In the new City of Enoch, the true believers will rejoice forever."

The crowd of dignitaries and their friends cheered.

Dr. Canaan rose and presented the two teenagers to the multitude.

King Samyaza continued. "We have just learned that Dr. Canaan and these two young men will be entertained by Enoch himself this afternoon."

Dr. Canaan pointed to the teenagers and waved excitedly. It was his big day.

"I am sure that with this success, Dr. Canaan will soon be exalted to the high rank of king that lately was made vacant by the death of our friend, King Ramuel. Perhaps this very night."

There was more cheering. The boys were excited too, although they couldn't understand what the big to-do was. As the crowd cheered Dr. Canaan bent down and explained to the boys. They were surprised to hear about their importance. "Wow!" they thought - just because we are here, Dr. Canaan might become a king.

As they returned to their seats, a paper was handed to Dr. Canaan by a messenger who came down from King Samyaza. It said: "Dr. Canaan, You are authorized audience with Enoch this afternoon at the time of the three o'clock sacrifice." It was signed by Yomyael, the secretary to Enoch.

"Come with me, boys," Dr. Canaan said. "We must hurry on now."

They waved good-bye to the throng and, entering the skyway once more, went on to the center of the City.

Jim could hardly wait to ask: "How come you went off with that girl, Jaydee? You just barely got back in time."

"She's real good lookin', Jim, but she can't talk. She uses a computer and it writes in our language.

"What do you mean, 'she can't talk'?"

"She can't say a word. She introduced me to her mother. That was her aunt who escorted us to her apartment.

"That's some story, Jaydee!"

"It's true. She was baptized same as us."

"No lie?"

"Really!" Jaydee was acting real defensive.

"You like her don't you, Jaydee?" Jim smiled and ran his right finger over his left twice and pointed at Jaydee.

"Yes, I like her a lot. What of it?" Jaydee said, blushing red as the two boys stepped from the skyway and followed Dr. Canaan onto the plaza.

Beneath the city center they were shown the dynamos that powered the City. Immense waterways ran through subterranean tunnels to the center of the City. After serving as a source of power, the water was pumped throughout the City to irrigate crops and supply drinking water.

Next, Jaydee and Jim inspected the central plaza where they saw the government buildings, the zoo and, above that, the temple complex. They were surprised to see the exotic animals in the zoo. They wanted to spend more time looking at the dinosaurs, but they had to hurry on. At last they came to the palace of Enoch.

A multitude of people were gathered outside the audience chamber of Enoch waiting for a chance to see him. There were people of every description. Many were dressed in exotic costumes of bright colors, decorated with gold and jewels.

Dr. Canaan and the boys didn't have to wait until all these people had their turn. The doctor and his guests were ushered into the presence of the Prophet immediately. It made them feel very important.

Enoch was surrounded by a group of uniformed men. Many were giants. They looked to be very strong.

Here was the richly adorned Enoch - the man John and Jack were told would soon put their boys to death. What sort of man was he really?

Chapter 5 The Seat of Power

John and Jack and their companions sat in silence and ate a meager lunch. Greuban and Hawthorn had been joined by the rest of their family. There were three more sons, two daughters and Greuban's wife, Sarah.

John and Jack visited with Greuban and his family after lunch. Greuban had a farm in a valley near the enchanted forest. He supplied small shop owners like Shuwa with fresh vegetables, eggs and meat. The older boys helped on the farm.

They were always in danger in the country, so he had kept the younger children hidden in the City with their mother. Now that the assassins had found them, they would have to move back to the country and take their chances.

After lunch Jack and John rested in a quiet corner while their hosts talked of ways they could escape and ways to rescue the boys. Their surroundings were light and well ventilated, but they were still in the heart of the rock which formed the island core of the city's center. Jack lay on one straw mattress and John on another.

"What do you think of these True Followers, Jack?" John mused.

"They're strange. They look to me like a bunch of fanatics."

"Daniel and Mahai seem to have our interest at heart. They genuinely care about others. Look how they have taken in Greuban and his family." John looked earnestly at his partner.

"I don't think Jaydee and Jim are in real danger. All we have is Daniel's word for it. You know how people exaggerate their fears."

Jack rummaged in his pocket and came out with a stick of gum. He offered some to John. John refused so Jack put the whole stick in his mouth.

"What if they're just trying to arouse our sympathy

for their cause? Look at that big to-do over the sacrifice - just because some woman gets all excited over her pet. Wasn't animal sacrifice an important part of the law of Moses? Was there anything wrong with that?"

"I got the impression that what we thought we saw was not what our 'friends' saw."

"What do you mean?"

"I mean that the object sacrificed may not have been a pet animal."

"You don't think it was a human baby, do you?"

"Maybe. I think we could draw that conclusion from what they said about the teenagers being little animals."

"You mean that is what Mahai and Daniel wanted us to believe."

"That bothers me too. We may become involved without a real understanding of the situation."

"It could be a set up. All those things they told us." Jack eyed his partner with his normal doubt. "That's probably a pack of lies."

John reflected some. "Did you notice any children on the streets or in the homes we passed, Jack?"

"No, come to think of it. That's a little strange for a city this big."

"The only children I noticed were at Greuban's house."

"I didn't notice any kids there."

"Oh, I just heard them once, and he went out and made sure they didn't make any more noise."

"That's why he went out. I thought he went out to tell his wife not to laugh at you."

"Something else bothers me, Jack."

"You got a world of bothers, John." Jack popped his gum.

"Remember the beggars."

"Yeah, I been meaning to ask; don't you believe

that the City of Enoch would have no beggars?"

"Jack, I'm flattered you remembered. It was years ago that we discussed the people of Enoch and I thought you weren't even listening."

"Well, maybe I wasn't listenin' with both ears, but now that we're here . . ."

"You're right on target. According to the book of scriptures there were no poor among them."

"Well, maybe they didn't do that all at once. They are givin' out a bowl of rice to each of those poor souls."

"Don't you see, Jack, the assassins, the lack of children, the beggars, and the persecution of the True Followers . . ."

"Oh, come on, John. You're trying to get me to think like one of them Followers wants us to think."

"No, I have just been sizing it all up. Maybe they are right." With that Jack turned over, popped his gum a few more times and closed his eyes until their host interrupted their rest.

In mid-afternoon, Daniel dispatched a few messengers and motioned for his guests to arise. Where the messengers came from neither John nor Jack could tell. Daniel led Jack and John into another dark passageway and they descended into the walls of the City once more.

Finally, they came to a slit of light in the wall. It was very narrow and must have been only a crack between two stones in the chamber beyond. What they could see of the palace inside was ornate and beautifully decorated.

The audience chamber of which they had a view was built of the whitest marble they had ever seen. The walls were almost transparent. Light streamed down from windows set in the middle of the ceiling where it rose high above the rest of the roof. Birds sang and nested there.

Braziers in high stands lit the floor all around the walls. In the center of the chamber was a shallow pool of water which was fed from a fountain flowing out of the rear wall. It ran over an Alex into the center. There it splashed down like a waterfall into the pool. Real trees grew in marble boxes in the pool.

The chamber was lined with precious metal and jewels. Figures were engraved on the walls in a triumphal parade of people. Around the throne, bright colored satins and velvets draped the walls and a canopy above the royal chair. Angels sculpted in bronze held the drapes of the canopy.

From their vantage point, Jack and John and their hosts could hear voices. One, which they decided must be Enoch's, sounded old and perhaps even feeble.

"If this is 649," Jack whispered, "wouldn't your Enoch be a young man?"

"Yes, he would be in his mid 20's."

The cackle of the old man interrupted their quiet discussion: "So, my dear Canaan, these are the young men you have brought us from the future." The voice of Enoch the great, echoed in the audience chamber.

Through the slit in the wall John couldn't see Enoch. Only Dr. Canaan and the teenagers appeared in his line of sight. The peephole through which John and Jack surveyed the audience chamber must have been just behind the city's leader.

"Yes, my lord, these are the boys who have come through the rift in time."

"Bring them closer so I can see their faces." Enoch was high above them and very large. He was dressed all in white robes embroidered with pure gold. Although his face was partially obscured by the shadow of the canopy, the boys could see that he was beardless and dark. His dark complexion was accentuated by a soft white velvet cap that he wore on his head.

He smiled broadly at Jaydee and Jim. There were few teeth in his grin. To them he looked like a kindly old man.

"He wants you to come closer, boys." Dr. Canaan nudged them forward as he spoke. Jaydee and Jim walked across the dais and started up the steps to the throne. Their eyes were not on the monarch. They were self-conscious and looked down as though they were being careful not to stumble.

They couldn't understand anything the Prophet said. "They are handsome looking lads. What are their names?"

"Their names are John and James," Dr. Canaan said.

"Oh, yes, James and John. Parents have such romantic notions." Enoch referred to the very James and John who were the apostles of the Savior. He had been briefed on the life of Jesus Christ as monitored by the probe on its visit to that time in the history of the earth.

"Are they brothers?" he continued, as the boys turned nervously away. Enoch took Jim and Jaydee by the hand and drew them up beside him. He cradled their heads between his gigantic hands one by one and kissed each of them in turn. The two teenagers drew away, not feeling comfortable with such demonstrations of affection, but the powerful man took them by the hand and drew them close again.

"No, they are friends," Dr. Canaan answered.

"Oh, how nice. Good friends, I imagine." The monarch released their hands and patted them on their heads. The boys started quickly down the steps. As they did so they looked up for the first time and saw a monitor like a huge TV screen in the canopy above the Prophet. Enoch could see their interest.

"Our guests have noticed my new toy, Canaan. Perhaps you should explain it to them." The leader smiled down benevolently on the boys.

"Yes, of course." Dr. Canaan turned to Jaydee and Jim. "This display that you see above Enoch's head is connected to critical localities around the City. At any moment he can see what is happening by simply adjusting the controls on his arm rest. It works for him just as the time probe worked for us." Then turning back to Enoch: "How long has it been installed, my lord?"

"Oh, only this week, I believe. I have made many discoveries since then." He smiled down on Dr. Canaan as if to say: "Ask me what I know."

"I trust all is well in the City of Enoch?" Dr. Canaan said.

"Yes, I will soon have it so." There was a look of triumph on the monarch's face. "I'm most pleased with your work on the time probe, Canaan. I am hopeful that we may soon start to transport our people to safety beyond the flood."

"We've accomplished all that we planned to do." Dr. Canaan wished only to impress the Prophet Enoch.

"How very good. Have you been able to send someone to their time to assure ourselves that it is safe?" There was a touch of urgency in his voice.

"Yes, your lordship." Dr. Canaan said.

"And do we know that the people there will be receptive?" Enoch's voice was probing.

"I will check that today," Dr. Canaan said nervously.

"Who did you send?" Enoch asked, almost as an afterthought.

"Your father volunteered to be the first."

"My father!" The Prophet gave a little sigh. "You involved my father in your experiments? "I know he is eager, but do you think this was wise?"

"Oh, it's very safe. You can see the boys are safe. Besides he is using a new device to protect him against dangers to his person. We are confident that no weapon can penetrate the invisible body shield that he is wearing."

"So, he's safe. My people can't all wear body

135

shields. Of what good is his visit to the future?"

"We have given him a radical new explosive unit. It has tremendous force and can clear an area of land ten miles across. He can use it to clear a place for the new City of Enoch. At the very least, he can make a big impression."

The Prophet sighed again. "He is an old man. How do you think he will take all this excitement?" Enoch wasn't happy. Jim and Jaydee could tell even though they couldn't understand.

"He is a strong man like your lordship. I thought you would be pleased."

"You should have asked. You have taken advantage of my family. There are other matters which trouble me about your project. Because of you, three other men have invaded our land from the future. While you have been enjoying a party with your friends, our city has been in grave peril. At this moment two of these men are roaming loose in our city and the other is being entertained by your associate, Dr. Zanhope. It is reported that these strangers have killed some of our citizens."

"Dr. Zanhope has reported nothing to me." Dr. Canaan was indignant.

"Nor to me. I have such high regard for his work too. He has always been very obedient, even more so than any of your brethren. They have not kept the covenant that they made when they came here. What I have learned does not bode well for the City of Enoch. Yomyael, whom I've trusted, has proven himself to be a great disappointment. Yet, I suppose I shall give him time to repent."

"How have you learned all these things? I know nothing of the three men, only these two youth." Dr. Canaan was beside himself with concern for his project.

Enoch simply pointed to the monitor above his head. "This tells me, and I have other reports. I need a moment to meditate on these problems. Please wait with my secretary. I may have some instruction for you before you leave."

Dr. Canaan and the boys were ushered out of the Prophet's presence. Their interview with the leader of the city-state was over. The teenagers were puzzled.

As the boys left the room, John and Jack's hosts motioned for them to follow in another direction. They led them through a very narrow passage, around a corner and to another tiny slit of light. Here they could see into an antechamber. Several people were seated around a man in a most elegant red embroidered robe.

"This is the evil Yomyael. He was originally a True Follower. He has had great influence with Enoch," Daniel said.

Yomyael sat at a table of marble decorated in gold. The usher bent over and whispered into his ear. He rose slowly, excused himself to the applicants in the room and moved to a position where he might be summoned into the monarch's chamber. Shortly he entered and shortly returned.

"His Excellency will see no more ambassadors today. Dr. Canaan, you and the two aliens will remain with me for a while."

As the foreign visitors filed out of the waiting room they showed signs of great disappointment. "I have been here six days already. I grow weary of this prophet Enoch," said one diplomat. Another added: "If he wants us to adopt his ways, he needs to show a little respect for our nations."

Once the ambassadors had left the room, Yomyael took on an air of stuffy overbearing.

The secretary indicated Jim and said: "King Arazyal informs us that this one asks a lot of questions and is not in accord with the customs of our people."

Jaydee and Jim couldn't understand the discussion but they knew that something was wrong and that they were in the middle of it. They feared that they had done something wrong and Enoch had found them out.

Until now, they had toured the fabled City of Enoch with pleasure. It was modern and efficiently run. They had come down from its heights on a skyway. They had gazed with astonishment at its eleven temple pyramids, its eight, mile wide concentric zones separated by successive defensive walls, the peripheral canal which made a perfect circle around the City, its gigantic waterways and generators.

They had seen the subways, the avenues that ran out from the center like spokes in a wheel connecting the ten surrounding pyramids and the palaces of the ten kings who reigned over the land. They had visited the government buildings in the city center.

They had marveled at the animals in the zoo. There seemed to be a complete collection ready to step onto Noah's ark at any minute, with animals of every kind. They had seen the communications tubes that linked the whole City. They had been told the city's history - how the river had been diverted and a lake drained and rebuilt into a city. They were impressed.

"Can these be the chambers of Enoch?" Jim asked as he looked around at the richly ornamented palace.

"Not the Enoch Brother Sloan has described," Jaydee answered.

"Well, maybe he doesn't know," Jim retorted.

As the two teenagers wondered, Yomyael continued in a much calmer tone. He said with finality: "You will never realize your ambition, Canaan, unless you capture these men and execute them." He looked intently at Dr. Canaan, adding: "and eliminate these two little alien time travelers as well!"

Behind the secretary, John turned to face his guide. "It's enough," he said. "We must rescue those boys at once. I know that this man is wicked."

It was probable that the old man seated on the palace throne could not be the prophet mentioned in the scriptures. Besides, God would never allow such wickedness to flourish for long at the door of His Prophet unnoticed and unchecked.

The interchange between Dr. Canaan and Yomyael had convinced him. With the prompt rescue of Jaydee and Jim in mind, John and Jack and their hosts withdrew.

But that wasn't all that transpired between Yomyael and Dr. Canaan. After a brief reflection, Dr. Canaan looked at the boys. He could see the fright in their faces. Had Enoch really made this demand? Had he lost his sense of right? Would he sacrifice their present success for a small problem?

He looked back up at the secretary. "Please beg the Prophet to be patient with me, my lord. I can see my error. I am conscious of the harm I have done. I see that we face great danger by the intrusion of these aliens. Before you and our Prophet I am nothing"

"Don't try to make excuses, Canaan. You probably don't have the talent for intrigue. My black order can round up these aliens without your help." Yomyael referred to the black robed assassins. These men operated like secret police, roaming the City at will. They were Yomyael's eyes and ears. It was they who tortured and killed Shuwa, the shop keeper. They would find the aliens and report back to Yomyael.

"That is just what I was going to suggest," Dr. Canaan confessed. "I am a scientist. My talents do not lie on the road of flushing out enemies of the state."

"I'm glad you realize that." Yomyael was calmed.

Dr. Canaan reflected momentarily. "You may not be able to find the other aliens, but if they are after these young men, as I feel they are, they may be tempted with bait."

"Are you asking me to spare the boys until we find the others?"

"Yes, in a way, at least till we capture the intruders.

Perhaps until the boys outlive their usefulness. They may be helpful in our continued investigation of the future." The doctor was pleading for time.

"I see, Dr. Canaan. You may be shrewd enough to be a king some day. I will give you one of them, but only one. The other must be turned over to the council." A benevolent smile spread over the secretary's face.

Dr. Canaan hesitated considering the situation. "If it please, your lordship, and I am allowed to continue to work with the remaining lad, the disappearance of the one must look like a kidnapping. The boy whom I keep must think that conspiring men have taken his companion. He must never know the truth."

"Very well. At least until he loses his usefulness." Yomyael rubbed his chin. "We shall see. Perhaps the inquisitive lad could be the first to go."

"As you wish, my lord." Dr. Canaan appeared anxious to escape the presence of the Prophet's secretary. An usher came from Enoch's audience chamber and whispered something in Yomyael's ear.

"Oh, by the way, Canaan, the Prophet asks about an invisible protective shield. Would you be so kind as to bring one for him to use. He has a little experiment of his own to conduct."

Dr. Canaan was surprised at this turn of events. "How soon would you . . ."

"Very soon, doctor!" The secretary interrupted. There was a touch of evil and intrigue in his voice.

"I am wearing one now. I can . . ."

Again Yomyael was abrupt: "Then give it to me now!"

Dr. Canaan reached into his pocket and removed a tiny instrument. Making some adjustments with the buttons on its face, he handed it to Yomyael.

"That's all there is to it?"

"Yes, your lordship. It is set to protect you from

any object that would threaten to penetrate your body."

"And what should I do when Enoch wants to use it?"

"Simply deactivate it here," Dr. Canaan indicated a red button, "and reactivate it there." This time a green button was indicated.

"Thank you! You and the little animals may go." It was more an order than permission.

Dr. Canaan felt he had met with disaster.

Chapter 6 In Peril for Their Lives

In the laboratory, Dr. Zanhope was facing his own disaster. First he had learned of the two men loose in the City, then Alex had lapsed into a coma, and now his daughter had fainted in his arms.

She was weak and hardly breathing. His natural concern was for his darling, Rachel, but he couldn't leave his patient either. "What can I do?" he said over and over.

He lifted Rachel onto a bed beside Alex's still body. As he did so she roused a little. Her eyes rolled around once and then focused on him. "Papa, am I dying?"

"Oh, no my child, you are just weak. You cannot die. You are all I have." For the first time in his life, Dr. Zanhope realized how true that was. His Rachel was everything. Since his wife's death, Dr. Zanhope had come to rely upon his daughter for a purpose in life. The fear of losing her was enough to cause him to want to change his ways.

His son gave him no joy. His heir was steeped in the tradition of the Watchers and had become a bully on the streets and now was one of Yomyael's chief assassins. This pained Zanhope deeply. He felt evil himself knowing that he had brought most of this sorrow upon his own family.

He hoped that somehow Rachel would escape the City of Enoch. Perhaps even with this young man. She was an angel of goodness, a light in his life. Now, faced with the prospect of her loss, Zanhope feared that death was her only escape. If so, he was not ready for it. He could not live without her.

Would God punish him by taking her? Although he had turned his back on the Watchers, he felt dirty and could not face his maker to ask for help.

"Pray for me, Papa." Her voice was soft and pleading. "Pray for the stranger too."

"I cannot pray. I am a wicked man." Dr. Zanhope

knelt and took his daughter's hand in his rubbing it to bring back the warmth.

"You can, Papa. Do it for us." With that his Rachel closed her eyes. Her breathing became softer and the color left her cheeks. Desperation brought Zanhope to spiritual knees.

"Oh, God," he began. "I am a wicked man. Forgive me. I left my post on the holy mountain and came away with the men who became the Kings of this wicked city. We have come to these people as though we were angels from heaven and have committed grievous sin. We have contracted with the son of Kajin to challenge your prophets, to find a way beyond the flood.

"Forgive me Father God. Restore the life of my only daughter. Bring back the life of this fine young man, too." There was silence for a while; then there was sobbing as the doctor prayed. Finally, he looked up with tears running down his face and beard.

"Dear Father, I of myself am nothing, but I ask these things in the name of thy Son, the Lamb of God."

Slowly he rose to his feet. He looked at his daughter and his patient, hoping to see a miracle, but there was none.

Suddenly, there was a knocking at the door. "Dr. Zanhope, are you in there? Please answer." There was urgency in the voice.

Drained, Dr. Zanhope softly closed the door to the bedroom, walked the length of the hall and crossed the living room. They would soon know anyway. Perhaps he could divert attention from the young man and his daughter. If he could only buy some time, they might recover and escape. He ran the metal key over the door and opened it.

"Yes," he said, looking through the crack of the partially opened door.

In that opening, the familiar face of his pretty

143

female assistant, Dr. Diane Lystra, smiled in at him. "I know, doctor, that things are not going well for you. There is a message to detain you here at all cost. We . . . your staff and I have chosen to ignore it."

Her words were a ray of sunshine in his dark world. "How did you know? Oh, I am gratified. It is so good of you." Dr. Zanhope was overwhelmed by the kindness. How much he had underestimated his people. They had worked tirelessly with him these past months and he had hardly noticed them. "Will you open the museum and have Asa check over the old gliders?"

"Yes, doctor, if that is what you want." Then she added, "Is there anything else you wish?"

"Please have him attach a hoist to the tower at the tenth pyramid so we may launch a glider to the west. Also have him fix two of the new rockets to the wings and . . . have him determine the direction and strength of the wind." There was worry in Dr. Lystra's eyes. Her brow furrowed but she turned and left. Quietly, somberly, Dr. Zanhope set the lock and turned again to his daughter.

He looked at the food on the table. An ounce of faith sprang up in his heart. If he could cause his daughter to eat something, maybe if the young man ate also, they would gather strength.

Dr. Zanhope filled a tray from the table with sweets and carried it into the bedroom. He was met only by silence. His daughter's face was still and white. The whole room seemed to be as cold as the tomb. Death was practically unknown among his people, yet he had seen it. He had experienced it with his wife. Even so, he refused to accept it. He felt such love for his daughter and a love had returned to him for his God.

He pulled a blanket over his daughter's body and one over the young man. Tabitha jumped up on the bed beside Rachel. She licked Rachel's face.

"Please dear God. Do not forsake me." Dr.

Zanhope held his daughter's hand. Still, he bowed his head. Perspiration appeared on his face. For an eternity he struggled with his prayer. There were minutes of extreme anguish; then, his heart felt a peace he hadn't experienced in many years.

Tabitha, who was resting near Rachel's head, stood, gave a little yawn and stretched. She jumped down to the floor and padded into the kitchen where she helped herself to what was left of breakfast.

Almost at the same instance, he imagined that he felt a little squeeze from his daughter's hand. Looking up he thought he saw a flutter of her eye lashes. Yes, there it was again. Her lips parted.

"Papa, I have had the most beautiful dream. I saw Mama. I saw a most wonderful man. It must have been the Messiah. He told me to come back to you. He said that the young man would come too." She looked questioningly toward Alex.

A broad smile broke over the doctor's face. His beard was wet and there were tears running down his cheeks. His gaze followed that of his daughter and he could see that Alex was stirring. He knew that God had heard him. He knew that the crisis was over.

* * *

At the very moment Dr. Zanhope's faith had returned, Dr. Canaan left the audience chambers with many misgivings. He had offended the great Enoch. He had let Enoch's father visit the future without consulting The Prophet. Worst of all, his staff was harboring people from the future. He, Dr. Canaan, would overcome his workers with an army if necessary. He would punish Dr. Zanhope. He would have him sacrificed along with the three men and the two teenagers if he could.

Jaydee and Jim were close behind Canaan. They

knew he wasn't happy and that something terrible had happened as they were rushed out. They didn't want to stay in the audience chambers. They were not sure that they wanted to be with Dr. Canaan. He was in such a bad mood.

They left the palace and walked to the skyway. In the shadows of the tower, with Dr. Canaan completely unaware, two men in black robes reached out and grabbed Jim and Jaydee and pulled them from his sight. Neither Jaydee nor Jim could scream. The men had a tight hold on their mouths. They carried them up the mountain to the temple. It was the time of sacrifice. A large crowd of people was forming near the base of the altar. A dark robed priest stood ready waiting for the sacrificial animal. The two men hesitated on the rim of the complex.

Suddenly the men with the boys ducked into a crack in the rock. It was very dark. They descended many steps into the depths of the mountain. They came out into a wet, misty cavern. It was mostly deserted. At the time of the evening sacrifice the people of the City were accustomed to gather at the temple.

Dr. Canaan looked up the hill to the temple. He was agitated in the extreme. To lose both of the boys was more than he could bear. He had been betrayed.

Jaydee and Jim were pushed into a tube car. The doors closed. The car flashed up the tube. It stopped several times but continued after every stop. There were few other people on the cars.

Occasionally, another black robed assassin would approach. The men who had captured the boys held their long knives over the throats of their captives. They spoke something the boys didn't understand to the assassins who met them. There was laughter and joking. People avoided them, but no one interfered. As their captors spoke, Jaydee and Jim felt that their voices sounded familiar.

At long last the car came to the end of its journey under the steps of a pyramid complex. The two teenagers were pulled from the car.

"Is this the place?" It sounded like the voice of Jaydee's grandfather.

"That's what they told us." Now the boys knew for certain. That was Uncle Jack!

"Grandpa!" Jaydee could contain himself no longer.

"Uncle Jack!" Jim addressed his captor. "Where did you come from?"

"We came through the rift like you did. Alex is here too," John said, pulling back his hood so they could see his face.

At that moment three assassins approached them with knives drawn. "This isn't a welcoming committee!" Jack shouted. John pushed the two teenagers behind them and Jack and John sprang on their opponents. The two men fought with their knives as though they had done this before. Jaydee was surprised to see how bravely his grandfather defended them. At the same time he feared for his grandfather's life. "If only grandpa had his gun!" he thought.

Just as John and Jack disarmed their antagonists, a company of police in black robes and red turbans approached. Their spears were at ready and their shields covered their left shoulders.

"Stop, assassins!" called their captain. "I arrest you in the name of the Prophet!"

The other three assassins grabbed Jim and disappeared down a narrow street. The captain gave a signal and a small part of his force pursued them.

John and Jack were quickly disarmed and Jaydee was taken aside.

"Leave me alone. This is my grandfather!" Nothing he could say seemed to be understood. John and Jack tried to communicate too, but to no avail. They were rushed off down the road. Jaydee was soon separated from his grandfather and taken back to the city center where he was ushered into the presence of Yomyael. With him was Dr. Canaan.

"Oh, my poor boy, what horrible things have happened to you? You must be frightened to death," said Dr. Canaan.

Jaydee didn't know what to say. "My grandfather's here. He and Uncle Jack tried to rescue me."

"He tried to rescue you? My dear boy, from what?" Yomyael said with confidence, as Dr. Canaan translated.

Jaydee was confused. He really didn't know what to say. Things were not right, but from what was he being rescued?

"Certainly you don't mean that those horrible assassins were your grandfather and your uncle?" Dr. Canaan asked.

Yomyael continued without regard to the boy. "I will give you a detachment of my black order to see you back to your laboratory, Doctor."

"Thank you. Your action was a stroke of genius," Dr. Canaan said, being careful to use a selection of words not in Jaydee's vocabulary.

"Really, I have his grandfather and uncle to thank for that," Yomyael smiled, knowing that Jaydee couldn't understand him.

* * *

John and Jack found themselves in a dark cold cell beneath the city center. They were beginning to suspect that they had been set up. They didn't trust their former host Daniel and were afraid that they had made things worse in their furtive attempt to rescue the boys.

"Where'd we go wrong, John?" Jack's face was nearly invisible in the dark cell.

"My guess is that someone knew where we were

148

going."

"Right. Either that Daniel is a rat or someone in his hole is."

"Well, we really don't know. Maybe they got caught and were tortured into telling the plan."

"Maybe these people are so ahead of their time that they have listening devices."

"Good point. We should be careful what we say. Let's give the True Followers the benefit of the doubt."

Voices were heard in the long corridor. Barred doors opened and closed. There were footsteps coming towards them. A very harsh light suddenly illuminated their cell.

"What have we here?" The voice was that of Yomyael. "Dark invaders from the future?"

The door was unlocked and opened slowly. "Chain them to the wall!"

Four men sprang into the cell and chained John and Jack to the wall. Jack resisted and was clubbed severely for his effort. Now there were six including Yomyael in the cell with the two men from the future. The four who had chained John and Jack were a matched pair of giants. They were not only tall but husky. They looked ugly and cruel and were very muscular. Their captain held a club.

"You have been charged with kidnapping. You will be tried by the Supreme Council and punished for your crime. I have no doubt you will be put to death."

"Have you caught the other assassins?" John asked.

"Interesting you should ask," Yomyael said, looking over his companions. "No, we have not been as fortunate with them. They seem to have slipped right through our clutches," he said with a sneer. "When we capture your grandson - and I'm sure we will - we have special purposes for him." Yomyael chose not to disclose that Jaydee was already in his custody.

John struggled in his chains. "What do you want

149

with my grandson?"

"Perhaps we will conduct a series of experiments on him or perhaps we will program him for a return to his own time. He seems pliable enough."

John was livid. He spit on the secretary.

"You pig! You shall live to regret this. For now we will use a little torture - a little experiment of mine." Turning to the captain, he said: "Call in the branders!"

The captain gave a command and three men with hot irons and a portable fire pot came into the cell. Now the room was rather crowded.

Yomyael took something from his pocket and transferred it to Jack's pocket.

"Now, who helped you in your attempt to take the boys?"

Neither Jack nor John said a word.

"Very well," Yomyael seemed only too pleased that they didn't give an answer. Turning to the branders he said: "Burn the one with the beard!" Jack tensed as the hot iron was aimed at him. The brand made a scorching sound and smoked, but Jack could feel nothing.

A second attempt was made to burn Jack. It also failed.

Yomyael laughed as Jack tensed, squirmed and then became puzzled. There was no doubt that it was hot. The whole room was warmed by it.

John also questioned this strange torture. He would have told anything to prevent his friend from suffering, but the two men followed a code - not to give in nor to expect their friend to do so.

Yomyael took a sword from the captain and came at Jack. He cut and thrust to no avail. Jack did not feel a thing.

"It truly works even as the little fat doctor said. I shall use it to take control of this sorry kingdom," Yomyael laughed.

Part III - The Path of the True Followers

Chapter 1 Rescue from Above

In the laboratory people were moving about with great energy. Machines were being dismantled, equipment was packed and notes and papers were being boxed for a mass exit.

Tabitha was adding to the turmoil by jumping in and out of empty boxes looking for mice or whatever. No one seemed disturbed by her antics; she was never in the way and they thought she was safe running free in the building.

Top security had been established. No one came in or out of the complex without the approval of Zanhope, or one of his two aides. Dr. Canaan's staff had literally been shut out with the exception of a few who were positively loyal to Dr. Zanhope.

In spite of these precautions, Tabitha disappeared from the laboratory shortly after the packing began. Rachel who had revived completely set about looking for her. She gave up on the second day. She reported the news to her father, but he was too busy to register much concern.

Doctors Zanhope, Lystra and Asa were having a running discussion while they boxed up documents in the office.

"We must establish a base beyond the power of the black order. We also must find people sympathetic to us." Zanhope looked into the eyes of his assistants Dr. Lystra and Dr. Asa. They were accustomed to matching ideas to Dr. Zanhope's problems.

"Once over the outer wall, we are in the domain of the enemies of the City. They have been bullied for years," Dr. Asa pointed out.

Dr. Lystra's eyes were flashing. She saw new hope

in the actions of her chief. "We must make friends or reach friends immediately. There are many who haven't completely abandoned the path of the True Follower."

"How can we communicate with them?" Zanhope demanded.

Lystra hesitated. She didn't want to alienate Zanhope from his daughter. She hoped the change in his aspect and the danger to his family had destroyed old taboos Rachel's father had instituted. "Rachel has friends among them. She thinks there is a network of Followers within the City."

"Good, have her try to contact them immediately." There was none of the old animosity in Zanhope's voice. "Have her send a message if she can. We need a rallying point to head for, maybe in the area of . . . Libnos. The prevailing wind is toward that city. Once the glider lands and you are among friendly people, you can use the time probe to bring our people and equipment out."

Lystra shook her head. "That should be you, not me, Dr. Zanhope."

"She cannot hope to work 'Lea' by herself and I couldn't either. You are the only one who knows its full potential," Asa added.

"Very well. I will go then." Zanhope wasn't going to argue the point.

"Rachel might also go. In case something happened to you, she has had more experience with 'Lea' than any of us."

Dr. Zanhope was hoping Lystra would say that. He didn't want it to seem like he was playing favorites. "Did you say there were two gliders in good shape?"

"Yes." Dr. Asa was sure. "We just need to be able to run them up the towers."

"Did Dr. Asa get the rockets attached firmly to the wings?"

"Yes." Dr. Lystra smiled. "I saw them. He did a

153

good job. They won't come off."

Dr. Zanhope thought for a bit as he sealed up a box. "We will need some diversion or defense to cover that action."

"What about the alien boys?" Lystra asked. "I don't mean to compound the problem, but we need to rescue them too."

"That might be just the kind of diversion we need."

"What do you mean?"

"If we use 'Lea' to rescue the boys we will cause a stir in a different part of the City."

"How can we locate them?"

"While they were here Dr. Canaan insisted on placing a tracking device in their clothes. Provided they haven't lost their shirts, we can find them."

"They should go with you and your daughter if we can free them from Dr. Canaan."

"The gliders are big enough for two," said Dr. Asa, "I propose we put the boys in with you and your patient in the second glider with Rachel."

Dr. Lystra summed it up by saying: "Since his recovery, Alex has shown a great deal of ingenuity. I think he would be valuable with you while you set up a base of operation."

"I concur. I understand he was some kind of pilot in his time." Zanhope picked up the wand which worked the time probe, the little brass ball that first brought Jaydee and Jim to the City. He turned on the switch. The master display lit up and the probe came to life on the table.

"What will we do once we are in Libnos?" Asa asked. "The black guard has power in Libnos. Even if we are among friends, we may be captured."

"In Libnos, we are building a machine that could carry us all out into the wilderness," said Dr. Zanhope, leading his assistants into the laboratory. "There, we might survive among the tent people."

154

Dr. Zanhope turned on the tracking device readout. A map of the Land of the Exile appeared on the screen. He zeroed in on the City and brought the magnification to "2". A red dot appeared toward the city center and another was approaching the laboratory.

"It looks as though the two boys have been split up, Doctor. Perhaps one got lost and the other is headed here with Dr. Canaan," Dr. Asa said.

"Very well. It won't be much of a diversion, but I will use 'Lea' to retrieve the boy who is headed here. Can you tell from the console which boy it is, Dr. Lystra?"

"It is chip J1. Which is that?

"That's Jaydee. Can you show me yet where 'Lea' is on the screen?" A second screen lit up showing what 'Lea' was seeing. Dr. Zanhope was using the wand to guide the little ball out into the City.

Dr. Asa took a pointer from the table and indicated a green dot on the first screen. It was 'Lea'. The green dot was rapidly approaching the red dot which represented J1 or Jaydee.

"I have him!" The two dots came together. On the second view screen there was a picture of Jaydee flying high over the City, for the little ball, upon reaching him, had literally hoisted the boy out of Dr. Canaan's clutches. Jaydee's face was an aspect of wonder and amazement. A moment earlier he had been sitting beside Dr. Canaan and four black robed guards. Without warning, he had been jerked from the car in which he was riding and pulled up and out into the open air.

"He looks a little frightened." Dr. Lystra said hesitantly.

"He ought to be. I just snatched him off the skyway right before Dr. Canaan's eyes. He looked surprised too."

Dr. Lystra pressed a lever on the panel and a section of the ceiling through which 'Lea' had exited opened much wider. "The boy will soon be here. Shall I bring him some refreshment? It might help to calm him."

"Yes," Dr. Zanhope said as a bewildered Jaydee dropped through the opening. The little arms of the brass ball were extended and its metal fingers were firmly attached to the boy's arms.

"How was that?" Dr. Lystra said rescuing Jaydee from the 'Lea's' arms.

"Scary!" Jaydee was happy to see Dr. Zanhope. Somehow he knew that this man was friendlier than Dr. Canaan.

Dr. Lystra offered a tray to the boy and he smiled up at her. "Thank you!"

As he calmed down, Jaydee gave Dr. Zanhope and his colleagues an account of the events in the city center. They were surprised to find that the other two men were Jaydee's grandfather and a friend named Jack who tried to rescue the boys. They feared for Jim who was apparently still in the hands of the assassins.

Jaydee asked for Tabitha. Rachel was sorry to tell him that Tabitha had somehow escaped her care. "In this city her life expectancy is probably more tenuous than Jim's."

* * *

Somewhere in the night Jim had fallen asleep. His captors had disappeared and he was shut in a room by himself. In the morning, a lovely young lady in her teens brought a tray of food. He thought he recognized her from the day before. She left before he could arouse his senses and ask any questions. He was hungry and ate.

About an hour later, Noni (that was her name he thought), returned for his tray.

"Hey, where am I?" Jim asked as she was turning to go.

The girl made a motion for him to be quiet. She

156

placed a piece of paper in his hand and left without saying anything. On the paper he read: "You are safe for a time. The assassins are gone and you are in the hands of King Samyaza. Don't be afraid. You have friends in the City."

What a cryptic note! What was going to happen to him? He would soon know. A man came about an hour later and escorted him into an elaborate room with a high throne. In front of the throne was a large heavy table. Some men were seated at the table talking. Others entered the room and sat at the table. Beside the place where he was told to sit, were two other chairs. John and Jack were ushered in and seated there.

"Where's Jaydee?" Jim whispered.

"We don't know," John answered. "We haven't seen him since we were captured. Where have you been?"

"I don't know. What are they going to do with us?"

"They're having some kind of trial where they have already decided our fate."

When the chairs at the table were full - there were twelve men - soldiers entered and stood beside the throne and the table and beside Jim, John and Jack. Finally, everyone rose and a man dressed in a bright red robe embroidered with gold entered the room by a door next to the high throne. John recognized the infamous Yomyael. He stood for a moment, taking in the scene and then sat in the judgment seat of Enoch.

Words were spoken and John and Jack were prodded to their feet again. At the same time a soldier next to Jim yanked him to his feet. There were more words spoken. A little man whom Jim hadn't noticed before was seated beside the high throne and was reading something out loud. After a bit they were permitted to sit again.

"What was he saying?" Jim whispered to John who was seated closest to him.

"We have been charged with kidnapping and you have been charged with teaching false and seditious doctrine. What did you say to them?"

"Oh, only that you shouldn't drink wine and that couples shouldn't prevent babies just so the wife could have a good figure."

"I see. They say that since we are outsiders we are what they call non-persons and can be sacrificed. "

"Non-persons?" Jim turned the idea over in his mind. "Is that something like a cow or a horse?"

"Exactly. We are non-persons because we are outsiders. We lack their cultural refinement. It makes it convenient to eliminate enemies without arguing about good or bad."

John paused and listened to the court some more. "They had wanted to call you a non-person under another provision of their law. They felt it would be poetic justice if you were judged under the same law you criticized.

"What is that?"

"This law keeps population in check. If I understand correctly, they identify children as non-persons until they can talk. A child is believed to have no personality until he or she begins to talk. Before that they are mere animals and can be sacrificed. Sacrifice under this provision, along with the potion to prevent babies, keeps the population down so they don't have to enlarge their city. The two ideas are part of the same law."

"But the law does not address ability to understand. Even though you cannot understand them, your ability to talk destroys their argument. They decided that since you can talk they can't classify you as a non-person under this law. Instead, they have judged you a non-person because you're an outsider."

"What difference does it make?"

"I guess it gives them a weaker case."

As the trial continued, John and sometimes Jack translated for Jim. Most of the talk seemed to be on the order of justifying what they had already decided.

158

Apparently, they had to show Enoch that justice was done.

Documents were brought and those at the table examined these papers. They talked in turn. Jim recognized some of the twelve as the judges at the banquet of the Kings. King Samyaza came in and discussed what Jim had said about wine; then King Arazyal came in and made a similar statement concerning Jim's philosophy for having families.

The Captain of the guard came in also and testified before the man on the throne about the assassins he captured. John and Jack weren't surprised to hear themselves denounced as common criminals - assassins. They had played the part, but they were sure that the jurors in this strange trial knew that the cloak of the assassin was really only a disguise they had used, and that the real assassins had escaped.

The Captain was commended for his brilliant capture. "Assassins are a constant threat to our community," Yomyael said. He avoided the fact that he employed them himself. "They do much harm and unfortunately few are brought to justice."

At long last, John and Jack and Jim were made to stand again and the little man at the small table read something.

"I'm sorry, Jim," John said as he was pushed away. "We've all been sentenced to death by sacrifice. I don't know what we can do about it."

Jim was guided back to his room. Almost as soon as the door was locked, Noni was there with her chaperon. She brought lunch. On his tray was another note, but this time she had written: "DESTROY THIS MESSAGE AS SOON AS YOU HAVE READ IT!"

"Can you help us escape?" Jim blurted out. Again she motioned him to silence.

He opened the note: "I CANNOT SPEAK TO YOU BECAUSE I HAVE NO VOICE. IF I COULD IT WOULD BE

DANGEROUS. PLEASE DO NOT ACT LIKE YOU KNOW ME! THAT WOULD LEAD TO MY DEATH. WE ARE TRYING TO HELP YOU AND YOUR FRIENDS ESCAPE FROM THE CITY. YOU MUST BE PATIENT."

Jim thanked her with a nod. Once Noni had left, he ate and then knelt down and prayed as he had never prayed before. "Where is the true Enoch?" he asked. "Why doesn't he come to destroy this evil city that has his name and is ruled by an imposter?"

After his prayer, he wondered what it would be like to be sacrificed. Would they cut him open while he was still alive? He remembered the story of Abraham and Isaac. What was it like for Isaac? What would it have been like if the angel hadn't stopped Father Abraham?

Jim heard a faint plaintive cry. He looked out into the corridor. Tabitha was there. Her back arched and she purred as Jim reached down to stroke her. Where had she come from? How did she find Jim? He looked to see if someone was in the dark passageway, but the cat was a lone visitor. There were no rescuers there.

Jim lay down on a pile of straw in the corner. Tabitha curled up beside him, purring as he held her close. She brought back memories of home and his family.

Jim drifted off thinking of a tune his mother liked. The lyrics kept turning over in his mind: ". . . and they called the wind Mariah."

He dreamed that he was on a dark mountain top. The wind was blowing. An old man with white hair and a white beard was repairing an altar of stone. A young man was helping him. When they had finished, the older man drew the boy close to him in the whistling wind and spoke to him. The young man answered. The man gave the boy a hug.

Jim thought they must be Abraham and Isaac. Isaac held his hands out and Abraham tied them. Then he lay back on the altar. Abraham drew a small knife from his cloak. Isaac raised his head and looked helplessly into the eyes of his father. Abraham kissed him on the cheek and ran his hand through the boy's hair. The boy lay back down and Abraham put the knife to Isaac's throat.

Suddenly it was light. An angel stood over Abraham and Jim could hear the call of a sheep that was caught in the bushes and he heard it trashing about. Abraham laid aside the knife and listened to the angel.

Without warning the hill grew dark once more. The altar vanished. In its place was a cross. A voice said, "Look." Jim looked up and saw himself hanging on the cross. Then he heard a cry of anguish. He looked below the cross. He saw a ram in the thicket struggling to free itself. He reached down to help the sheep, but when he did, it changed. In its place he saw a man who was suffering great pain. Jim took his hand to lift him up, but the man disappeared. Jim's attention was drawn again to the cross. He saw the man hanging there in his place. The man was the Savior.

Then he heard a voice say: "I am the resurrection and the life; he that believeth in me, though he were dead, yet shall he live." Jim felt a great longing.

He awoke. His chest felt warm. At the same time his hands and feet were cold. The dream had been so real.

It gave him consolation. He was not alone. He knew that Heavenly Father cared about him just as Abraham had cared about his son. If he and Jack and John were to be sacrificed in the days to come, he knew God would be with them.

* * *

In quite a different time another sacrifice was in progress. An altar had been constructed in Uncle Jack's back yard. Grandpa John's prize bull had been killed and its less palatable parts were being consumed by a hot fire.

161

Enoch's father had dressed out the rest of the carcass and was preparing to roast it in the fire after the burnt offering was finished.

"All great father of earth," he prayed, "accept this sacrifice in gratitude for my safe arrival in this strange time."

He was very tall. His hair and beard were long and he was wearing a long sheepskin robe. As he prayed with his hands stretched out toward heaven, he looked like a prophet of old. He was so intent that a throng of men surrounded him without his knowledge. They had guns and seemed determined to capture him, but they waited patiently for his prayer to end.

As he finished, one stepped forward, like David addressing Goliath and said: "Are you Jack Cavanaugh?"

"Jack Cavanaugh?" The giant seemed to mimic the intruder. Then, as he gazed around the circle of men, he laughed. His laughter was very loud. To Stanley Conover, it sounded threatening and wicked.

Enoch's father advanced on the little man with right hand extended in a gesture of greeting, but Stanley didn't see it as such. Frightened he ordered his men to fire. There was a volley of shots. They seemed to skip and zing off the surface of the giant. The crowd withdrew and Stanley with them.

The giant fumbled with a little box he had hanging at his side. This inspired another volley of shots. He spoke but no one understood his words. Shortly though, another voice sprang from the box at the giant's side. It said: "Why do you attempt to harm me?"

As Enoch's father continued, the men realized that the strange voice from the box was a translation of the giant's words. From the translation and the negative effect of their bullets they realized that they were dealing with an advanced and powerful being.

"This can't be Cavanaugh!" Stanley exclaimed.

"This giant must be from another world."

"He seems friendly enough," another man said.

"Of course I am friendly," the giant said, as if in answer. "If you will join me, we will soon eat a feast of peace." As these words were translated the group put away their weapons and settled around the father of Enoch. They also put aside their fears and approached him, accepting his extended hand and attempting to make polite conversation.

The meat was cooked and proved to be tender and tasty.

"Where did you come from?" someone asked

"From the City of Enoch," the giant answered.

The men knew nothing of the City of Enoch, but considered that it must be a city on a distant planet. They knew that the air force had recently removed a wreck of some sort from Jack's yard and began to suspect that the story of a plane crash might have been a cover for the truth. No doubt this man had come in a space ship of some kind and the Air Force was keeping it a secret.

Stanley began to see the opportunity for power in the arrival of the giant.

"In my tongue, I am called Kajin," the giant said. "I come as an ambassador to establish a great city here. We will make you our brothers and live in peace with you."

"We are your brothers," Stanley volunteered. He didn't know about this peace business, but if he could make friends with this stranger and learn how he operated, he was sure he could become a man of power.

Meanwhile, the giant was examining a pistol. One of the men showed him how to fire it. Kajin was soon firing the gun and reveling in its potential. He would have to take some back with him when he returned to the City of Enoch. Stanley's men couldn't imagine how a pistol would be of any value to a man who was bullet proof, but they were delighted that they had something which the giant felt had merit.

"Bring me many of these instruments!" Kajin commanded. "We can use them to defend our new city."

This was an easy order for Stanley. If he brought many guns to Kajin, he was sure it would establish his friendship and cement their relationship.

With the advent of Kajin came new direction for the pro-Castro men under Stanley Conover. He listened intently as the alien spelled out the plan of the City of Enoch.

He trained his men in the new order. They learned the ritual sacrifice, the greetings afforded a brother, and the pledge of sacred silence. All of these were adapted to the pattern Stanley felt most beneficial.

Trained in the order of Kajin ala Stanley, the men melted into the community to indoctrinate, organize and provide for the overthrow of the present government. Their job was to make way for the new governing city of the Americas.

* * *

While Kajin was preparing the way for the City of Enoch in America, Yomyael was fast corrupting the seat of power in the past. The same protective device that made Kajin awesome in the future would soon make Yomyael invincible to the antediluvians.

"My dear Samyaza." Yomyael smiled at the highest king of the land without rising from his chair. "What brings you to my humble abode?"

"I believe you summoned me." Samyaza strode up to the secretary, his robes whirling around him as he advanced.

"Oh, yes, I believe I did. How terribly thoughtless of me to forget."

A bit irritated, Samyaza stopped in front of the little cleric and asked: "By any chance do you remember

164

what for?"

"Yes, of course, you have something I want." and then as an afterthought: "Oh, do be seated!"

"I have something YOU want?" There was great rancor in the King's question. Nevertheless the King sat as invited.

Yomyael rose, circled the King, and said: "Yes, it is true. I want the boy. I let you have him for the period of the trial, but something has come to my attention that leads me to believe that you will not release him to be sacrificed. You may even allow him to escape."

"Rubbish, Yomyael! He is secure and there is no way he can escape. Nevertheless, on one thing you are correct. I don't feel that he should be sacrificed. I think you go too far. This boy is different. He has great intelligence. There is no need for this killing. He isn't a threat."

"Your words helped condemn him!"

"I did not imagine that you had death in mind."

"What if I told you that Enoch required it?"

"I could hardly believe that, and I won't turn him over to you until I can have a word with Enoch."

"You are a stubborn old man!"

"I was once your leader!" King Samyaza rose from his chair and stared Yomyael full in the face.

"You have lost the stomach for leadership. It is in my power to rule now."

"Nevertheless, you shall not have the boy!" the King declared and started for the door.

"Oh, I think so."

Samyaza half turned. "What do you mean?"

"I had hoped that you would give me the boy without threats."

"Threats?" The King faced Yomyael again.

"Your daughter, Noni, has been seen with the boy."

"So? She takes him his food. It is harmless. If anything she might induce him to see things in the correct light."

"Probably not."

"Why do you say that?"

"She has been plotting his escape. She is a traitor and should be executed."

"That's impossible. She can't even speak. She is mute."

"Yes, she is mute. That is something we have ignored for far too long."

"You can't apply the law to her. She can communicate!"

"Yes, she can communicate. Read this little love note!" Yomyael triumphantly handed the King a sheet of paper. It was Noni's note to Jim. King Samyaza read the note. The color drained from his face.

"You see. She is a traitor."

"I see," he said, handing the note back to Yomyael. "You have won this time, Yomyael, but I shall have my revenge!" With this King Samyaza stalked from the room.

* * *

In the countryside just beyond the City of Enoch a small band of men was gathering. It was dark. Dense clouds had obscured the sun. Lightning flashed across the sky.

"When will they come, my master?" A very dark heavy set man addressed Mahai, Daniel's father. Mahai had organized forces in the countryside to help in the evacuation of refugees from the City of Enoch. The two men were leaders of the group. All eyes were upon them.

"I don't know, my friend. They will come when they come. We must be ready."

"I have gathered all of my men. Yosep is bringing his group tomorrow. There are still others farther away who have agreed to help."

"They will be needed. I pray that we will not have to fight the black guard."

"We have stopped a contingent on its way from Libnos to Enoch. They have with them bags of a strange black substance. It is not food. It tastes vile. They claim to be bringing this stuff to a Dr. Canaan. What shall we do with them and their black dust?"

"Send them back, but keep their dust in case they try going another way and we don't see them. This Dr. Canaan is an enemy to our cause."

"We have built shelters from the storm as you have asked."

"It is good."

* * *

As the army of True Followers had readied themselves in the countryside, Dr. Zanhope and his people had finished their preparation also. There was now time to think about alternatives and contingencies.

Jaydee found the doctor in a reflective mood. "Where is Jim, Dr. Zanhope?" The doctor was seated in the laboratory with Tabitha beside him. She had returned just as mysteriously as she had left.

"Last time I looked he was in the area of King Samyaza's palace." The screen over the doctor's head came alive as Zanhope pushed some buttons. The large map of the City flashed on the screen. "There. . ." The doctor pointed to a place on the map, but seemed startled by something he didn't see. There was no tiny beam of light in that area. Instead, a light was flashing in an entirely different part of the City. "They've moved him. It looks like he is now in the area of Yomyael's quarters."

"That isn't good is it, Doctor," Jaydee guessed.

"You are right, Jaydee. I think he is in great danger."

"What can we do?"

"Well, when we first experimented with our video surveillance, we installed one in Yomyael's apartments to demonstrate how they worked. At that time Yomyael learned something that caused him to have his wife beheaded. Let's see if our monitor is still in operation."

The doctor made some adjustments on the control panel beside his desk and the screen suddenly changed. The map of the City disappeared. In its place was a clear video of a living room. A man was writing at a small table. He rose as someone addressed him from behind. As he got up, a man and a small boy came into view. Just then Dr. Zanhope tuned in the sound.

"Ah, it is working," the doctor said. Dr. Zanhope and Jaydee could now hear and see what was happening in the living room of the evil secretary.

On screen, Yomyael knelt down and took the boy by the hand. "Dear child, where have you been?"

Jim couldn't understand him, but the tone of his voice sounded solicitous. "Can you help me?" Jim said.

"The poor boy," Yomyael said to himself. "I am the only one that can help him now."

Just then the man who accompanied Jim drew a knife and drove it down towards the back of the kneeling cleric with great force. He recoiled with a gasp of alarm. His arm and the knife in it were repelled without effect. The assailant stumbled back and dropped his weapon.

In surprise the man said: "I didn't know you wore armor."

Yomyael rose, observed the bewildered man and called out for his guards.

An army of servants and guards entered the room.

"Take this man to the dungeon immediately," he said to one of the soldiers. "Have him beheaded and send the head to King Samyaza. No, wait. I will send him a message with the head. Wait for the message." Turning to one of his servants he said: "Take this brat to the dungeon too. Put him in one of the most secure and dark holes you can find."

With that Jim was yanked out of the room as if he were the assassin, and the would-be murderer was dragged away kicking and screaming.

Yomyael returned to his table, sat and wrote and then read aloud: "Dear Samyaza, for your treason you will pay handsomely. You will give me your daughter for a wife. If ever you think of such treasonable conduct again she will die quickly at the hands of him who has severed the head of your servant." He signed it: "Yomyael."

With that he laughed. "I am invincible!" Yomyael disappeared from the screen, prancing from the room clutching the note.

As the video faded on Yomyael, Dr. Zanhope translated the words of the note for Jaydee. Now, fully comprehending what he had just seen, Jaydee grasped Dr. Zanhope by the arms and pleaded: "You can't let Yomyael do this to Noni. She's my friend."

"I know. We shall have to work hard to overcome this evil before they break down our walls."

Outside Jaydee and Dr. Zanhope could hear the continuous thundering blows of the battering ram.

Chapter 2 Escape of the Captives

Dr. Canaan attempted several times to gain entry to the laboratory complex. It was futile.

Everything was out of control. His life depended upon order and discipline.

Unless he could enter his laboratory, he could not use any of his equipment. Years of progress were sealed behind the doors of his workshop.

A troop of a thousand soldiers had surrounded the building and were looking for any opportunity to enter. More troops were on their way. Dr. Canaan knew that nothing they had could give them access to the complex. He had planned it well and Dr. Zanhope had added a few innovations of his own.

Most of the outer ring of the City was mined with tunnel networks designed to provide shelter for the defenders of the outer walls and a means to harass the invading hoard should an enemy breach the outer river or the walls.

The laboratory had no such tunnel under it, but work was underway. In addition, battering rams and other engines were being employed to destroy the thick walls of the laboratory. This would all take time.

He had sent a messenger to the laboratory in Libnos to bring back some of the high explosives which had been produced there. This too would take time. Meanwhile, he would return to the city center to witness the sacrifice of the two alien men and the disruptive Jim. This would be a fitting example for those assassins and radicals who would disrupt the public peace and defy the Prophet.

As he arrived at the central city plaza, a large crowd was gathering. The event had been widely advertised through the city's communications network.

Dr. Canaan worked his way as close as possible,

170

but the crowd was too thick. Finally, he climbed into the heights of Mount Armon where he had an excellent view of the plaza called Paradise.

The priest had laid out several knives on the altar. Smoke curled up around the mouth of the dragon. There was going to be a lot of painful cutting before the sacrificial animals were burned. Large animals always gave more opportunity for theatrics. Theatrics impressed the multitude.

Here came the priest and his assistants. There were extra temple guards too. Next came the little animal and the two bigger animals. The young one was to be first.

Just as they were about to begin, a dark figure appeared on the steps of the pyramid near the altar. First one individual and then another pointed up to the man on the pyramid. Hush filled the plaza.

"Fellow citizens of the City of Enoch, today we bring you the evidence of the success of our fine municipal system. These animals which we present to you for sacrifice have threatened our fair city with spiritual corruption and criminal lawlessness. The one, yes the little animal, has been sent here by an alien race as a false prophet to teach us to ignore the elements of our sacraments and to indulge in meaningless propagation and overpopulation. These teachings, if allowed to continue, would spell doom to our way of life. I say death to the alien!"

A cry of "death to the alien" rose from the crowd below. "Long live Yomyael, the right hand of Enoch the Prophet!" Lightning flashed across the sky blinding the crowd. It was followed by a clap of thunder so loud and near that it sounded like a cannon going off in the square. The clouds were growing very dark. There was a moment of silence.

"The other two, the larger ones, come to us as assassins cloaked in black," Yomyael continued. "They

171

have murdered on our streets and kidnapped one of our young people!"

Jack spat and said half to himself: "Shucks man, we were only trying to steal your little false prophet."

John looked over at Jack. "This is no time to joke around, Jack."

"Death to the alien!" Yomyael repeated.

"Death to the alien!" The crowd echoed.

Jim looked up the steps. He wondered where his rescuers were now. How would they force their way through this crowd? How would they ever reach him?

Yomyael finished his speech and motioned for Jim to be brought up the steps to the altar. Two soldiers took him by the arms and dragged him to the top of the stairway kicking and squirming. He was tied to the altar just in front of the burning dragon.

John stood with his face down. For just a moment he prayed, then lifting his head, he shouted: "Wait!" It was the voice of a man so determined and dynamic that no one could ignore it.

Then with a perfectly clear tenor voice he began to sing.

He sang for Jim who was about to die. He sang for Jaydee who he hoped would escape this evil city. He sang for his wife whom he expected soon to join.

His powerful voice which he had not used in years boomed into the plaza, intriguing the masses gathered there. Resolutely he sang: "Oh Lord my God, . . . "

The priest put down his knife. He seemed fascinated by the religious fervor of John's song. He turned and listened. The crowd was silent. Slowly, they turned one by one to look at the lone man standing there, his hands tied while he sang for the boy.

". . . How great thou art." Jack was proud of his friend as he finished. The song cooled the excitement of the spectators. Many felt a spirit of compassion. Some slipped away.

John seized the moment to state their case: "Citizens of the City of Enoch. I beg you to look at the innocence of this lad you are about to sacrifice. Does he look like someone who has come to destroy your way of life? He has only sounded an alarm which you yourselves should have done years ago."

More left the plaza. Here and there some shouted, "turn the boy loose!"

John continued: "Our only crime is that we have tried to rescue and protect this lad and his companion. Now, we ask you to join us and free this boy."

The crowd began to be unruly. Arguments could be heard among the throng.

This was too much for Yomyael. He was starting to lose control of the masses.

"It is a trick. Do not be swayed by this interloper. He was taken in the very act of banditry. Kill them all now before your very minds are infected with this evil!"

The crowd was easily returned to their purpose. The Priest took up his knives and raised them above his head, turning every way so the crowd could see. The feeling of compassion brought about by the song John had sung was gone.

"Kill!" they shouted in larger and larger numbers as their lust for blood returned. The priest brought down his knives and concentrated on the sacrifice. He tore open Jim's shirt.

John turned his head. The knife was raised. The priest made little motions describing the cuts he was about to make.

Jim screamed. Then, suddenly out of nowhere a furry ball ran up the back of the priest and planted itself on his head. The priest dropped his knife and reached for the furry mass.

It was Tabitha. She was not idle. She clawed and

scratched at the priest's face dodging his hands while he shrieked in desperation.

At last the soldiers grabbed the cat. The priest again took up his knife. His look was determined.

There was blood on his face, but this time he motioned for the soldiers to give him the cat. He laid Tabitha across Jim's bare chest and started a majestic sweep of his knife.

At that instant, there was a buzz. Something shiny flashed across the plaza, struck the knife from the priest's hand and lifted the priest high over the crowd. Tabitha fell from his grasp and the ball dropped the priest full into the mouth of the dragon.

There was a scream and a sizzle. The mysterious ball rose above the heads of the crowd. Tabitha scampered from the plaza as the mysterious ball took the stage.

"Way to go, 'Lea'!" Jim shouted as lightning filled the sky and thunder drowned his words.

The little round ball sent the guards sprawling down the steps, sawed the ropes that bound Jim to the altar and cut the ropes that bound both John and Jack. Lightning crackled along the cables to the skyway and spat upon the supporting tower, giving a voice of authority to the little ball.

At first the crowd drew back with a gasp. It appeared to them that a new god had entered the arena. Rain began to fall. There were sizzling sounds as the rain pelted the burning dragon before the altar.

"The god of flight is angry!" some said.

"It is a false god! The dragon god is angry," shouted Yomyael. "Kill the sacrifice!"

The crowd took up a chant. "Death to the alien!" With each repetition, the spectators gathered courage. They began to press in on the two men and the boy.

Behind the crowd there was a sound of creaking iron. Here and there was a ringing sound like a dull bell.

Shouts of: "Haw! haw!" were heard. This was followed by trumpeting and roaring and bellowing and screeching.

Huge wild animals encouraged by the shouts of their keepers and thunder and lightning, surrounded the crowd, pressing in on them as the crowd had pressed in on John and Jack. The masses gave way and ran until John, Jack, Jim and Yomyael were left alone in the middle.

John could see Samyaza, opening more cages in the zoo and prodding the animals out into the plaza. Why was Samyaza helping their escape. The plaza was dominated by giant carnivores. Terror was the order of business.

"Come back!" Yomyael shouted, but his voice was lost in the confusion. The people ran off the plaza, into the trees and over the edge of the city center. Some jumped into the chasm below. Others ran right into the path of the hungry flesh eaters and were quickly dispatched.

"Do not be afraid!" Yomyael shouted. "I will save you!" With that he ran down the steps past Jim, John and Jack right into the open mouth of a saber toothed tiger. The animal closed its huge jaws around the little secretary.

"Come on, let's get out of here!" John picked Jim up and hurried across the plaza as though it wasn't covered with wild animals. Jack followed. He ran into a few animals on the way, excused himself and was soon close behind.

As they reached the edge of the fleeing crowd, they looked back, expecting to see the bloody remains of Yomyael being tossed about by the tiger. Instead, the tiger had dropped the impervious cleric beside the altar. Yomyael was saved by the little protective device in his pocket. Dr. Canaan, who had been watching from a distance, now gained courage and ran to Yomyael's side. He took the secretary by the right hand. Lifting his arm in the air, he shouted: "Long live Yomyael, right hand of the Prophet!"

To those who had seen the boasting secretary

approach the tiger, it was a miracle. Rain was pouring over the plaza. Lightning and thunder highlighted the triumph of Yomyael.

At the same time the animals were either milling around or occupied with meaty human morsels. The crowd had stopped, and observing from a safe distance, turned to look at the invincible Yomyael.

"Hail, Yomyael, right hand of Enoch!" they shouted.

"Quickly!" Daniel and several other True Followers appeared behind the time travelers to encourage them to escape. "Come quickly! There is no time to delay."

Yomyael called a soldier to his side and pointed out the route of the escaping sacrificial animals. Then he turned to Dr. Canaan.

"They are of little importance now, Canaan. I am invincible. I will soon replace Enoch and you can be my right hand man."

"I am flattered, my lord."

"You will serve me well. How soon will you be back in your laboratory?"

"I don't know, my lord. I have explosives on the way."

"Explosives - very good," Yomyael was thinking. Explosives were the new weapon. He could conquer the world with them.

Chapter 3 Soaring and Sailing

Most of the soldiers had been called to the inner city to round up the animals which Samyaza had released. A small contingent of soldiers was still quietly undermining the laboratory. They had been looking for a soft spot in the floor, but there was none. Dr. Canaan had promised them a new wonder weapon to make a hole. Nevertheless, they continued to dig, looking for a certain spot he had described for them.

With the relaxation of the siege, Dr. Zanhope had sent the little brass ball to investigate. The grounds around the laboratory were empty. He checked thoroughly for a trap. There appeared to be none. He did not know at the time that the diggers were resting. All was silent and dark in the hole beneath the building.

"Let us make our escape now, Doctor," Asa said.

"We'll send a crew out first to ready the gliders. Dr. Lystra, are my daughter and the two aliens ready?"

"Yes, Doctor."

"Dr. Asa, you go out with the crew. If the soldiers come back, we can use 'Lea' to help you out." Dr. Zanhope was excited.

"Yes, Doctor." Dr. Asa led his crew out the door in the direction of the tenth pyramid.

The tenth pyramid was not far from the laboratory. Beside it was the museum of the gliders. A high metal tower joined the museum. It was part of the skyway system. Dr. Asa's crew attached a pulley to one of its lateral cables. It was their aim to lift the gliders to this point, fire their rockets and release them to soar over the city wall, across the peripheral canal and out into the country side.

All of the pyramids that surrounded the City were built for defense as well as for worship. The outer wall of each pyramid which faced out of the City was nearly perpendicular. These walls were met on either side by the high inner wall of the City. From this high place soldiers could direct the defense in times of siege. Below the wall and the pyramid, the mile wide peripheral canal acted like a moat to deter invading hoards from approaching the city.

Today, there was no siege. There were no soldiers on the pyramid. As the four who were to man the gliders left the laboratory, they could hear shouts and machinery in motion. They ran in the direction of the noise not knowing what to expect. There, they could see Asa's people in their white smocks surrounding what looked like a giant bird. Its wings were outstretched and it was chained to a cable that ran up the metal tower beside the pyramid.

Suddenly, the soldiers who had been undermining the laboratory came out of the hole they were digging and faced the doctors and their crews. Their knives and spears were at the ready.

Dr. Zanhope took an instrument from his pocket. He looked directly at the soldiers and pointed the instrument at them.

"With this new weapon, I can turn you to dust in a very few minutes."

The soldiers withdrew and formed a protective shield around their leader. He and they debated the wisdom of advancing. They spoke in hushed tones lest the doctor, whom they knew for great feats of magic, might disintegrate them.

While they were standing in this circle protecting their leader, the doctor had his daughter climb into a glider. Alex got in with her.

"Remember my instructions?" the doctor said to the young man.

"Yes," Alex said confidently.

Another glider was being brought as Alex and Rachel were drawn up the tower. At the top, the rockets were ignited and the glider was released and darted away, caught by the wind and propelled beyond the outer walls of the City. Alex was a good pilot. After the rockets gave out, they drifted and soared in the wind.

They passed over the canal and the locks that took ships down to the river Oban and into the valley below. Here and there they felt the wind rising from the valley. It lifted them up, up high above the surrounding hills.

Rachel was thrilled. She had never been so high before in her life. Even when she had climbed the highest peaks in the west with her father she hadn't been able to see so far and feel so free. It was inspiring.

The wind squeezed through cracks in the cockpit. It whistled around them. Yet, they seemed to be standing still, motionless in the air. She felt like an eagle drifting in the misty grey sky.

She looked down as they slipped sideways. Below, she could see the river winding through the valley. It dropped away through lock after lock until it came to the distant flat land near Libnos.

Beside the river a road ran down the hill. At first it wound through the valley taking the same course as the river. When the road and the river came to gentler slopes, the two travel routes parted and a dark forest stood between them.

The wind's current slackened. The glider fell several feet. Rachel caught her breath and gave Alex a big hug as he guided their ship from the seat in front of her. For a moment she had forgotten the confusion and conflict behind her. She even forgot her father.

The successful flight of the first glider changed the picture for the soldiers left back at the pyramid. It diminished their fear of the doctor's secret weapon. Knowing that the doctor might be the next to climb into the great bird and that if he escaped they would face a torturous death from the Secretary of State, they advanced again. Sudden disintegration was preferable to a slow and painful demise.

Again Dr. Zanhope pointed his "weapon" at the valiant soldiers. This time the round ball from the ground beside him took flight and ran into the first three with such great force that they collapsed in front of their comrades, causing most of them to fall in a heap. Those who were conscious withdrew again dragging their fallen companions.

Dr. Asa and another man stripped off their smocks and, taking up the knives of the fallen soldiers, took a position to defend Dr. Zanhope and the rest of the crew. "Go, get into the glider!" Dr. Asa shouted as he and the other staff member engaged the soldiers in combat.

More staff members joined the ranks and the fighting became sore. Dr. Zanhope maneuvered his little ball into the turmoil. "Lea" fought well, but when the soldiers saw that they didn't disintegrate, they gathered courage.

"You must go on the next glider, Jaydee," Dr. Lystra said.

The crews were still fighting and other men were coming from the hole to join them. Jaydee didn't want to go. He picked up a long knife that one of the dead soldiers had dropped. He was going to fight too.

"Come on, Jaydee!" Dr. Zanhope encouraged. "We've got to do what Dr. Asa says!"

Dr. Zanhope and the boy entered the second glider and were carried up to the top of the tower. As they reached the top, more of the soldiers came out from below the building and drove the doctor's staff away from the tower so they couldn't release the second glider.

"Here, Jaydee," the doctor said, handing him a huge metal cutter. "Climb on top and cut the cable. Jaydee was scared, but knew that if he didn't they would never escape. Taking one last look at the soldiers and the doctor's staff below, he climbed out, wrapped his legs around the mooring device and cut the cable.

There was a sudden jerk and the cable broke loose. Jaydee dropped the cutters. Dr. Zanhope fired the rockets and the glider soared free of the tower. Dr. Zanhope was skilled with the glider also, but it was all Jaydee could do to hang on.

The wind tore at Jaydee's clothing and stung his face. His arms ached and he was afraid to look down. After a while he was able to swing down into the cockpit.

He closed the canopy and began to enjoy the beautiful view all around him. On the west he could see tall snowcapped mountains. Gentler slopes on either side gave way to rocks and boulders beside the river.

As they descended, the trees captured Jaydee's attention. Both Dr. Zanhope and the boy became fearsome that the trees might claim their flying machine.

They twisted and squirmed, trying to stay over the road. They didn't fly as far as Alex and Rachel, but landed in a green field beside a dark and mysterious forest in the flat lands. They were free of the City of Enoch.

* * *

Elsewhere others were struggling to extricate themselves from the evil City. Black guards were pouring into Paradise Plaza as John, Jack and Jim escaped with the True Followers. Daniel was their leader. The soldiers were restoring order, rounding up animals and looking for the sacrificial victims.

The True Followers and their guests were no longer safe in the dark recesses of the rock hideaway. Even though many of the soldiers were mauled and eaten by wild animals on the loose, many more were able to control the beasts and bring them back to their cages. They had found the access behind the bear cage and were exploring the passages used by the "fanatic" sect.

Meanwhile, Daniel was leading his charges into the

181

depths of the City. Jim felt a small hand take his in the dark and give it a squeeze. Somehow Noni had found him. She had Tabitha in her arms. It was reassuring to be near Noni, but he felt guilty for Jaydee's sake.

Her father, King Samyaza had participated in Noni's rescue. He feared what Yomyael was about to do. He didn't want Yomyael to take his daughter into his household. The idea that he would marry her was repugnant. Once he had helped rescue Noni and the aliens, he was concerned about his own safety.

"Let me go with you!" he begged the True Followers. "I am truly a traitor now. Yomyael will seek me out and torture me to death!"

"You are a double traitor. You have betrayed the faith and now you turn your back on your false prophet. If it weren't for your Noni, we would just as soon leave you behind to die." Although Daniel's words were tainted with mercy, his voice was full of rancor. He did not trust Samyaza.

Jaydee's grandfather was heard in the dark. "Where are we going?"

Daniel called back over his shoulder as he cautiously led the group down a flight of stairs. "The City is undermined with a network of tunnels. The secret works of darkness come together in these subterranean passageways and the chambers that branch out from them in all directions. We will follow the tunnels to the outer wall. Then we will have to climb to the top of a pyramid and go down a rope into the canal."

"Into the canal! These kids will have a hard time in the water. How wide is the canal?" John complained.

"It is a mile wide." Daniel had just turned a corner and his face picked up light from torches which appeared out of the gloom now and then along the route.

"They won't survive that!" Jack growled.

"If we are lucky, there will be a boat waiting for

us," Daniel said and the group moved on quietly. King Samyaza couldn't be silent for long. Moving up beside Jim, he touched him lightly on the shoulder.

"My boy, I am truly sorry about the trial and the trouble my testimony caused."

Jim couldn't understand and gave a little shudder. His memories of King Samyaza at the trial were not good.

"He can't understand you!" John said. He was none too polite because he remembered the trial also.

"Oh, I forgot."

"I know you have helped us, but your testimony at the trial was unnecessary. Jim is a decent boy. There are few like him in our world and from what I can see, there is no place in your world for boys like him."

The King cowered a little but wouldn't be stifled. After a while, he tried to talk to John again. "Would you tell the boy that I'm sorry? If there is anything I can do to make up for it, I will."

John ignored him. He was having troubles of his own. Neither he nor Jack had had much of a moment of peace since they came through the rift in time. He was worried about his grandson Jaydee. He blamed King Samyaza for some of that worry.

The King tried again to speak to John. "Did you hear me? Please tell the lad that I am sorry."

Daniel became provoked at this. He dropped back to talk to Samyaza. "Leave them alone, you hypocrite! All that you have in mind is your own selfish passion. You and your friends are to blame for the wickedness of this whole city. You came down here as missionaries. You seemed like holy angels to these people. Instead you became fallen angels and upheld the human sacrifices and false practices of their leaders. You deserted your holy calling and indulged your lusts. You are directly responsible for the situation we are in and the plight of this boy. You have driven the righteous people out or put them to death. Now, leave us alone."

King Samyaza was visibly wounded by what Daniel said. Seldom had anyone spoken to him so rudely. Only Yomyael could be so reproachful to a king. He had stood up to Yomyael for Jim's sake. Standing up to Daniel was a different matter. He must be diplomatic.

"I will be quiet. No doubt you are right."

"I have no doubt. One day there will be a resurrection and you will come to judgment for your evil ways!" With that, Daniel took his place in the lead. His face was red. He was angry and no one missed it.

They walked in silence for a long while. Finally, John turned to the King.

"It's all right. I will talk to the boy. If you are sincere, you can help by just being a friend to the boy and help wherever you can." There was steel in John's voice.

"I see you are put out at me also. Why is that?"

"There are several reasons, Samyaza. Neither you nor your people have made us very welcome in your city. We came here to see that my grandson and this boy returned to our time safely. You tell me why that is such a problem."

"We are just different than you."

"Oh, there are people in our time like you. They will do anything for power and prestige. I have met people in your city who do not seem much different from those in our time."

"You think my friends and I are bad?"

"Yes, and I think that Jim has put his finger on part of the problem. You adjust reality to suit yourselves. You call little children who can't talk yet 'animals'. You have decided that since they aren't human, you can sacrifice them to your god. You excuse yourselves by saying that if you allowed them to live, there wouldn't be enough food to satisfy the real people. This isn't a good excuse since you and your friends and all who follow you live in luxury."

King Samyaza was silent for a long time. "You feel we have no right to make our own laws and govern according to our desire."

"On the contrary, we respect your right to govern. It is just that the rights of your little ones are as important as the rights of your kings. Consider your daughter. She doesn't talk. Would you sacrifice her?"

"Oh, no, she's special."

"How long would it take you to discover that every individual is special?"

"I hadn't thought . . ." The King appeared to be moved by what he heard.

"Isn't there some spark of feeling in your heart?"

"Yes, I suppose so, but I haven't felt much in the last forty years. I have been so busy with the City and the great plans we had." Little by little the King revealed his inner thoughts - feelings he ignored for a long time.

As the group continued through the tunnel, Jack engaged Daniel in a similar conversation. Jack wasn't as successful as John in swaying Daniel's feelings. He could not get Daniel to soften his position. Daniel was strong in his hatred of the Watchers.

"Do you believe what you said about the resurrection and judgment? Will we all be judged for what we've become? What if King Samyaza has truly repented and you still can't forgive him? How will the judgment go with you?"

Daniel was silent. He knew that Jack was right, but he could not admit it. His feelings would have to cool. Jack decided to let it go. He knew that Daniel meant well.

There were other things to occupy Jack's thoughts and the imaginations of his companions. Now and then little eyes peered at Daniel's followers from dark corners. Rats. Tabitha wriggled away from Noni and chased through the darkness, ridding the path of the pests. Behind them they could hear occasional noises - footsteps and voices.

185

They guessed that the soldiers were following them.

Suddenly, out of the shadows ahead a large creature waddled up - its huge mouth hissing as it came. Rows of sharp teeth gleamed at them in the semi-darkness. Its scaly back sported a hard saw-tooth ridge. This giant grey monster had chosen a downward path when the cages were opened in the zoo and was following the tunnels under the City. As Daniel's followers came closer, Daniel spoke and the reptile was calmed.

"Don't be afraid," he said to his followers. "He recognizes me as his caretaker. Follow closely! Don't talk and especially don't scream!"

Tabitha had returned to join her human hosts. This time Jim held her.

They slipped by the monster without another sound, each person trying to step in the tracks of their leader, each afraid to disturb the commanding presence Daniel gave.

Shortly they heard screams and cries from their pursuers. The creature had encountered the soldiers in the dark.

As they crossed a feeder passage, two people joined them. One was rotund like Samyaza. The second was tall and slim. Daniel knew them. The former was Noni's mother, Abigail, and the latter was her sister, Ruth. They attended his congregation. Jim recognized Ruth as the woman who had escorted Jaydee and Noni the day of the banquet.

Turning to Noni's mother, King Samyaza grumbled: "What are you doing here?"

"I have as much right to help our daughter escape as you!"

"You'll only be a hindrance.

"I doubt that!"

"But you are old and fat!"

"Have you looked at yourself lately?"

The passage began to rise slightly. It was evident that the tunnel followed the contour of the land above. As the group began to climb, King Samyaza began to pant. He wasn't used to much exercise. Noni's mother was large also but the hard life she led made her equal to the task.

"Look at you," she chided. "You can barely keep up. What have you been doing these past ten years?"

The King was silent. He was caught between the criticism of Daniel and the harangue of the wife of his youth.

Something fluttered by in the dark overhead.

"Watch out!" The lumbering King took a defensive position and hovered over his wife.

"It's a bat!" Jim shouted.

Noni became hysterical. She couldn't voice her alarm but waved her arms about her head, sweeping the air for the flying rodents.

Tabitha caught one creature as it dived toward Noni. She fought it to the ground and clawed and bit it to death.

Without warning another bat dived into Noni. She was struck down and slumped to the floor. It was caught in her hair. It screamed where she couldn't. It squealed as it tried to free itself. Other bats disappeared at its cries.

Daniel moved rapidly to Noni's side. "Don't move!: With one stroke he decapitated the giant creature. As all looked on horrified, he carefully extracted the talons of the dead animal from Noni's hair.

"I think we should rest a while. Let's move into this passage on our left."

At this point King Samyaza took Daniel to one side.

"There is an apartment near here where we can hide."

"Are you sure of your way?"

"Yes I have been here many times. It was the place of our brotherhood meetings before we found richer quarters."

"Is it safe? Is it used?"

"No one uses it now. It's vacant."

"Lead on then."

They followed Samyaza out of the dimly lit tunnel into a side corridor and then through an opening in the wall of the tunnel. The opening wasn't obvious. They immediately turned left and after a few steps they turned right and then left again and entered into a dark cell.

The chamber Samyaza led them into was about twenty feet square. Daniel lighted a torch. He held it for just a minute so they could see most of the room.

The ceiling and walls were hung with dark drapes of some kind. There were benches around the room and a large table in the middle. A pole rested in the middle of the table and supported the drapes above like a huge tent.

Golden medallions decorated the drapes above at the points where it was tied. Brightly colored shields hung around the walls. Once they got their bearings, Daniel extinguished his light and they all sat quietly on the benches in the dark.

Noni sat very close to Jim. She was shaking uncontrollably.

"Maybe we should pray," Jim said.

"That is good. Would you ask the boy to pray for us?" Daniel said to John. He moved close to Noni and put his arm around her. Her mother was also very near.

"Jim, Daniel says for you to pray for us."

Jim opened his mouth, but nothing came out. Daniel and the others waited, but still Jim could say nothing.

"There is something wrong." Daniel lit a torch, looked around and then put it out again. "Have there been human sacrifices in this room, Samyaza?"

"Yes. At the last there may have been."

"Let's leave this place at once."

They were about to leave the room; however, in the main tunnel they had left behind they could hear voices. The soldiers were moving on ahead. The little group sat in silence waiting for the soldiers to move on. Noni continued to shake.

Suddenly, Jim felt a sharp stabbing pain in his hand. "Something bit me!"

Daniel lit his torch again. "It was a scorpion." They could all see the insect scurry away.

Daniel was quick. He tore a piece of cloth off his shirt and made a tourniquet for Jim's arm. Ruth agreed to watch the tourniquet and loosen it every ten or fifteen minutes.

Then Daniel smeared some strange black ointment on the bite from a small jar he had in his pocket and made a bandage. "This will draw the poison out."

The ointment eased the pain a little. "Oh," Jim said. "It hurts worse than a bee sting." He complained from time to time, but was brave and did not cry.

King Samyaza found the scorpion in a nest with others and killed them all with the handle of his knife. The ladies felt calmer.

"Thank you, my husband."

"I'm not . . ." The King broke off, looked over at Noni and reconsidered what he was about to say. "You are welcome, my wife."

John and Jack moved about the cell further verifying that there were no other surprises looming in the dark corners. The scorpion sting delayed them a little longer. Noni still seemed agitated. Everyone began to become concerned.

While the pilgrims were scurrying through the tunnel, they were warm, but now that they had rested, they began to feel cold. Everyone shook a little.

Daniel stood. "Come with me, we can rest a little farther along. I know another place."

It seemed forever before they came to another opening in the wall. Here, they entered much the same way. Under Daniel's torch they could see a clean room painted white. There were few furnishings. Benches were in rows, one row behind another. At the far end of the room were three chairs behind a small table.

"What is this, Daniel?"

"It is our chapel. The spirit is right here. Jim can pray."

The little party prayed, meditated and rested. There was peace in the little chapel. No one shook even though it was cold. Ruth began to sing softly to herself. Soon Abigail took up the hymn and Daniel followed. The melody was so special that John and Jack began to hum the tune.

Jim's hand still hurt a lot. He could not understand the song. He looked at King Samyaza who had not joined the rest. He was sitting with his head down. Occasionally he wiped his eyes with his sleeve. The music had stirred something in his heart. The hymn trailed off as softly as it had begun.

Ruth loosened Jim's tourniquet and checked his bandage. Daniel looked at Ruth. In the torch lit chapel she looked attractive to him. She wasn't especially beautiful, but he admired her for her spirituality. She was forever serving others. He thought of her as the ideal Follower, but they were always too busy to become acquainted. Today was no different.

"We must go on. Our friends will be waiting for us and the soldiers may discover them."

"But why can't we take the tunnel we were in?" King Samyaza questioned.

"No. I have an alternative route. It isn't pleasant. We will go by the detention center."

The King gasped.

Daniel put out the torch and everyone reluctantly followed him out of the cell. At least they weren't climbing as they crossed from one route to another, but soon they turned and headed uphill again. King Samyaza hung back.

"Come, oh fat king," Abigail said.

"I am coming, oh wondrous lump of clay!"

Abigail was hanging back also. By continually chiding the old king she caused him to give the walk his best effort.

Chapter 4 The Captive Women

Up ahead the tunnel grew light. Torches were attached to the walls on both sides of the passage. As Daniel's little band of followers drew closer to the light they could see arms and hands extended out from the wall as though the wall itself were alive. Moans and screams could be heard.

Approaching nearer still, the group could see that the arms were thrust through window-like holes in the walls. They extended into the tunnel, their hands reaching and grabbing at the air. Only a very narrow place in the center of the tunnel was open to Daniel's group to go by.

Because of his size, King Samyaza was afraid to pass through for fear of being touched by the out-stretched hands.

"Make way for the King!" he shouted.

This only made his progress more difficult.

"I want to touch the King!" said one.

"We are your loyal subjects!" said another as he extended himself as far as he could into the passage way.

"Give us some bread!" called a hungry inmate.

They snatched at every member of the group, calling them lord and king, little king or princess as the size and person dictated. All came through without a scratch, but as Samyaza and his wife came along, it was different. They were scratched and patted and turned about at every window by the hands that were extended through the holes. Finally, it seemed impossible. Daniel retreated, leaving the others up ahead and came back to the spot where the King and his wife were having trouble.

"The King desires to set you free!"

"Set us free!" They murmured.

"What are you saying, Daniel! They will tear me to shreds?"

Daniel looked full at King Samyaza and repeated.

"You want to let them go free, remember?"

"Oh, of course I do." Samyaza was less than animated about the idea.

"There is a condition. You must go back the way we've come. We came from a great celebration." Daniel knew that the celebration was still in progress, but he had not been part of it. The rest was a fabrication. " It is the King's invitation that you join the happy throng in a great birthday feast."

"Of course!" said the King thinking of the party he had attended. Why not? It would send these unfortunates off in another direction.

"Yes!" said the prisoners. "We'll go to the celebration!"

"Whatever you do you mustn't follow the King. He'll be going on to invite others." Daniel lied. With that He opened the doors and freed the people.

Some attempted to come at the King and his wife, but most of the prisoners simply passed them by and started out toward the city center. Those that remained were discouraged by a long knife that Daniel drew.

"Come on. Let's see what the celebration is all about!" As they left, they pulled torches off the walls and paraded off behind the others. What a commotion they made as they went down the passage. An army of black guards couldn't have passed through them to pursue Daniel and his followers.

Daniel again took up the lead. At last they came to a place where the tunnel began to level out. It was below the highest point in the City. Here they encountered women weeping in cells along the wall.

"Who are these women? John asked Daniel.

"These are the women who are depressed and lonely for the loss of a child who was most likely sacrificed. Many blame themselves because they could have escaped into the country side but chose to remain.

193

They cannot forgive themselves."

"It is true," Samyaza' wife added, staring hard at her husband. "There are also women here who took the potion to avoid babies. See, they are slim, but eventually the potion has made them unhappy forever."

Daniel opened the doors for them also. Some came out right away; others lingered. They went up and down the passages in all directions. They moaned or talked to themselves. Some even sang.

Ruth had compassion on those that remained and urged Daniel to see that all of them got away before the guards came by and locked them up again.

"We should hurry," King Samyaza scolded. "If we stop to run all these women out, we'll be locked up ourselves!"

Abigail wouldn't put up with this attitude. "Stop your complaints, your royal highness. If you had any backbone these women wouldn't be here in the first place.

Ruth found one woman weeping in a corner of the cell. "What are you crying about, dear?"

"Eunice. It's too late for Eunice. They already took her."

"Who took her?"

"They took my sister away this morning. She thought they were going to let her go back home with her husband."

"But who took her? Where did they go?"

"The priests of the dragon have taken her to the surface to prepare her for the ceremony."

"They call it a party," King Samyaza interjected.

"Yes," Daniel said. "That's what they call it." By now the woman had stopped crying and was wiping her face with her sleeves.

"What is your name?" Ruth asked.

"Barbara."

"Well, Barbara, let's see if we can find your sister."

Soon Daniel's group came to the end of the tunnel. They climbed up a stair way and into the fresh air. They expected to come into the broad light of day, but found the fragile light of nightfall tinted the sky. The lights of the City shone here and there.

Ahead of them was one of the pyramids of the City and beside it one of its gates. The gate was under heavy guard and there were many people on the pyramid.

"Go up one at a time. When you reach the temple at the top, hide among the worshippers. Wait till I come with the rope. We'll try to rescue Barbara's sister before we go over the side."

King Samyaza vouched for each member of the group as one by one Daniel's followers started up the pyramid. Some lingered on one terrace or another to rest, smell the flowers or touch the trees. Jim and Noni reached the top first. They were followed by Jack and John and the rest.

"What exactly is this?" Jack asked.

Barbara had reached the top a little before Jack. She surveyed the surroundings and said: "This is the ceremony I told you about. Eunice must be here someplace if they haven't sacrificed her already."

On the top of the pyramid, people were sitting on pillows or squat chairs in an open air building much like a Greek temple. Some were seated around small tables spread with little snacks and drinks. All were dressed in fine jewels and lavish clothing. Men and women were engaged in quiet conversation while a half naked woman danced on a pedestal in a light in the middle of the gathering.

John took in the activity at the top of the pyramid and sat down to wait. "Come on, Jack. You need to blend."

"Blend with what. All they're doing here is gawking at a pretty lady on a pedestal. It looks to me like a burlesque show."

"Well, can you think of something better to do?"

For a minute the dancer disappeared along with the light. It gave an eerie sensation. "Hey, look at that. She disappeared!" Jack was surprised.

"It must be a holographic image." As if to prove John's point the image reappeared.

"Why do they use a holographic image?" Jack said.

Just then one of the "worshippers" strolled up to the image and tried to put his arms around it.

"That's why." John answered. John was reminded of his wife, Eleanor, as he watched the dancing girl. How he missed his sweetheart. It had been a long time since he had held her in his arms. He knew they would be together in eternity, but eternity was far away at the moment. His mind wandered.

Jim and Noni were off to one side with Ruth. She loosened the tourniquet on his arm. She removed his bandage and examined his hand. The redness was gone. She applied more salve and a new bandage.

Jim wondered what the worship was all about. Noni somehow knew when he turned to look at the image. Each time she would cover his eyes with her hand.

"Why are you doing that?"

Noni shook her head, letting him know that she disapproved.

After some time, Samyaza's wife reached the top. She was followed by her husband. He was panting and sweating. Just as he reached the top, the music and the dance of the image changed. Moved by her charm, the audience in the little temple began to sway and chant. They clapped their hands to the music.

"Don't look!" said the King's wife.

"Oh, it must be the exciting part of the worship!"

"Just don't look!" she repeated. The King sat down and gazed off into the last rays of sunset. The clouds which had brought a violent storm earlier in the day, were bright with orange and red. It was like fire in the sky. There was just a small patch of the clearest blue on the horizon.

"I don't remember it being so beautiful," he mused. His wife glanced at him, thinking at first that he was looking at the image. Then she followed his gaze to the sky in the west.

"Oh, the sunset. Yes, it is!"

Just then Daniel reached the top. He crossed the flat temple base, and tied his rope to a pillar. Only a few of his followers noticed him. He looked down the steep side of the pyramid. In the distance a fishing boat had broken away from a large flotilla of boats and was bobbing around in the middle of the river.

"We are ready," he signaled to the boat, and then turned to his group and beckoned.

"How will we lower Noni and her mother?" the King asked as he approached Daniel.

"You shall see."

"But what about Eunice?" Barbara cried.

Just then a tall woman dressed in a splendid gown walked onto the pyramid. She was escorted by men in blue-black robes. They were headed for a curtained enclosure at one side of the pyramid. Eunice's countenance was radiant, but beneath the makeup on her face one could see that her cheeks were hollow. Her body swayed rhythmically to the music, but she also shook and moved about drunkenly.

Barbara ran up to her and took her by the arm. "Eunice, don't go with them!"

"They are taking me to my baby! I'll see my baby again. Isn't it wonderful?"

"No, Eunice. Your baby is dead. Don't you remember? They're going to drug you and then they will kill you just like they did your baby."

"Oh, no it's a party. We're going to have little cakes and wine and listen to the music in the garden of earthly delights."

197

"Eunice, that's not what it is. It only looks like a party."

"They're going to show me the way through the shroud of the eternal world and into the chamber of the bridegroom."

The priests were hesitating. They glared at Barbara. She was interfering with their ceremony, but they dared not agitate their followers or the woman they were about to execute. "Stand aside, woman! You are keeping your friend from the stairway to the eternal presence."

They pushed Barbara away. She fell backwards and stumbled over some of the guests. As they did so a rotund man approached them striding through the throng of worshippers, his long robes dashing platters and cups of wine to the floor and breaking them as he went.

"This woman will not be sacrificed today!"

"But your worship. She has been prepared. She wants to go to her child. "

Samyaza would not be placated. Turning to Eunice he said: "You do not want to know what happens in the chamber of the bridegroom or up the stairway to the eternal presence!"

Eunice looked bewildered. "But I want to see my child."

Barbara had picked herself up and put her arm around her sister. "You will only see your child if they kill you, Eunice! That is the truth."

Eunice wavered. Barbara took her hand and led her away from the startled priests. The worshippers seemed not to notice the little drama between the priests, their charge and their antagonists. The attention of the party guests was glued to the image on the pedestal. The priests melted away as Daniel gathered his followers around him. Everyone came except John and Jack. The boat out on the river was sailed closer.

"Come on, John!" Jack urged.

"Just a minute."

"You shouldn't look at that anyway. Come on." John didn't move. The swaying motions of the dancer and the music had mesmerized the onlookers.

"John!" Jack repeated.

By now all of Daniel's followers were looking at John. The boat was right below them. The priests were beginning to notice Daniel's group.

Jack shook John. He did not respond.

"He has fallen into the worship of the image!" Daniel said with alarm.

As if she understood the situation, Tabitha sprang from Noni's arms and ran to John. She climbed up into his lap and pawed his chest until he put his arms around her and looked down.

When he looked at the cat he thought of Eleanor, of his love for her, his loyalty to her and his desire to be with her in the eternities. John rose with Tabitha still in his arms. He moved as though he were in a trance at first and then slowly walked with Jack over to Noni. He handed Tabitha over to her. He was his old self when he reached the group.

Quickly Noni was lowered down to the waiting boat with Tabitha securely in her arms, then Abigail and the fat King. At last all the other men and Jim were safely in the boat.

Just as they began to row away, spears and arrows began to fall around them. Shields were thrown up to protect the women. King Samyaza was too big a target to miss and an arrow struck him in the shoulder. He cried out because of the unexpected pain, and then continued to express his hurt with a low moan.

Abigail carefully cut out the arrow and stopped the blood with a few pieces torn from her petticoat. Daniel gave her some of his black salve to use in the dressing.

"Thank you." The fat king was noticeably touched.

"There wouldn't have been enough material on

skinny girls to do that!"

"I know." He smiled through his pain.

The men of the fishing boat quickly rowed out and into the mass of other fishing boats at anchor in the channel and disappeared among them.

It wasn't any too soon as a warship put out on the canal. Its master hailed the fishing fleet.

"Have you seen a fishing boat come this way from the pyramid?"

"I'm sorry - have we seen a fishing boat? They are all around us."

"No, no - one from the City?"

"Oh, have we seen one from the City?"

"Yes, have you seen one?"

"No, we are busy fishing, we don't pay much attention to the City - sorry."

A man from another boat nearby answered: "I think it went over to the shore." There among the reeds, a fishing boat was anchored. It had been there for a long time, but it answered the description, so the warship was maneuvered to the other side of the channel.

It was growing dark and the fleet began to lift anchor. That night, instead of heading to their usual harbor, the fishermen sailed around the City to the river Oban where it runs down towards Libnos.

There, under cover of darkness, Daniel's friends separated their boat from the fishing fleet and entered the lock that would take them down to the next level in the river. As the water was let out into the next level they moved ahead. The lock was shut behind them and as the water let out ahead, they went down one more level. Finally, they reached the River Oban and sailed on their way to Libnos.

There was a moon that night. For a while it was pleasant to stand by the rail and watch it shimmer over the water. This was the first chance that Daniel and Ruth had to become acquainted.

At first their conversation was general.

"What do you see out there in the darkness, Ruth?"

"I was looking off to the west where I was born."

"Where was that?"

"Oh, up there on the holy mountain."

Daniel was surprised. "Really, what was it like?"

"I didn't know how wonderful it was. From where we lived we could look over and see the Garden of Eden. It was so beautiful that I did not realize how splendid our own part of the mountain was. I always wanted to be in the Garden."

"How far away was it?"

"It's just a few miles. You could see the Tree of Life and the Tree of Knowledge of Good and Evil. They were different from the other trees. The Tree of Life had a bright white fruit."

"I thought all that was symbolic."

"Oh no. On our own peak we had some of the same flowers that bloomed in the Garden. Only the fruit was scarce. Mama said that everything grew naturally in the Garden, but we had to work hard to keep things up where we were."

"Did you know Samyaza and the other Watchers there?"

"Yes, they were our heroes. They performed all the works of the Temple. They taught us to be righteous and look forward to the Messiah."

"Did you have any idea that they would change the way they did?"

"No, but they talked a lot about how they could gain access to the Garden of Eden. That was when the idea for the gliders started."

"You mean they were planning to fly their gliders over into the Garden."

"Yes, they worked very hard on those gliders. They

thought that was all they had to do. When Father Adam heard about their idea, he sent his son, Seth, to talk them out of it. There were many meetings in the Temple. Everyone was excited to see Seth, but Samyaza and the others did not like to hear what Seth told them. They said that he was a very old man. They thought that he was not in touch with the modern world.

"What did he tell them?"

"He explained that they were not ready to enter the grounds of the Holy Garden of God. He said that it was for those who wore the crown of righteousness. This would not be possible until the Savior came and paid the price."

"So they rebelled and came down to the people in the City of Enoch?"

"No, but they started to watch the people below. They went down to the low ledges and watched the valleys of Shulon below where Adam used to dwell. They began to think of ways they could use their gliders and then something strange happened."

"What was that?"

"An army came to the foot of the mountain one day. It was a very unusual army. The army played loud and haunting music. The men of the army shouted for the Watchers to come down and join them. They brought horses and had horse races. The people in the army looked like they were having fun. It was always like a big party."

"So did the Watchers mingle with them?"

"Not at first. Genun and his army were there for many days. In the evening they danced and drank and their women entertained. The women wore feathered costumes and painted themselves with bright colors."

"I have heard of Genun. He and his evil army roam the countryside and kill and pillage."

"We did not know that at the time. I was young and was attracted to the festivals below."

"You were?" Daniel was shocked and amazed that

202

Ruth would be fooled.

"Everyone thought that Genun's army was exciting. Some of the men wanted to go down and investigate. We were told not to think of it, but finally a small party did. They never came back. They became part of the army of Genun. They took some of their women to wife. They adopted their customs. It was then that we discovered that the people of Genun's army were killers and robbers. They thought that if they could weaken our forces on the mountain, they could take control and pillage us."

"Were you frightened?"

"Of course. It was then that Samyaza started talking about missionary work among the people below. Only he said that it would not be good to go to the people of Genun as the others had. The leaders of the Watchers would fly their gliders down the mountain to the City of Enoch."

"How did you come down? Did you come in a glider too?"

"Oh no. We came later when they sent for us. We followed the river Dabadan from the Holy Mountain all the way to the City. There were at least a hundred of us."

While Daniel and Ruth had been talking, Jack and John had been listening intently nearby.

"How long ago was that?" John interjected.

"Nearly forty years ago."

"That can't be. That would make you about sixty. You don't look a day over twenty."

"Thank you."

"Ruth, how old are you?" Daniel asked.

Ruth blushed. "Sixty-five"

"You're not too young for me then."

Jack and John both looked surprised.

"And how old are you, Daniel?" Jack asked.

"I was just eighty last month." This startled the aliens. They would have thought Daniel was in his early thirties.

"Where were you born, Daniel?" Ruth continued with more interest.

"I was born in Libnos. My parents were attracted to the teachings of the Watchers in those early days. They came to the City of Enoch when it was just an island."

"We've met your father. What became of your mother?" John asked.

Daniel dropped his head. "She was sacrificed along with my sister ten years ago." Daniel turned and put his hand on the rail.

Jack put his hand on Daniel's shoulder. "I'm sorry. I'd no idea. I can see now why it'd be hard to forgive a man like Samyaza."

It was becoming late and the two foreigners went below to leave Ruth and Daniel to reflect on the past alone. Ruth moved very close to Daniel and put her arm around him.

They did not talk much - just looked off into the darkness.

* * *

Earlier in the day on the road to Libnos, Alex and Rachel struggled in high wind to modify the glider. It had been built to be transformed into a sail plane. They had disconnected the wings and were attempting to reattach them in an upright position.

"The wind is too hard right now," Alex said.

"We can't wait long."

"I wonder how your father is doing."

As if in answer, the second glider, now converted, came speeding by. Jaydee waved from the cockpit. They couldn't stop.

Behind them several men came running. At first, Alex and Rachel thought they were pursuing her father and the boy, but they stopped when they reached Alex and Rachel.

"We have come to help!"

Two men took the plane and held it steady while four or five others hoisted the wings into place and tightened down the anchoring bolts.

"Thank you!" Rachel motioned for Alex to board and got in herself.

"You are welcome!" The helpers soon disappeared into the brush and the next gust of wind picked the sail plane off the ground a little and sent it down the road.

"At this rate," Alex shouted, "we'll soon be in Libnos."

Rachel was pleased with the way in which Alex handled the glider and sail plane. In the short time she had known him he had been very courteous and grateful for all she had done for him. As they flew along at great speed she reminisced about the life they could have together. She felt a little dizzy.

Alex was having a good time. "This is truly reckless," he thought "-a glider turned into a sail plane."

Without warning, the road dipped and the plane went out of control.

"Watch out!" The machine left the road, was pulled out into a field and smashed on some rocks. Alex crawled out of the cockpit but Rachel did not move.

Alex reached into the plane again and took Rachel's arm. He felt for a pulse. He couldn't find it. Looking down at her innocent face he realized how special she was. He examined her for an obvious injury, but there was none.

He stood up and looked around. He could see Dr. Zanhope and Jaydee down the road a little. They had crashed too. He waved frantically.

Jaydee and Dr. Zanhope were running towards him. Jaydee arrived first. He quickly sized up the situation.

"She's not hurt is she?"

"I don't know!"

"Is my daughter all right?"

"I can't find a pulse!"

"Please say she's not hurt."

The doctor examined his daughter quickly but carefully. There were no marks. He felt for a pulse.

"There is a weak pulse. Maybe she has a concussion." He brought out a small bottle and held it near her face. She coughed and pushed his hand away.

"What are you trying to do, kill me?"

"She's ok!" Jaydee shouted.

Alex lifted her gently from the cockpit and laid her on the ground. She put her arms around him and gave him a kiss.

"Hey! You're all right!"

"We'd better be on our way then," Dr. Zanhope remarked. "These hills are none too safe."

Alex started to pick Rachel up again.

"I can handle it. Let me down."

As Alex set Rachel on her feet, they discovered that an army of ragged and evil looking men had crept around them unnoticed.

Ignoring them, Dr. Zanhope started out to return to his sail plane, but they stopped him.

One man, taller than the rest, stepped towards Alex.

"The girl is mine!"

Another man challenged him.

"You always get the good ones."

"That's because I'm the leader."

Alex addressed the second man. "I would make a much better leader than him. Let me lead you."

"But then you would get the girl."

By now Alex was standing between the two men. His movements were quick. Both men were soon lying on the ground in great pain. The rest of the mob moved in. No one paid any attention to Dr. Zanhope. He ran to his sail plane in no time. He got the controller for the mysterious ball and quickly activated it. The ball flew straight and sure. One head after another was dealt a tremendous and surprising blow. Those men in the back of the mob couldn't determine how one man could dispatch so many of their comrades. They broke and ran.

"That was brave, Alex." Rachel looked admiringly at her hero.

"I didn't have a chance," Jaydee complained.

Within minutes the four were on their way again. Dr. Zanhope carried his kit and the controller and Jaydee got to carry the ball. Alex and Rachel carried the rest of the equipment.

Chapter 5 Flood Waters in The City of Enoch

Enoch sat in his throne mulling over the events of the past days. He had learned that Yomyael hadn't repented and couldn't be trusted. He had reviewed the judgment of the supreme council. The charges against the two men appeared correct. It was clear from the report that they had murdered a shop keeper and still another man without provocation. He wished that he hadn't relinquished his seat to Yomyael. It set a precedence that might encourage this ambitious man. Besides, the judgment of the boy named Jim was severe. He would have liked to have examined Jim himself.

There was a noise in the antechamber. Yomyacl and Dr. Canaan entered unannounced and unbidden. Worse, Yomyael carried a long knife. Automatically the soldiers beside the ruler's throne barred the way.

"What is this, Yomyael? Are you adding treason to your crimes?"

"I seek only to execute judgment. You are no longer fit to rule!"

Enoch noticed how uncomfortable Dr. Canaan looked. He didn't seem to be a part of this conspiracy.

"And you, Dr. Canaan, do you feel I am unfit?"

"Your majesty, I haven't examined you. Perhaps at your age . . . "

"You are sealing your own doom, Yomyael. I have been most lenient with you." The Prophet waved his hand and the room was suddenly full of guards. They came at Yomyael from every direction. Dr. Canaan stepped aside and they surrounded the little secretary.

"Will you still defy your prophet?"

Yomyael raised his knife and plunged through the soldiers massed around the throne. There was a scream of pain and confusion, but as the mass drew back only soldiers lay bleeding and moaning.

"You are next, false prophet!" Yomyael vaulted up the steps. As he did so, a strange thing happened. In his anxiousness to climb the steps and strike Enoch, Yomyael failed to notice something drop from the folds of his robe - something which had rested securely in his pocket only moments before.

Yomyael was confident, but the guards at the throne were fearful of their own lives. They struck out at him with desperation. They put every force they had behind their long knives. They struck again and again.

Yomyael's destruction was complete. What the tiger couldn't penetrate on the day before was torn asunder in an instant. He fell with surprise and futility before the throne of Enoch.

Dr. Canaan hurriedly retrieved the instrument that lately rested in the secretary's pocket. Swiftly he adjusted the mechanism. Almost unnoticed he dropped it into his own pocket.

There was one who saw. Enoch was high up and could observe all. As the soldiers took Dr. Canaan by the arm, he noticed that the doctor didn't resist - that he seemed anxious to leave.

"Let the doctor stay a while. I have something to say to him."

Dr. Canaan smiled nervously: "How can I serve your lordship?"

"We came very near a disaster today, Dr. Canaan. Now, I shall need a new secretary. I need someone I can trust and someone who can offer me technical support."

"If I can be of service in whatever way . . ."

Enoch cut Dr. Canaan off. "I sense that you were caught up in Yomyael's treachery by chance. I want to believe that you are trustworthy. Can I count on you in the future, Dr. Canaan?"

"Yes, your lordship. I shall not falter."

"Give me the device. It will be safe with me, and,

Dr. Canaan, don't make any more of these little charms. They may lead others astray."

Dr. Canaan readily drew the device from his pocket, adjusted its controls and handed it to Enoch. He rightly determined that it wouldn't be destroyed, but would soon be the only such instrument in the world.

"Now, return to your laboratory and bring my father back today. If you demonstrate your loyalty in this, I will make you my right hand."

"I will obey!" Dr. Canaan was pleased. He felt washed clean in the blood of Yomyael. His dreams were indeed realized, for to be the secretary of Enoch was to be more powerful than a king - even more powerful than a judge.

More than ever he must gain access to his laboratory. It didn't matter to him that the boy and the men had escaped. Apparently, this meant nothing to Enoch either. It didn't even matter when he reached the laboratory and found Dr. Zanhope and his staff had escaped.

All that mattered was that he activate the time mechanism and retrieve Enoch's father. He had news that Zanhope's staff had pilfered some of the equipment and were somewhere secreted in the City. So long as the time travel equipment could be found, he could manage. Perhaps later he would miss the expertise of Dr. Zanhope. Perhaps later he would have regrets. Now, he must please his leader.

"Where are the men with the explosives?"

"They have come, Doctor, but they were delayed by a strange army on the road."

"Was it Genun?"

"No, they only took their packages of explosives."

"That is strange! So, how did they get more explosives?"

"They went to Libnos for more and returned by another route."

"Good! We shall start at once. Have you found the place?"

"Yes, we think we have."

The doctor climbed down into the hole and assured himself that the spot was right. He set the explosives in place. Everyone retired to safety and then the doctor himself set off the charge. Those who were present said the laboratory itself lifted into the air. There was a muffled roar and then a momentary silence.

Lastly, there was a rushing sound - like the thunder of a water fall. Around the hole, loose dirt shot heavenward followed by a geyser of water hundreds of feet high. The blast had breached the wall of the City and had penetrated into the surrounding canal.

Dr. Canaan and his crew ran for high ground. There was a scramble to climb onto the roofs of the houses. Many were lost in the torrent. In the wake of the first flood, the laboratory rested at anchor. Like Noah's ark it rode the waters securely.

Part IV - Escape from the City of Enoch

Chapter 1 Voice of the Serpent

On the river Oban, Jim awoke to the realization that the pain he had experienced the day before had disappeared. The tourniquet had long since been discarded and now the sting of the scorpion was gone.

He had not slept well. The sway of the boat and the poison of the scorpion had worked to keep him tossing and turning all night.

Now there was a new sensation. The passengers on the little fishing boat felt a rush of water driving them down stream. Then, without warning, the river channel became dry.

"What happened?" Barbara's question brought the whole party to the rail.

"It doesn't matter; we must flee into the woods." Daniel, always the leader, hurried his little group off the boat, into the mud, up the bank and into the forest.

Noni had questions but was unable to voice them. She clung to Tabitha and showed her frustration by hesitation and frantic movements. Jim took her by the hand and led her on, giving her confidence and security.

They rested in the shadows of the forest. This was a strange forest for Jim. Vines seemed to come down from the trees and reach for the ground. Some grew all around the tree trunks like serpents. "What a good place for snakes to hide," Jim thought.

Below the trees the bushes and grass were tall. Sounds of creatures rushed among the shadows and, often as not, a little forest animal would be interrupted in its rounds by Daniel's retreating caravan.

It would be a long trek to Libnos and they needed to conserve their energy. Rations and water were passed around. Before long the group was expressing astonishment over the behavior of the river.

John and Jack took Noni aside and began teaching her the fundamentals of sign language. Before long Jim became interested and he too learned some of the rudiments. This was good.

As the group continued their journey, Noni and Jim practiced. Jim took Noni's hands and helped her learn the signs by shaping them in her fingers. Although she couldn't see what she was doing, she soon was able to express herself so Jim could understand. At least what she communicated was in a language he could learn in no time.

This not only made the time pass fast but it took their minds off their worries and helped to calm Noni. What she felt underfoot told her that they weren't walking on paths that were used from day to day, but rather fresh trails trampled out by her comrades as they went through the forest.

After several hours, they came to a little stream. The sun was shining through the foliage and bees were mixing the pollen from one flower to another in a grassy meadow. Noni felt the sun on her face and could hear the sound of the bees. She became calm, even happy.

"We shall rest again here!" Daniel commanded.

"How far are we from Libnos?" John asked.

"I should say about three or four more hours of walking."

King Samyaza, who had been lagging behind as usual, wandered up.

"Why do we go to Libnos? Yomyael has his black guards there also."

"We have friends there - besides that is where John's grandson will be; Dr. Zanhope and his daughter have taken him there."

"Oh, I like Dr. Zanhope. Has he gone back to the old faith? He seemed always to be uncomfortable with the reformed ritual."

"Samyaza, I hope that you have seen the error of your ways too."

"Well, Daniel, this journey has reminded me how difficult the old ways were."

Abigail sidled up at that point.

"If you weren't so soft from the new ways, you would enjoy this little hike."

"How would you know, oh lovely mountain?"

Noni and Jim were running about the meadow. Jim would run ahead and make funny noises and Noni would try to catch him by the sound of his voice.

Jack had sat on a log that lay near the stream. Tabitha jumped up on the log also. Perhaps she was anticipating a warm sun bath in a little patch of light next to Jack. Notwithstanding her goal, the minute she landed on the log, she immediately began sniffing and examining its surface.

John was approaching Jack, when the log began to move. Jack thought he had loosened it and that it was rolling into the stream, but this wasn't the case.

Feeling insecure, Tabitha ran down the log away from Jack. Jack got up and, as he did so, one end of the log rose. On its end was a hideous head. As luck would have it, this was the end Tabitha was running toward. For a second she was almost head to head with the creature and the two hissed back and forth at each other for what seemed like eternity. Then, Tabitha sprang from the log and streaked for the nearest "real" tree she could find. She climbed to the upper branches and peered nervously at the suspicious log below her.

The opposite end of the log freed itself from the surrounding grass and swept up into the air also, twisted and coiled around Jack's body. He was helpless.

John slipped Daniel's knife from his belt and was bent on freeing his friend at all costs.

A voice sounded in John's head. "Would you cut off the serpent's head to save your friend?" John stopped, knife in mid air. This was indeed a strange serpent.

"I am ok," Jack assured John. "Actually, I feel quite comfortable. It has been cold during our journey and I am now warm and toasty."

"You see," said the voice, "I am your friend too."

Daniel took the knife from John. "We must kill this evil beast before he infects our minds."

"Oh, but I have always been in your minds, and killing this wretched creature won't stop me."

"What is it?" Eunice asked.

Daniel gave in to the serpent's persuasion and put away the knife. "It's, no doubt, that same serpent who beguiled our first parents."

"How clever you are, son." the monster replied. "The serpent is my obedient servant."

"What do you want?" John asked.

"I want only to serve you and . . . to be served by you," said the snake, releasing Jack.

"What can you possibly do for us?" King Samyaza was genuinely curious.

"Well, for beginners, I can tell you that there is no more reason to fear my servant Yomyael. Your escape was quite unnecessary."

King Samyaza smiled and gave a little sigh. "I suppose I could return to my kingdom?"

"Oh, your chances would be very good. You might even succeed in the secretary's position as Yomyael never could. You could do nicely, as Dr. Canaan has lately succeeded only in drowning the City. You could be a kind of savior. Your seeming repentance would serve you well."

Samyaza began to ponder the possibilities.

"And what would you do for me?" Jack asked.

"Well, besides having the serpent warm your body from time to time, I believe I know where there is a very rich deposit of gold near here."

The serpent knew Jack's weakness.

"And for me?" Abigail asked.

"I am afraid there is little I can do for fat ladies who like to have babies. I am not in that business; however, perhaps I might see that you never go hungry."

Abigail thought deeply. "What of my daughter?"

"Now there I could work a miracle, but alas the girl has already rejected any help from me. She, like her aunt Ruth, is wholly dedicated to the Messiah. It's a pity but some people are particular about where their miracles originate."

John confronted the serpent next. "There is nothing you could do for me either. I reject you outright."

The serpent coiled itself tightly and stood facing John as though it was about to strike. Its eyes flashed. Its jaws worked and its tongue moved in and out as it hissed.

"So, you are immune to me are you? You don't believe in my power. Remember how you were impressed by the image in my temple?"

John's expression froze. He was experiencing something that none of the rest could. Perhaps he heard the music of the temple and saw the dancing image. He threw his hand in front of his eyes. "Stop it!"

"Sorry, I was only demonstrating that I could entice you too."

Jim was puzzled by the whole adventure. "What would I fall for?" he asked in a taunting way.

"Oh now, that is a hard one. Young men, especially those your age are terribly hard to manage. You are a very unusual boy at that. You are all full of good thoughts and noble aspirations."

"Have I really stumped you?"

"Oh, by no means. You see, I know that you like Noni a lot. You wish more than anything to hear her talk and be able to communicate, but she refused my help. Now, if you were very obedient to my wishes, I could make it so you might read her mind just as well as you can hear my words. "

Noni was very disturbed by this revelation, and shook Jim's arm and when he seemed not to respond, she shook her head.

"Enough of this," Daniel interrupted. "We are losing valuable time."

"Time is a thing I can help you with. I can help you reach Libnos right away."

"So, if we give in to you, we won't have to walk through this dismal forest. What will we do, ride on your back?"

"Well, that is possible, but I have a better plan."

"And what crime must we commit to gain this advantage?" Daniel queried.

"Oh, don't rush me. You know, young man, you have great impatience and greater hatred."

Daniel beckoned. "Let's be off, folks. This discussion is leading nowhere. We shouldn't even listen to this liar."

"Wait, I can see I've hit a sore spot. What I ask is very simple. In the valley just beyond this fringe of trees is a family I loathe. Now, they have a cart and lovely horses. If you would just take the horses and cart, it would give you suitable conveyance to Libnos. It would punish their insolence and serve me well. If the little king should want to return to the City of Enoch it would serve him too. After you were through with it, you could send it back. All you need do is a little borrowing."

"Is that all?" Daniel seemed to be agreeing to the idea. This alarmed the rest of his group.

"No, there might be a little chore from time to time

- nothing serious. I would reward you accordingly. Oh, Daniel, Daniel, your mind is so closed that I cannot tell if you agree!"

"It is because I will never do your bidding." Then turning away from the serpent, Daniel motioned for the group to follow. "Those who are for the serpent may stay. Those who are for the Almighty may follow me."

That day seven valiant pilgrims and their leader made a choice to follow their maker. They left the primeval tempter alone in his forest. Each met his or her trial alone, but together they were strong.

Even Tabitha met her trial. It took a lot of coaxing to bring her down from the tree, but Jim and Noni prevailed.

As they continued on they discussed how it might have been when Adam and Eve faced the tempter alone - how he had found them separated in the garden and broke down their meager defenses. Alone and with very little understanding of the consequences, the magnificent seven and their leader might have buckled too.

The flat lands around Libnos were not really flat. Actually, gentle hills and valleys swept through the dark forest near Libnos. So it was no surprise to the little group when they emerged from the forest to find a valley below them. In the center of this peaceful little valley were farm buildings surrounded by fruit trees and garden plots.

What shocked them was a mob of riffraff chasing cattle and killing them. In every direction they looked, men were butchering sheep and cows and plucking chickens. Daniel recognized the killing for what it was - the plundering of a small army of villains. There was no opposition to the men and little leadership.

Daniel drew his long knife and Jack and John fell in behind him, with King Samyaza reluctantly bringing up the rear. Tabitha pranced out before them, swishing back and forth in the tall grass as though she led the group. Jim was left behind to protect the women. As soon as the army of villains saw men coming at them they scattered, leaving carcasses and booty on the spot.

Daniel and his well organized militia found the farm buildings deserted. There was no sign of family. The defenders, if there had been any, had escaped without leaving a sign of their existence.

When Daniel decided that it was entirely safe, he motioned for Jim and the women to join his small troop. King Samyaza was in a barn getting into a cart which was hitched to a fine black horse, when Abigail found him.

"Where are you going?"

"I'm going back to the City of Enoch where I am a king."

"Is that how you want Noni to remember you - back with your friends, sacrificing human beings?"

"She is safe now. She will be glad of that."

"I thought you had changed your feelings and that perhaps you wanted to be a True Follower again."

"It is too hard."

"So, you're going to steal this family's horse and cart and do as the serpent persuades you?"

The King was silent, but he stepped down from the cart and moved away.

"Well, suit yourself. I won't stop you. You better be quick though, because I'm going to tell the others." With that Abigail left the barn.

Samyaza stood silently for a moment. Then, he knelt down on the hay beside the horse. "Oh, God, forgive me for my dishonesty. Forgive the murders that I have caused to be committed in the name of religion. Help me to choose the right. It is so hard for me. Give me a new heart. Let thy spirit take hold on my life so that I will not listen to the serpent's voice." His words broke off and he started to cry.

Above the King, in the loft of the barn, a women

and three children heard his prayer. They were moved by his plea and prayed also.

They knew that they were now safe. They knew that good people had come and saved them from the army of ruffians.

As the King finished his prayer, the woman let down a ladder and began coming down. Her three little children followed. King Samyaza looked up in amazement. He realized that had these children been seen in the City of Enoch, they most assuredly would have been sacrificed.

Just then, Abigail returned with Daniel and his followers. The woman ran to Abigail and melted in her arms. She had been through a terrible ordeal.

Turning to her husband, Abigail asked: "Would you have robbed this poor woman?"

"I changed my mind."

Daniel was not convinced. "I am glad this woman stopped you before you did something ugly." He looked over at the woman and her three children gathered around Abigail. "Where is your husband?"

"He has gone with my two oldest sons and some other brethren to help some True Followers escape from the City of Enoch. I have another child up there in the hay. He has a bad fever. Can you do something for him?"

"We can pray for him," Daniel responded.

"Oh, thank you. I hoped you would be one of us. I hear there is a doctor with the group coming from the City of Enoch. Perhaps he could treat my son."

"We will pray for him. After, if I may borrow your horse, I will go for Dr. Zanhope and the others."

"I would like that. Maybe my husband could come home."

I will leave you in the protection of these good people. Daniel looked questioningly at King Samyaza. "Are you staying, your highness?"

King Samyaza looked back with sadness. He

nodded yes. He mumbled something about being sorry. He truly was. He was glad he had made the right choice.

* * *

In another place people were also choosing sides. All around John Ferris' farm strangers were gathering to see the giant alien. For various reasons they saw his arrival as salvation to their unrelated causes.

"Is it Jesus Christ?" one asked.

"Oh, I don't think so. Maybe he is a representative. I hear he comes from the City of Enoch."

"The City of Enoch. Hallelujah!"

Stanley's army had grown considerably. They had recruited far and wide. Jack's farm was crowded with tents as far as the south pasture. John's place had become a parking lot for a most unusual array of vehicles and armored cars. From all over America malcontents had come to vow their allegiance to the strange giant who couldn't be killed by bullets. They brought with them a store of guns and ammunition that could defy an army.

Kajin was happy. He saw that the force that was gathering came from divergent views, but he was sure everything could be sorted out when Enoch and his followers arrived to found the new City of Enoch on earth.

Meanwhile, the County Sheriff was trying to keep some kind of order until the Governor would advise what to do. Alex's Clodbusters had adopted a policy of wait and see. They weren't inactive though. They were gathering auxiliaries from all over the state.

The Governor, on his part, had activated an MP company and alerted all National Guard units in the State.

"I am sorry to have created so much excitement!" spoke the little box at Kajin's side.

"Not to worry, big guy." Stanley tried to reassure him.

"What do you mean?"

"Oh, it's all right, Kajin. Everything is under control."

Just about every hour someone wanted a demonstration of Kajin's invincibility and he obliged.

Often as not someone would just pop off a few rounds, endangering anyone who happened to be nearby.

Stanley had ordered his men to keep their distance, but he wasn't against the demonstrations. He liked the publicity it brought. He had also informed the newspapers that the Air Force was trying to hide Kajin's space ship.

The press was taking pictures and asking questions. The leaders of various groups were giving speeches and reporting their views on the situation.

In Congress, healthy debates were flourishing on the floor of the Senate and the House. Local law makers were alarmed at the proliferation of arms and encampments around the alien leader. Some felt he was a religious crackpot. Others said he was a threat to the local and national government.

Lately, several prominent religious leaders had arrived. At first they were snubbed by Stanley's guards and didn't gain access to the alien from the City of Enoch. After three attempts, Kajin noticed them and asked who they were.

He graciously gave them an interview. They asked many questions. When the interview was finished, the ministers decided it was a hoax and that Kajin was a freak. "After all," they said, "the Bible said nothing about a man named Kajin from the City of Enoch coming to the United States."

According to the newspapers: "A large group of believers is organizing. The members of this group are calling themselves 'Enochites'".

Meanwhile, Kajin performed the daily sacrifice and supplication as was his custom. Stanley and his group rejoiced in the opportunity to participate in these rituals. Daily they initiated more and more to their new order. Kajin was an eloquent speaker. His views on how to get from others what rightfully should belongs to you were not unique. His methods were exciting to the have-nots who were not willing to work.

Shortly before dawn on the fourth day, Kajin was strolling in the meadow. Some of Stanley's men were trailing him and Stanley was talking to Kajin about prospective sites for the new City of Enoch.

Just as they reached the neighbor's orchard, Kajin raised his hand as a signal to halt. He pointed to the spot a few feet in front of him and said. "I declare this to be the site for the new City of Enoch."

As Stanley was turning to face Kajin, a shot rang out. There was a gasp and Stanley fell dead at Kajin's feet. There was silence. The giant simply reached down and picked up his friend and carried him back into camp.

The bullet wasn't intended to kill anyone. It was just a doubting person's desire to make sure - to see for himself, if Kajin was really bullet proof. Stanley's men didn't see it that way. They caught the gunman and mercilessly cut him to ribbons with their bullets.

Not long after, some Clodbusters came upon the gunman's riddled body and reported it to Sheriff Kline. His deputies took plaster impressions of the foot prints around the scene and examined the area for other evidence.

About this time, Stanley's body was taken to the local undertaker and, because of the nature of his death, was turned over to the County Coroner. Questions were asked at Jack's place. Stanley's companions were close lipped about the incident. They said only that an assassin had done it. Their attitude was surly. Something was said about the Sheriff not keeping order.

From that time on Stanley's followers developed a bitter and ugly way of dealing with fortune seekers and visitors to the "City". Frequently, hard feelings flared up and people were pushed about.

Kajin could see the explosive nature of the situation. Maybe this wasn't the right time for the City of Enoch. Perhaps a few years later would be better.

The Clodbusters also had ideas. They wanted to move in with the Sheriff's department and arrest the "Pro-Castro underground" that Stanley had left behind. They were joined daily by many radical groups and were becoming a massive military threat. Since the Enochites had joined, Stanley's followers had grown to over 5,500. Tense incidents occurred almost every day. It was impossible to keep order in such a large group. The sheriff's department could not foresee the problems that arose.

No one knew quite how it started, but the next day while Kajin was inspecting the mine shaft to see if there was any sign of his being zapped back to his own time, a fight broke out in the camp. Someone began making threats and then one of Stanley's followers began firing. Jack's farmhouse soon became a place of defense.

Below ground, Kajin could hear the shots. He knew that no one could be firing at him. This was no demonstration. He rode the lift to the surface and climbed into the shed at the top.

As he came through the door of the shed, bullets hit him from all sides. There were two armed camps. Sheriff's deputies had returned fire and called in support from the MP Company located nearby. The Clodbusters had responded. Many of them were already deputized.

Kajin moved slowly across the opening between the shed and the farm house. He was impervious to the bullets. When he reached the farmhouse, he shouted to be let in. The nature of his attempt frightened the attacking hoards. It was feared that Kajin might have secret weapons as well as immunity to their arms.

Armored personnel carriers were brought up and

fifty caliber weapons were fired. Before the battle was over, Stanley's followers were all destroyed and the farm house was burnt to the ground. Kajin emerged from this mess as the only survivor. He wasn't happy.

Neither was the Governor. How would he answer to his people? How would he answer to the people of the United States. In Congress debate became hot. Three Senators were dispatched to investigate the fiasco. Their conclusion: "The National Guard acted with excess of force."

More than fifty men were dead. The press made a big issue of the problems in the State. Everyone was disturbed throughout the country.

Kajin retired to the shed and thence to the mine shaft. He was wondering if some form of retaliation wasn't in order. He felt powerful in his protective shield. He didn't understand this alien race. He took out the land clearing device that he had brought from the past and decided that tomorrow he would clear the area around the place he had designated.

* * *

Zanhope, Rachel, Alex and Jaydee had just settled in the shelters prepared by Mahai's men, when Daniel arrived. It was agreed that Zanhope and Greuban would leave at once and the rest of Mahai's army would follow early in the morning. Greuban, it turned out, was the owner of the farm and the father of the boy with the fever.

Zanhope took the black stuff Mahai's men had confiscated from Dr. Canaan's troop. He thought it might come in handy if the ruffian army returned to the farmhouse.

Daniel was happy to see his father, Mahai. They exchanged hugs and information about the travelers.

In the morning when all were gathered at the

farmhouse, Zanhope announced that Greuban's son was better. Helpful herbs gathered in the forest had been boiled and made into a broth and the fever had broken.

It didn't appear that the ruffians would return, but just in case, Dr. Zanhope and Alex had prepared a new weapon to drive them away. "Lea" would drop small packets of powder mixed with clay over the heads of the invading army. These could be ignited by a small triggering device. The defenders hoped these tiny missiles would scare the army away and Mahai's men would not have to fight.

By noon, the travelers were ready to resume their trip to Libnos and were in the middle of their goodbyes when the ruffian army returned with still others they had gathered in the neighborhood. Mahai marshaled some of his troops around the valley farm and Alex and Daniel took others up into the woods just above.

Neither group had to fight. Before the villains were close enough to do battle, Dr. Zanhope went into action with "Lea". "Lea" swooped down on them dropping bag after bag. In between bombing runs, she dived down and bashed in a few heads. The confusion this caused was enough to drive the ruffian army away for good.

Some of Mahai's militia stayed at the farmhouse, though, to lend a hand helping Greuban until they were sure the villains would not return.

Barbara and Eunice decided to stay also. The two of them had taken a liking to the calm sweet spirit of Greuban's family and their help was welcome on the large farm.

Chapter 2 The Golden Chariot

Enoch's patience was wearing thin with Dr. Canaan. First, the City of Enoch was experiencing a flood almost equal to the great flood to come. The only part of the City saved from the deluge was the central island and the mansions of the Kings and the pyramids on the perimeter of the City. Second, his father couldn't be returned from the future. Third, Dr. Canaan couldn't enter his laboratory. It was sealed.

On his part, Dr. Canaan dared not show his face in the chambers of the great Enoch. He had determined to track down Dr. Zanhope and bring him back in chains. Never much of an innovator, Canaan was reluctant to admit that he was nothing without his cohort.

Now, the chips were down. He needed Zanhope and Zanhope was gone. He wasn't only gone, he was insubordinate. There was a rumor abroad that Dr. Zanhope had gone back to the old beliefs. Even so, there were ways to persuade a "True Follower" to cooperate.

Dr. Canaan had traveled all night. His horse was lame. The doctor had feared for his life three times during the journey. Twice he had seen strange lights on the road. Once he got off the road and nearly fell to his death into a chasm. He was in fear for his life.

As he led his mount through the gates of Libnos, he was a most weary traveler. He went straight to the Libnos factory that he and Dr. Zanhope had started. Workmen were just arriving.

"Dr. Canaan," Burbos Josie addressed him with surprise. "Did you finally receive the supply of explosives?"

"Yes, and with it I blew up the City of Enoch."

"You jest?"

"I wish."

"What do you mean? You haven't started a private

war with the Prophet, have you?"

"Worse, everyone is against me."

"This sounds intriguing."

Canaan ignored the comment and looked around the compound. "Dr. Zanhope hasn't shown his face here has he?"

"I haven't seen Zanhope in several months. Is there reason to believe he is coming here? I should like to see him. I have had some trouble with the aero plane."

"He may come here. If he does, you will not give him access to the aero plane for any reason! Further, Burbos, I want him put in irons and kept until I return." There was rage in the doctor's words.

"Just a minute." Burbos called over his assistant. "Budmore, Dr. Canaan says that we are to put Dr. Zanhope in chains if we see him." Burbos turned back to Dr. Canaan. "There, is that what you wanted?"

"Yes!"

Dr. Canaan stalked off leaving the two men to puzzle over the reason. What could their friend Zanhope have done to deserve this kind of treatment? Burbos turned back to his assistant. "He doesn't want us to let Zanhope near the aero plane. Do you think all this has something to do with our little experiment?"

"Possibly. Still, there must be more to it that we haven't heard."

"He spoke of blowing up the City of Enoch. Maybe Zanhope has gone mad and caused Canaan to do something stupid."

"If you ask me he is always doing something stupid."

"Yes, that is true enough. Let's go to work."

* * *

In the hut of Tumic Bar, twelve visitors were huddled for the night. It was cold in the City of Libnos. The wind whistled through the streets. A white dusty clay blew down the alley. The buildings, mostly made of that same white clay, were nearly all dark. The twelve were alone. Tumic, their host, was out. His wife was busy in the kitchen brewing warm cider and baking cakes. Tabitha was curled up beside the fire.

Dr. Zanhope presided over the little group. "We have come this far. Tomorrow we will bring the rest here and take over the aero plane."

Daniel hovered in the background now. He had more time to concentrate on his relationship with Ruth. He was no longer the leader. Perhaps he was the spiritual advisor, but no one had asked his advice.

He hoped his father would join them tomorrow. Daniel's father and many other True Followers were keeping watch tonight throughout the City. Alex had organized them into a militia of secret police and taught them some of the methods he had learned in the CIA.

"What is the aero plane like?" John asked.

"It is copied after one of your small defense bombers." Zanhope's eyes flashed. "It can carry a small amount of freight or passengers. It will be just right for our purposes."

"Is it complete?" Alex could hardly wait to try it out.

"I haven't seen it. They told me it was nearly ready months ago, but I couldn't come over here to help make some of the components for the engine."

"Can I help?"

"No doubt you could."

Rachel and Noni soon lost interest in the discussion. Rachel took Noni by the hand and told her how she felt about Alex. Noni could only nod and shake her head, but that was sufficient for Rachel. Abigail and her sister helped in the kitchen.

Jaydee and Jim had been talking nonstop since they

all arrived this morning. The rest of their group slept through the day, but Jaydee and Jim talked.

Now, it was Jaydee's turn to be jealous. He had thought of Noni as his girl. His first love so to speak. Nevertheless, he did not want to mar his friendship with Jim. They reviewed the events of the past days with infinite attention to detail. It was homecoming.

Tumic had slipped into the kitchen from the back of the hut and was serving his guests the hot cider and cakes when there was a knock at the door. Hush fell over the group. There was apprehension that they had been talking too loudly and had been discovered by one of the black guard. Gingerly, Tumic opened the door a crack to see who was there in the shadows.

"It is I, Burbos Josie."

"Come in Burbos."

Looking around the room, Burbos spied his friend Dr. Zanhope in the group. "Oh, Dr. Zanhope, Dr. Canaan here and is looking for you. He wants us to put you in chains. What have you done?"

"Burbos, my friend." The two men met and gave each other a hug and a pat on the back. It was clear that Burbos wasn't interested in bringing Dr. Zanhope to justice.

The little hut was crowded beyond comfort. Presently, Daniel, King Samyaza, the two boys and the four women were left alone with Tumic and his family while the four other men retired to Burbos' cottage to plot and plan.

A dark figure watched the home of Burbos. He saw Burbos go out and he saw him return with the three men. He had sent an accomplice to follow Burbos to the home of Tumic and he knew that there was a large group in his hut. It was time to report to Saluki.

* * *

Saluki sat brooding over a large bowl of steaming

230

hot soup. He swished his spoon through the mixture examining each hot vegetable. Strings of chicken interrupted the green and yellow chunks. He dipped a spoonful from the bowl, blew across it, and tested it with his lips.

"It's too hot, wife!"

"I told you."

"I know." He emptied the spoon back into the bowl and placed it on the table.

He was disappointed. Why did women always make things so hot. Everything had to be hot enough to burn. He was forever in need of time and here he sat delayed by a bowl of soup.

There was a knock at the door. "More interruption," he murmured. He rose, pulled his collar up tight around his neck and opened the door.

A man dressed in black slipped through the crack and pulled back his hood showing a mess of bright yellow hair. It was his shy.

"Juju! Has Zanhope shown his face?"

"Yes, master. He is in Burbos' house now with two strange men and the rest are in the hut of Tumic."

"Did anyone see you?"

"No one is about. It is too cold and bitter out."

"I shall tell our visitor that the doctor has come to Libnos. Wait here; I'll be right back."

Juju wandered around the room. He tested Saluki's soup. His back was to the door. It opened and two people entered without his knowing. When he looked around to see if anyone had noticed his indiscretion, he saw the two men for the first time. They wore hoods and didn't remove them.

"Who are you?"

"Don't cry out! The house is surrounded." The two seated themselves at the table and motioned for Juju to sit also. When Saluki returned with Dr. Canaan, the three were sitting quietly.

"What?" Dr. Canaan sputtered.

Saluki was angered. Looking at Juju, he sprang forward, reaching for the two men. Saluki stopped in mid air. He faced two knives hastily drawn from under the cloaks of his uninvited guests.

"Sit down, my friend. You too, Doctor!"

Juju looked across the table at his master. "They say the house is surrounded."

"By whom?" Dr. Canaan demanded.

"Your friends from Enoch's city, Doctor." The tall stranger spoke. "Your friends seek retribution for your acts of unkindness. I understand that you have flooded the City and have failed in your attempt to return the Prophet's father."

"Who accuses me? I demand to know who you are."

The tall one threw open his hood.

"Dr. Zanhope!

"This is a poor joke." Dr. Canaan sputtered.

"It's not a joke, Canaan. You were going to have me in chains. Is that a joke?"

"Well, you sealed the laboratory."

"And so you tried to blow it apart."

"I needed the time travel equipment."

"You don't need it."

"How so?"

"I have the ball with me. I can bring Kajin back whenever you want."

"Then do it!"

"There is something I want in return."

"What?"

"The aero plane."

"So take it. If you have this house surrounded what is to stop you?"

"I need fuel. I need your authorization."

"It will do you no good. The engine is incomplete."

"I can complete it now. I have an alien who knows about these things."

Dr. Canaan looked over the second man. "Who is he?"

Alex pulled open his hood.

"This is the man." Zanhope announced.

"Bring paper, Saluki!"

"But, Doctor. We cannot let them take the aero plane."

"Without the engine it is nothing." Canaan wrote as he spoke. He handed a note to Saluki. "You shall have the fuel tomorrow, Zanhope."

"Don't try to interfere, Canaan! We have agents all over this city."

"I shall await your success," Canaan said with a sneer.

"I'm sure," Zanhope countered. The two visitors withdrew from the table and left. Dr. Canaan said nothing. He felt cheated. He abandoned his host with his helper and climbed the stair way to the second floor disgusted.

Saluki pointed to the door. He did not need to say a word. Juju rose and went out into the night.

Finally alone, Saluki tested the soup. It was cold.

* * *

After King Samyaza had drunk his fill of cider and supped on cakes, he leaned back against the fire and began to snore. His wife, Abigail, and her sister, Ruth, came out of the kitchen with Mrs. Tumic.

"Where did the men go?" Jim asked.

"They have gone to the home of Burbos Josie to plan our escape to the tent people," Rachel answered.

"Perhaps we should bring the rest of Dr. Zanhope's staff here tonight," Jaydee said.

233

"It would be a little crowded," the others laughed.

"Yeah, I guess so."

"Tomorrow will be soon enough. We have word from them that they are safe. Alex has done wonders organizing the local men here and in Enoch's City to spy for him."

"How did the staff escape from the soldiers?" Jaydee asked.

"When you and my father flew away, the soldiers went after you. Doctors Asa and Lystra led the staff to Dr. Zanhope's house."

"That would be the first place I would look."

"In the flood and all the commotion since, no one has thought to look there. Now, they have been trapped in the second story by the flood waters. We will time shift them tomorrow."

"You'll what?" Jim didn't understand the term.

"Time shift them. We bring them back or forth in time a little and move them here. It's tricky."

"I'll say. This whole experience has been tricky."

Noni came over to Jim and made some signs to him. Jaydee was surprised.

"Hey, what is this? What did she say?"

"She says that she likes you."

"Oh, yeah! After all you two have been through together, she likes me." Jaydee said with sarcasm.

"Well, she says she likes us both, but she thinks you're very brave."

"Hey, teach me some of this stuff. I want to make sure you didn't just make that all up." Jaydee was provoked.

Noni smiled and made some more signs.

"She can still understand everything you say, Jaydee."

"So teach me!"

The three young people were soon busy with their hands. Jaydee especially liked the experience because Noni took his hands and showed him how to hold his fingers to make the various signs.

Abigail shook King Samyaza awake.

"What!"

"You were snoring."

"I always snore when I'm full."

"Come talk with us for a while."

"What about."

"Rachel cannot believe that you have changed."

"I haven't."

Rachel joined Abigail and the King at the fire. "Father says that you are going to reunite with the True Followers."

"Well, it would be foolish right now not to. Nevertheless, I really do miss my horses."

Abigail screwed up her face. "And your skinny wife?"

"Not as much."

"Be serious, my husband."

"I am. I miss the whole thing. I miss the horses, the food, the music, but I see now that you and Noni have the best of it all."

Rachel put her arm around the King and gave him a little hug as she stood above him. "That's sweet."

"Like I said, I'd be foolish not to."

* * *

"It's too small!" Zanhope had just seen the aero plane for the first time.

"That's what I tried to tell Dr. Canaan, but he wouldn't listen."

"Where did this design come from? It's totally different."

"It was in the second book of plans you brought me."

Alex was admiring the bright golden outer shell of the little interceptor. "It's beautiful!"

"But it won't begin to carry our people."

"Maybe we could move you and you could use the ball to move the rest."

Saddened, the doctor stroked his beard. "Yes, it will have to do. Let's start with the rest of the engine now."

The three men went into the office and Alex supplied the remaining details that were needed to make the jet engine work. In three days the aero plane was ready. Alex took it up for a trial run. Everything was perfect. The sound of it was exciting. It roared smoothly into the sky. Alex felt it was better than anything he had yet flown.

Dr. Canaan and Saluki were also excited. They did not interfere. They were content to watch from the sidelines.

Saluki had studied the plans and operations for the fighter. He was a bright young star in the evil doctor's following. Little escaped his attention. He would someday fly the bright golden chariot.

Dr. Zanhope had brought Kajin back as agreed and Dr. Canaan had sent the giant time traveler on to the City of Enoch alone as a peace offering for the Prophet.

Dr. Canaan asked a mechanic for details he missed. "Was the armament installed?"

"Yes. It has been tested too."

Chapter 3 Doctor Canaan's Revenge

"It's gone!"

John was first to see inside the hanger as the three men approached the open door. Sure enough, the bright golden interceptor wasn't there.

The shop foreman and his assistant tried to explain. "Dr. Canaan took it. He and Saluki came just ten minutes ago. They came at us from two different directions. We couldn't stop them."

John, Jack and Alex stood dejectedly trying to figure out what to do, when Dr. Zanhope, Burbos and Tumic arrived.

"Where is the aero plane?"

"They got it, Doctor." Jack said.

"They? Canaan and his lackey?"

"Yes."

"He doesn't know how to fly it."

"Saluki does. He has been studying the plans for months."

"We've been double crossed, gentlemen."

"What will you do, Doctor?"

Doctors Asa and Lystra walked up just then. This was to be their first viewing of the aero plane.

"It's been stolen, my friends," John said. "What should we do?"

Dr. Lystra, always the one to put things right, had the first suggestion. "You told us that you undid all the chaos Kajin caused by lifting him out of the future before he started making trouble. Right?"

"Yes, what are you driving at?" Zanhope asked.

"Well, we caused an airplane crash in the future which I think should be undone."

"What airplane crash?" Zanhope was puzzled.

"The one where the probe got wedged in the cockpit and caused the pilot to panic."

237

"Oh yes, on the farm where the boys from the future found our probe."

"Yes, we could undo that crash."

"I think I see what you suggest." Zanhope said. "We could retrieve that plane before it crashed and bring it here. That would nullify the crash and give us a means to escape."

"Splendid!" Alex cut in.

Dr. Zanhope was excited. "Exactly. Let's do it, Dr. Lystra."

Dr. Asa was full of questions. "Where would you pick it up? Are you just going to take it out of the air before it crashes? How do we land it?"

"One thing at a time, Doctor."

"I could take the pilot's place," Alex suggested.

"That won't do," said Lystra. "The pilot would still be in trouble for ditching his plane."

"Why don'tcha take the crew and all?" said Jack.

"How do we bring them out of the sky?" Dr. Asa asked. "Hijack them?"

"They don't have to come out of the sky." John explained. "We just put our people in the plane. Once they're in the plane and pilot finds himself in a strange time, we'll convince him to help us. Is that hijacking?"

Jack didn't beat around. "Yeah, it is."

"That's never stopped us in the past . . . er should I say, future," John added. "Besides, we're undoing a wrong."

"Two wrongs don't make a right, though." Dr. Zanhope was trapped in his new found desire to do the right thing.

Dr. Lystra could guess his problem. "But you're restoring what we have destroyed. I say: do it!"

Burbos asked the key question: "What do you say, Doctor?"

Dr. Zanhope stroked his beard nervously. "Let's go ahead. We'll just have to convince the pilot that it is better than the alternative."

"Who'll do the convincing, Doctor?" Lystra asked.

"That will be Alex's job. He comes from the future." Zanhope scanned the sky. "We have just one other thing to worry about. Where is Canaan with that deadly interceptor?"

* * *

Dr. Canaan was having the time of his life. Saluki was also enjoying himself. They flew and flew until the aero plane was almost out of gas.

"We must go down, Doctor."

"Take it down on the road near Enoch's city. I have just the place to keep it. There is a wood near the road to Libnos."

Canaan didn't dare to approach Enoch until he could show that he had something of great use. He would demonstrate the fire power of the aero plane and then he would come home. Saluki made a perfect landing - well, nearly perfect for an amateur.

Dr. Canaan soon had help brought from the City and the plane was sheltered in the woods. He signed a requisition for gas. This was a commodity which only the rich and noble could obtain. The kind he needed was very rare at present but he had developed a factory in nearby Obelsail. The needed fuel would come before dawn. He planned to destroy the factory in Libnos then.

Dr. Canaan followed the men into the woods as they rolled the sleek little plane into the shadows and into a meadow near a little brook. Dr. Canaan sat down on a log to rest and Saluki joined him. A shelter was soon put together for the aero plane and the two men. Comforts were brought from the City of Enoch and a fire was built by the little stream.

"Dr. Canaan." A voice seemed to come out of

nowhere.

"Did you say something, Saluki?"

"No, Doctor. Maybe one of the workmen did. I thought I heard something also."

"Doctor, it is I, the prince of flight." The log on which they sat moved and the two men were soon mesmerized by fright. The head of a giant snake was bobbing and weaving before them, holding their attention.

"I hate to do this, but it does work. Most people imagine that my words are their own thoughts. Worse yet they think they are hearing the Almighty speak to them even though they are too wicked to hear him at all."

"Are we hearing the snake, Doctor?"

"I don't think snakes talk."

The voice sounded in their minds again. "You are right. It is your old friend."

"You say you are the prince of flight?" Dr. Canaan asked.

"Yes, I had hoped you would realize that I am he."

"What can you do for me?"

"Well, I thought you might like to know that your old comrade, Dr. Zanhope, is going to try to escape by aero plane tomorrow."

"How can he do that? We have the only aero plane."

"Oh, well, he is going to steal one from the future."

"That would be perfect." Dr. Canaan said.

The serpent stopped swaying. "How is that?"

"We can shoot him down and demonstrate the value of our new weapon."

"Good. That is a great idea, Doctor."

Saluki, still mesmerized by the serpent, finally ventured a thought of his own. "If you are the prince of flight, what can you do to make us fly better?"

"Let me see. I shall promise you both that you shall go up when you want and shall not come down until you are ready and that you shall feel no pain even though your aero plane should crash."

"What kind of promise is that? Why can't you make us a promise so we can't crash?"

"All right, I shall promise that you, Saluki, shall never crash."

" That's more like it!"

Chapter 4 Never to Crash

Major Colin Bailey shared Saluki's desire to never crash, but, as we know, he did. On the other hand, Dr. Lystra suggested that Dr. Zanhope undo the crash by catching the C119 in the future before the crash. He also was to bring the C119 into the past and use it for their transport to the western wilderness. Zanhope did this by sending "Lea" forward in time to find the C119, drag the probe and airplane back into the past and time-shift his people and equipment aboard the airship. Now Major Bailey was to have a whole new future, or is it past - one which would make him wonder if he was immune to crash.

At the instant that Dr. Zanhope found his airplane in the future, Bailey experienced a series of frightening lightening flashes and thunder claps. They were brighter and louder than any he had ever seen or heard. Moreover, the center of this disturbance was right behind him in the cabin. He felt sure his cargo was pounding holes in his craft, but there was no rocking or pitching to go with these seeming explosions.

Major Bailey turned the controls over to Captain Deven King and started back into the cabin to investigate the commotion. In the dim light of the cabin, he could see many people seated in the passenger slings. Cory Thurston, his load master, was removing his headset as he approached the Major.

"When did all these people come on board, Sergeant Thurston?" Bailey shouted over the drone of the engines. "Our manifest doesn't show them."

"That's what I was coming to see you about," Cory shouted back. "I was blinded by some brilliant bursts of light and they just appeared out of nowhere."

"And loud explosions?"

"Yes, Major, very loud."

"Impossible! I saw the light and heard the noise

too. It was too near." Major Bailey looked around at the people suspiciously. "You'd think this whole cabin would be blown apart."

"Yes, sir."

Bailey focused again on the Sergeant. "Is this a joke, Thurston?"

"No, sir."

One of the passengers rose from the canvas bench along the side and came up to the two crewmen. "I'm Alex Goodrich, CIA." Alex flashed a badge in his wallet. "Perhaps I can clarify things, Major."

"Please do."

Alex pointed to the one of the ports along the side of the cabin. "If you will look out your window, you will find that the terrain below is really unfamiliar."

"At this altitude, I doubt I could tell anything about terrain."

"Then, check for ground signals."

"This does look strange, Major," the sergeant said, as he looked out the ports on the side. "A while ago we were traveling in clear blue sky. Now we are in a dense cloud cover."

"That can't be. There was clear sky all around when I left the cockpit."

"See for yourself, sir."

The Major looked. "I don't see what that has to do with all these passengers."

"Major, you are now in a time in the history of the world when only one other plane has flown."

"What do you mean?"

"I mean that the sky all around you is nearly 7000 years younger than when you started out this morning. These passengers have been beamed on board your ship from that time and we are traveling into an area where there are no airstrips or flight patterns established."

"You CIA weirdoes think we'll fall for anything.

You've hijacked my plane!"

"I'm afraid you are right."

The Major slumped down in the seat Alex had just vacated along the wall of the cabin. He refused to believe. "What do you want? I don't know how you got here but what do you want?"

"We just want you to drop us off about 500 miles from here. I have a chart if you would care to look at it."

"What would I do with a chart? I'm not a navigator. I don't even have one on board. We are just on a routine flight going home." The Major suddenly looked shocked. "Oh, no, the cargo!"

"What is it, Major?" The load master knelt down so that his head was at the same level as the commander. "What about the cargo - you mean the box that we were asked to bring along?"

"Yes." Major Bailey's concern was that his new passengers might be after the cargo for some reason.

Now Alex was interested. "What cargo are you talking about?"

"I can't tell you. It's top secret. Stay away from it!"

"Major," a voice came over the intercom.

"Captain King is calling for you, sir."

The voice came again. "Where did all these clouds come from?"

The Major responded with a firmness that was second nature to him. His jaw tightened. It was the feel of command. He must make the best of the situation. He must find a solution. Perhaps he should destroy the plane - now. He got up and vaulted up the ladder to the cockpit. When he got there, Captain King was calm.

"Sorry to disturb you, Colin. I just got spooked when all these clouds appeared out of nowhere."

"It's nothing, Steve. Just try to climb above it." Major Bailey settled down into his seat and pretended to know what he was doing. He must not lose his cool.

"Unidentified plane at 11 o'clock, sir." Sergeant Thurston voice came over the intercom.

Alex was at his shoulder. "It's Dr. Canaan."

"Who's he?" Bailey asked somewhat subdued.

"He's not a friend."

"What's going on, Major? Where did this civilian come from?" The pilot queried.

"CIA, Steve. I just found him and his friends on board. I think it has something to do with the cargo."

The little interceptor crossed their path again. It was traveling at a terrific speed. Suddenly, the golden interceptor turned on the C119. It came right at them, leveled its guns and fired. The flying boxcar was no match for the fighter. Instinctively, Major Bailey pointed the ship down, taking evasive action. The passengers were thrown about in the cabin. Tabitha broke away from Noni and crouched under the bench along the side. She growled intermittently.

Luckily the interceptor fired only conventional weapons. Bullets ripped through one of the wings and across the right fuselage, bringing all of the passengers to their feet. Jaydee drew Tabitha from under his seat and clutched her snugly, reassuring her with a purring sound. In the cockpit, sweat popped out on Major Bailey's brow. He was concerned for his passengers. "Sit down and fasten your seat belts."

At that moment the fighter made another pass. This time there were some solid hits on the outside of the cabin.

Thurston surveyed the passengers seated along the sides of the cabin. "Is everyone ok?" he shouted.

Almost everyone nodded nervously. Tabitha struggled to free herself, but Jaydee constrained her. He held her to his face and hummed gently in her ear. She relaxed.

Daniel bowed his head and began to pray out loud. Ruth and Rachel followed suit. It didn't matter that they were all praying out loud. Little could be heard in the din of the engines as they labored to bring the plane out of a shallow dive.

"Open that box, Sergeant," Major Bailey shouted into the intercom.

"I'm on it." Thurston, who was now standing in the middle of the plane, turned and strode to the rear of the cabin. He broke the seals and opened the box marked "top secret". Inside were launchers and missiles. They were marked "heat seeking" and "experimental". "What now Major?"

"Can you open a jump door and shoot that guy down with one of those missiles?"

"I can try."

"Do it!" Major Bailey's urge for self preservation had gotten the best of his devotion to duty.

Seeing what Sergeant Thurston was up to, John jumped to his feet. "You can't shoot that thing in here. It will fill the cabin with smoke and flames and probably set this old crate on fire!"

"We can use 'Lea'!" Zanhope sprang into action and came to the door, carrying the ball and the controller.

After what seemed like ages, the three men found the right combination, armed a missile and sent the little brass ball out the jump door with it. "Lea" flew a few yards away from the C119 and aimed her projectile at the little golden interceptor as it swept by. There was a burst of flame and smoke. The rocket shot out at the target, locked on to it, and, describing a long curve, followed the interceptor on its third run at the Flying Boxcar.

Saluki had seen the missile fired. He didn't try to fire at the C119. He must have seen the missile following him and passed under and behind his target. For a second Sergeant Thurston saw the missile head straight towards him, then, for some reason, it exploded.

"Oops! I dropped the launching mechanism," Dr.

246

Zanhope said bringing "Lea" back with some trepidation.

"You must have dropped it right in the path of the missile," said Sergeant Thurston. "That was a happy accident."

"It could have happened because of our prayers," Jim added.

Another missile was fitted to the little brass ball and she took her position just as the interceptor came around for a forth pass. This time the rocket followed the plane with great tenacity.

Saluki, on his part, tried everything to lose the rocket. He dived, did barrel rolls and slips.

Somewhere in the busy maneuvers, Dr. Canaan found a moment to eject. His chute did not work well, but he fell into a large pine tree.

Saluki would not give up. He stayed with the ship. Finally, hoping to climb beyond the range of the missile, he headed up straight for the sun. The speed and the stress worked a hardship on the little interceptor. First the wings failed. Then the tail section dropped off. The golden chariot began to wobble. At last the engine stopped, but the little rocket pursued with devilish accuracy. There was a tremendous explosion and a huge fireball.

An audible sigh of relief was heard over the intercom coming from the cockpit. Captain King who had never been in an air fight, gave Major Bailey a little pat on the back.

Bailey smiled slightly. "Are there any more of your friends out there, Goodrich?"

"No. You just shot down the only other plane in this time period."

"How far are we from your drop zone?"

"I calculate about one hour on this bearing."

"Good."

"None of these people have ever jumped before, Major. If it's all the same, I'd like you to take the plane down and land."

"Look, CIA man, your people never fired one of those missiles before. It seems to me that they could jump for the first time."

"Well, it's not that simple. We have women and children and equipment. I doubt you have enough chutes for them all and you surely don't have cargo chutes for the equipment."

"What's the terrain like?"

"Most of it is lowlands. I'm sure we can find a place."

"Ok, ok."

Everyone was elated until Daniel noticed that Mahai, his father, was just staring straight across the cabin at him, his eyes glassy. Daniel got up and crossed the cabin. He ran his hand in front of the old man's face. There was no response.

Daniel sat down on the bench beside Mahai. He unbuckled his father and cradled him in his arms. He touched something wet on Mahai's back. On the pad behind his father where his back had been pressed against the wall of the cabin, there were several small holes.

The look of horror on Daniel's face told the whole story. Some of the bullets that had entered the cabin during the fight had struck Mahai in the back.

Zanhope tested his pulse. There was none. Mahai was dead.

Dr. Zanhope closed Mahai's eyes and Dr. Asa helped Daniel lay the old man on the cabin floor. Sergeant Thurston helped them strap him in place. No one spoke.

Daniel rose and looked out one of the ports. Below, a sea of grey-blue shadows was interrupted by islands of dull grey-green. Daniel wept.

Ruth stood, came up behind him and put her arm around him. He turned and she held him to her shoulder. No one remembered much more about the flight.

* * *

Dr. Canaan worked himself free from the giant tree in which he had landed. The foliage was thick and soft. With effort he lowered himself from layer to layer until he was only about fifty feet from the ground.

"Never come down until you're ready," he murmured. "All right I want to come down."

The branch he was riding gave way at that instant and he fell into the snow below. It was cold but soft.

The promise of the serpent or whatever it was rang true. It hadn't been painful. He supposed too, that Saluki would never come down. There was nothing left of Saluki to come down or for that matter there was nothing of the little interceptor.

He could no longer hear the C119. He vowed that he would get even. Somehow, someway he would deal with Dr. Zanhope in the future. If he had to track him to the end of the world, he would have vengeance.

Chapter 5 The Pilgrims of Enoch

Sirock Shum left his tent to check on the cattle. He was bare headed and wore only a light jacket of sheep skin. He had long blond hair, a handsome reddish beard and sported an elegant tan. The sun had been hot that day but it would soon be cool.

He, his wife and his sons had lived in the wilderness for many years. They had fine families. They lived a peaceful existence away from the difficulties of civilization.

It would soon be dark. His dog, Moke, joined him on his nightly rounds. Where was that dog? Maybe he was chasing a rabbit.

Soon he could hear the dog baying. Sirock guessed that he had found live quarry. The sound came closer.

There was a rustling in the brush. Something small dashed past Sirock in a great hurry. It scurried up the tree behind him. There in the tree was a long haired cat. Sirock did not recognize the feline.

Moke appeared, panting and barking. His mouth was frothing. He worried the cat in the tree for a bit and then turned to Sirock disgusted with the chase. Something else was bothering him.

Moke looked up at Sirock and barked. The dog seemed anxious to lead him somewhere. Sirock followed.

In a little hollow called the flat place, he saw a large shadow where he hadn't seen any homes or buildings before. Coming closer, he could see people gathered around an object that he couldn't identify. It was a strange house, if that was what it was. It had large hard awnings that were attached to long booms. It stood on tree trunks which ran down into wheels. There were wind mills attached to its booms. It definitely didn't belong there.

"Hey, you people. You can't live on this land. It belongs to the people of Sirock Shum."

A tall man with a beard rose from the group that was seated under one of the awnings and came towards Sirock.

"Do you know me, Sirock," he asked. The man's features were in the shadow and Sirock was looking into the setting sun, but he could recognize the voice. Someone he hadn't seen in many years had that voice. He began to walk faster.

"I know you!" he said. "I know you." It was his son, Zanhope. He hadn't seen him since he left the holy mountain. How did he know to come here?

Zanhope put out his arms and the little man fell into his embrace. "Father, please forgive me." A girl followed. "This is Rachel. Do you remember little Rachel."

"Yes I remember." The red bearded man extended his hand to the girl. "Come, Rachel, meet your grandfather." They all embraced and laughed.

Turning to his son again and holding him at arm's length, Sirock smiled.

"You are forgiven, son. Are you clean now."

"Yes, papa. I am clean. I have forsaken the evil of my past. May I bring my friends to meet you?"

"Yes, son, your friends are mine."

Sirock met them all. "Where is your wife?" he asked.

"She was sacrificed by the Enochites."

"Oh, I am so sorry. She was a wonderful woman."

Sirock's love for his son was extended to his traveling companions. He sent for tenting to drape around the inside of the strange house, blankets to warm its occupants and food of every description to grace their table. They couldn't have a fire in the cabin, but they all had warm blankets and the drapes on the walls shut out the cold of the night.

He gave orders to make the strangers comfortable but his son and granddaughter he took to his own tent.

When they entered the tent and his wife recognized them, she couldn't contain the joy she felt.

His faithful sons were notified and came home to see the prodigal. They spoke of the time, now long past, when they all lived on the holy mountain and how the army of Genun had come with their beauties and their horses to tempt the sons of God.

In those days, Zanhope had gone with the 200 wayward. They had left on the pretext that they would teach the Gospel to the sons of Cain who in the Adamic tongue was known as Kajin. Shum had left the mountain in shame for his son. He had taken all his young brothers on a long trek out into the wilderness hoping that they wouldn't follow their brother. It worked for him. They were all here.

Zanhope had been the star of the family - his father's gem. Now, even he had returned. Zanhope, on his part, had grown with experience. His experience had caused him to grow strong. Once he had changed for the better, that strength made him a leader.

His younger brothers still looked up to him. They made a place for him in their hearts. He could have his old birthright if he wanted.

* * *

Major Bailey was a good host. He quickly became acquainted with his brood of passengers. He was concerned about their comfort.

That first night, Major Bailey introduced himself to all the visitors, taking time to learn about each one.

"Now let me see, you are Dr. Zanhope's first assistant, Dr. Lystra. Are you a medical doctor or a physicist or what?"

"I am sorry to bore you, Major Bailey. We don't specialize. Doctor is a title we borrow from your culture. In our time it means mastery of all the sciences."

"I see. Then you are a doctor of science in its broadest sense."

"Perhaps. Certainly not so broad that I can fly one of your aero planes."

"Airplanes," Major Bailey corrected. "They haven't been called aero planes in ages."

"Oh, you see how naive we are, Major."

"Not at all. You may be beautiful and innocent, but certainly not naive, Doctor." Dr. Lystra blushed. She was excited that Major Bailey could be so warm and polite.

Turning to King Samyaza, Major Bailey called Captain King to his side and asked Dr. Lystra to translate for him.

"Captain King, meet King Samyaza."

"I think we've met already."

"Oh, you've met. Next you'll tell me you are related."

"With a name like King, we must be."

"Well, perhaps you can tell me something about King Samyaza's kingdom."

"No, we hadn't talked about that."

The King laughed. "Really, I am a king without a kingdom, Major. I have left all that behind."

"And you did that all for this charming young lady."

Noni smiled.

"I realize that you can understand me but cannot talk."

Noni nodded.

"She has been that way since birth, Major," Abigail said.

"You must be Noni's mother. What a charming lady you are. I hear that you are almost exclusively responsible for the upbringing of your daughter."

Turning to the King he laughed: "Is that because being a king is such hard work?"

"No, Major, it is because I have made myself too busy. I owe a lot to Noni's mother and I am trying to make amends."

"Nobly said, King Samyaza," Major Bailey repeated: "Nobly said."

So the evening progressed with all going about in blankets and addressing one another until all were acquainted in the cabin of the C119, 907.

Despite the conviviality, Jim and Jaydee were secreted in one corner having a hard time making a big decision. Although Jaydee's grandfather wouldn't hear of it, both Jaydee and Jim were speculating on staying behind when the C119 flew again and returned to its correct time and space. Both of them had been smitten by Noni. Both had romantic notions about the immediate future.

Alex had a similar problem to deal with. He was meditating in another corner. He knew he loved Rachel. There were no romantic notions about the future for him. After the CIA, he had been alone as far as family goes - not that he had always been single. He had married, but in each case life had dealt him a cruel blow. Those nearest and dearest to him had been mysteriously taken. Call it paranoia, but he was sure that his enemies had found him out and caused strange accidents to take his loved ones away. In retirement, he had formed his Clodbusters as a protective shield against this enemy. Here, in the past, and isolated among the tent people, he could think about safely raising a family.

Major Bailey interrupted his concentration: "Hello, Mr. Goodrich, I'm sorry I got so upset at you today. It was a bit much to understand all at once."

"I could have made it easier, Major. I guess I was afraid there wouldn't be time before we were attacked."

Captain King was right at Major Bailey's elbow. "There almost wasn't. By the way, Colin, that was quick evasive action on your part."

254

"Yes," Alex added. "You handled that C119 like a fighter plane."

"That old second nature takes over I guess. Speaking of you though, Alex, what are you doing over here all by yourself?"

"Oh, I've just been thinking about going home."

"Is there any question? I mean you just can't abandon the CIA, can you?"

"Oh, that. Actually, I'm retired. I just flashed my Deputy Sheriff badge to get your attention."

"Oh, well, it did the trick," Major Bailey said. Then changing the subject, "So, you might not feel an attachment to the twentieth century?"

"I see something here which might bring a lot of peace to my life."

"Something like Dr. Lystra?" Captain King suggested.

"As a matter of fact, a young lady named Rachel."

Major Bailey smiled broadly. "Zanhope's daughter. She is a beauty."

While all the celebration went on in the cabin, Major Bailey had arranged for Ruth and Daniel to spend the evening in the cockpit. It wasn't so warm and it was a little cramped, but it gave them privacy. Here, Ruth could talk to Daniel alone and try to ease the hurt he felt over his father's death. Here, they also sorted out their future. Major Bailey was pleased that he had acted on a suggestion of King Samyaza - an idea that King Samyaza wanted kept secret.

There was another who wanted to extend comfort to Daniel. Sirock Shum wanted to have an elaborate funeral for his old friend, Mahai. He had known Daniel's father for many years. Daniel wouldn't hear of it. His father was a quiet person and a spiritual one. There would be only a solemn ceremony beside the grave.

Samyaza had a suggestion for this also. Upon

Abigail's prompting, he asked to have the privilege of digging the grave. As he said, "In this way I can develop a few calluses on my hands and soften my soul in the process."

Like Ruth and Daniel, Cory Thurston had found a private place toward the end of the cabin. Here in the upward sloping space around the giant cargo doors he was reading his scriptures by flashlight. Jaydee and Jim were poking around looking for their own privacy when they found Cory Thurston behind a large blanket hung to shut out the cold in the rear of the cabin. Outside the protective barrier, he had wrapped up in a parka and was deep in thought, oblivious of his surrounding and the teenagers.

"What are you reading?" Jim asked without hesitation.

"Oh, I've been reading a little about this age in my Bible. There isn't much though."

"What does it say about the City of Enoch?" Jaydee asked.

"Let's see. Oh, here it is. I'll read it to you: 'And Cain knew his wife; and she conceived, and bare Enoch: and he builded a city, and called the name of the city, after the name of his son, Enoch.' Is that what you wanted?"

Jaydee was shocked. "That's not what it says in our Bible."

"Oh, really. What does it say in your Bible?"

Jim, who had been as shocked as Jaydee at first, recovered his composure. "It is the same in our Bible, Jaydee. I remember seeing it. It's just that we don't ever talk about that Enoch and his city."

"That explains a lot of things. We must have been in the wrong city."

"I heard you had a bad time of it. What was it like?"

From that point on, Jaydee and Jim had an avid listener. Cory was a great student of the Bible. Their experiences made it come alive for him.

As the boys unfolded their disappointment at not meeting the "true Enoch", Cory opened the scriptures to them. They poured over the time covered by their visit. Cory pointed out that it would not be for many years yet that Enoch, the seventh from Adam, walked and talked with God.

Jim shared what Brother Sloan had told them in Sunday School class and Cory registered surprise at Jim's perspective; nevertheless, he questioned where all this information came from. He had heard of Jewish tradition that spoke of "fallen angels" marrying with the daughters of earth people. Jaydee and Jim's firsthand experience with the "Watchers" gave him a new understanding of the passage that spoke of "the sons of God" taking wives of the daughters of men. The three had a spirited discussion far into the night.

* * *

The next day another lively discussion about Enoch began. John and the fugitive King reviewed their experiences in the City of Enoch. John shared his understanding of the Enoch who would walk and talk with God and King Samyaza told of the prophecies concerning the young prophet to come.

"How did you ever happen to believe that the son of Cain would lead you back to God?" John asked as they cleared a space for some buildings close to the airplane.

"I suppose we wanted to believe it. We seemed to be wasting our lives away on the Holy Mountain. We saw a chance to do exciting things. His city seemed like a good place to start. Besides there were certain inducements."

"Such as?"

"Well, they had horse racing and parties. Granted, they were wild and vulgar, but we felt we could fit in and perhaps change things a little later on."

"What about the sacrifices?"

"At first we saw only animal sacrifices. We were used to this. Then, there were punitive executions for horrible crimes. Leaders of rival armies were captured and savagely cut apart and their bodies displayed as a warning. We heard of similar executions performed against the people of Enoch."

"So, you thought that was all right?"

"Yes. I don't know what the next step was. Many of our people, who had been raised on the Holy Mountain, complained of the harshness of these executions, so we began to call them sacrifices. We told them that God had required it. It was the same with other things too. When we wanted to make changes to improve our circumstances, we told the people that God commanded it. We pretended to have revelation the same as Adam and Seth had.

"You lied to the people?"

"Yes, when that happened, we stopped worrying about right and wrong. We began making up our own laws. Anything we wanted became good to us."

"What was the covenant you made with the son of Cain?"

"We swore upon our own heads that we would execute people as we saw fit to further the cause of Enoch."

"That was his covenant?"

"Yes, when we couldn't call them sacrifices, we had private executions or sent assassins to murder in secret."

"How do you feel about this now?"

"Terrible. I doubt that the Lord will ever forgive us.
"But you hope?"

"Yes." Samyaza looked away, out across the open spaces. All around them men were working. It was becoming hot. The King was sweating.

That day some of the men began improving a

runway. At the same time, John and Jack and some of the doctor's staff began building a large permanent enclosure for those who would be staying with the people of Shum. This later would become Zanhope's new laboratory.

King Samyaza and his wife, Abigail, and Noni would fill another apartment. Daniel, Dr. Asa and the other male members of Dr. Zanhope's staff, another, and lastly Ruth, Dr. Lystra and the female members of Dr. Zanhope's staff would have an apartment of their own.

Ruth and Daniel waited anxiously for the chores of the day to end. They were often seen in the evening, walking among the gentle hills and talking. On these occasions, Moke and Tabitha could be seen racing along, playing tag in the tall grass and through the bushes.

King Samyaza and his wife also took an evening walk in the sunset. "Why have we never done this before, good woman?" the King asked.

"I suppose you didn't want to be seen with me." Abigail answered.

"Nonsense, I was too busy."

"Is that why you never came to call on me and Noni and never gave me any house money?"

"Oh, that. I guess I thought that the other Kings would ridicule me. You were big with child then and, when Noni came along, I was afraid for her safety."

"You thought all this out when I was expectant?"

"Maybe. It was a dangerous time and I was their leader. For all of that, I am sure to pay. I am sorry for the way I treated you. You did not deserve it."

Samyaza was truly penitent. His remorse was not all that he carried.

One evening while waiting for Ruth to finish her work in the makeshift kitchen, Daniel walked up the hill to a small plot of ground Sirock's people had set apart for a cemetery. He found Samyaza sweating over the grave for Daniel's father. Daniel was tempted to say something mean.

Instead, he walked down the hill to the tent of Sirock Shum for water and brought it up to Samyaza. He thanked the former King for his kindness and frankly forgave him.

Through all these experiences their host was not around. Those first days, Dr. Zanhope spent most of his time with his family. He visited with his brothers and their families and introduced Rachel to her uncles and aunts. This took them far out into the wilds. During these trips, Alex missed Rachel.

Left to themselves, Zanhope's guests thought of their own relatives. "When will we be going home?" John asked, laying down his hammer. He was anxious to take Jaydee back to his mother. It had been a week now since they had stepped into the past and his daughter would wonder if Jaydee didn't come home on the weekend. He was concerned also with Jim. He had heard rumors that the boys were thinking about staying here with the tent people.

"The runway is almost ready," Jack said, "but I heard something about a lack of sufficient fuel."

"It would be impossible to get any out here." John measured a cut and drew a line across a rough board. Taking up a saw he quickly cut the board to size.

Jack helped John lift the board into place. "Maybe they could just cause us to appear in my south pasture."

"That would be novel." John began nailing the beam down. "They wouldn't need a runway for that."

Jack was matching John's action on the other end of the board. "It's better than a crash."

"How would it be explained?" John asked.

"Oh, I'm sure the Air Force would come up with something."

"You're right there."

"Why are you so eager to go home?" It was Jacks turn to ask a question. "This is a great place for fishing."

"I'm worried about Jaydee and Jim. The longer they spend here with Noni, the harder it will be to tear them away."

"I see what you mean."

* * *

At that moment, Noni and the boys were having a good time in a little mountain camp just above Sirock's tent. They had borrowed some ponies and made a lunch and rode up among the rocks and woods to a stream that Jack and John would find full of fish later.

Jaydee was helping Noni off her mount and Jim, who had lagged behind, was just joining the two. Actually, they had raced to the top of the hill and Jim had lost the race.

"That's not fair. You have the better horses."

"You're just not good with horses, Jim."

Noni shook her head in a way that told Jaydee that he had said the wrong thing. She led her pony over to the brook and dipped her hand into the cool, fresh water.

"It's nice isn't it?"

Noni nodded.

The three were soon swishing through the grass and chasing each other among the trees. Finally, they sat to rest and eat their lunch.

Jim remembered their experience in the enchanted forest. "There's no giant snake here," he laughed.

Noni smiled a bit and then, upon reflection, frowned a little.

"I guess the voice of the evil one is always with us," Jim confessed.

"That must have been a frightening experience for you," Jaydee said.

"It was for Noni. She was afraid I would want to read her mind."

"That would be a bother. She wouldn't have any private thoughts."

"What are you thinking, Jaydee?"

Noni turned to Jaydee along with Jim, anticipating his answer. She wanted to know what he was thinking also.

"I guess that I'd like to stay here forever."

"Don't you miss your folks?" Noni signed.

"Yeah." Jaydee said. He turned to Jim. "How about you, Jim?"

"Now that you mention it, I miss them very much."

"Who's going to be here to ride with Noni when we're gone?" It was as if Jaydee had read her mind.

"I guess there are other kids."

"Not close friends."

Noni bent over and kissed Jaydee on the cheek.

"What about me?" Jim frowned.

Noni gave Jim a kiss too, but it wasn't the same to him. He disliked being second.

Jaydee jumped up. "Let's see what is farther up."

"You're on!" Jim sprang to his horse. He felt challenged. He didn't wait for Noni to climb on her horse as usual and he didn't help her. When Jaydee had extended this courtesy, Jim was far up the canyon.

They followed Jim for a long way. He was always in sight, but never close enough to catch. Jaydee tried several times to slow him down and make him wait, but he seemed spurred on by a devil.

Jaydee was growing weary of this game. He could see that Noni was tired.

"We're turning back," he shouted as loud as he could. Jim seemed not to notice. Jaydee reined in his pony hoping that Jim would see that he wasn't going on. Noni followed suit.

They waited there for a long time, the wind blowing softly around them. It was growing cool. Jim was out of sight.

Noni was frightened for Jim. She drew her mount close to Jaydee and took his hand, urging him to go on with her. They rode slowly. Jaydee kept looking carefully into the canyons that opened onto the trail they were following. Finally, they stopped again. They waited. Nothing.

* * *

Jack and John had left their work for the day and succumbed to the warm sunshine. They dug some worms and made some fishing poles and then started up the same little brook that had enticed the youth. John hoped they would run into Jaydee and his friends.

"You know, John, it really doesn't matter when we leave here. Zanhope can always drop us back close to the time we left home."

"I guess that's right. Too bad we didn't have something like that going for us when we were working people. We could have taken a vacation and not lost a day of work."

"Say, this looks like the place where the youngsters rested. See the way the grass is pushed down?"

"This looks like a scarf. It must be Noni's."

The two men settled down in the selfsame spot where the young people had been. It was comfortable. They baited their hooks and dropped their lines into the brook. John was distracted. He took off his shoes and put his feet into the water.

"That looks like a good idea. If we catch something, we can just wade right out and take it in."

The water felt good. Jack had soon pulled in several fish. John was not doing quite so well. He was focused on his grandson. Things were growing serious between Noni and the boys. Even though they could take an endless vacation here in this western paradise, each day they lingered meant that he was losing the battle to bring Jaydee home.

A lone horse appeared on the horizon. John looked

for a rider, but saw none. The horse was coming quickly down the canyon. It galloped past the two fishermen and headed for the camp of Sirock Shum below.

"Which one was that? Jack asked.

"It looked like one of the horses the kids took."

"I hope nothing has happened to them."

John rose. He laid his pole aside and put on his shoes. Before he could follow suit, Jack was left alone at the fishing hole.

"Wait for me!"

John walked with urgency in his pace. Jack had a hard time catching up with him. The two men walked for a long ways.

"There they are," John said with a sigh.

"It's only two, John. See, there are two horses and two riders."

"You're right, Jack. It looks like Jaydee and the girl. What could have happened to Jim?"

"You don't suppose they got in some sort of argument over the girl, do ya?"

"Oh, don't be silly, Jack. Kids that age don't have those kinds of feelings."

Jack stopped and waited for the horses to come closer. John was still walking fast when he intercepted Noni and Jaydee.

"What happened?"

"Jim got a bee in his bonnet and took off. We couldn't catch him."

"Did you see his horse come back?"

"No. Did it?" Jaydee was shocked. He turned as if he was going back.

"Don't think of it, son. Give me your horse. You climb on with Noni and ride back to the camp. You and Jack put together a search party. I'll ride on now." Jack heard the last of John's remarks and understood.

"Get on young man. You two alert the camp. Have

them gather some warm clothes and supplies. I'll be there directly."

* * *

It was misty in the high country. Jim was stirring where he fell. He could see a white horse and rider coming out of the fog. He was a little dizzy and his vision seemed blurred.

The rider was young, about twenty-five. He was handsome and had a close cropped beard of the most excellent black and dark wavy hair. He wasn't tall in the saddle. On his horse he carried a blanket. Behind him followed a pack animal of some kind that Jim didn't recognize. It was small and limber and was loaded with many hides. The shale along the path shifted and cracked as they approached.

Jim tried to stand, staggered some and finally steadied himself on a nearby sapling.

The man dismounted and offered a small flask for Jim to drink from. Jim took it and drank. His mouth had been dry. Now he was refreshed.

Pointing to himself the young man said: "Kanoki!"

"Your name is Kanoki?"

"Yes." That seemed clear enough. Maybe if this man knew yes and no, they could communicate some.

"My name is Jim."

"Yes."

"My friends will be looking for me. Can you take me to them?"

"No."

"They are down in the valley." Jim pointed, but the man ignored him. Instead, he took a cloth from his pocket, smeared some evil smelling black stuff on it and touched Jim's head with it. It really hurt.

"Ouch!"

Kanoki motioned for Jim to hold the cloth on his head. The pain started to subside.

Jim's new friend took the boy by the hand and led him into the shelter of the nearby trees. He sat him down by a large rock and tied up his beautiful white horse. Now Jim could see that the horse had faint grey spots.

While Jim sat looking on, Kanoki gathered dry twigs and wood and built a fire against the rock. Jim felt dreamy and he dozed. When he awoke he found that the young man had built a comfortable lean-to around him.

He gave him a blanket to wrap up in. Then, he knelt in prayer. Jim knelt too. There was a long silence.

A small deer appeared nearby and could be seen in the opening in front of the lean-to. From his sitting place, Kanoki quietly drew a bow, fitted an arrow and shot the deer. Jim fainted from exhaustion. When he awoke the venison was roasting on the fire and the deer skin was covering the lean-to. It dripped on Jim but he didn't mind.

Kanoki prayed again. This time Jim prayed too. He was very thankful for Kanoki and prayed that Noni and Jaydee wouldn't worry.

They ate, wrapped up in the blanket and slept. Jim dreamed. He dreamed of Kanoki on his white horse. He thought he saw him climbing up into the clouds on that horse. The sun was shining on him brightly. He could hear voices singing. Then he woke up. He was alone. It was still dark. He could hear a wild animal roar somewhere in the woods. Then, it stopped.

Kanoki came out of the darkness. He was carrying something heavy. He skinned it and hung the hide over a make-shift rack he had built near the fire. He carried the animal off and returned shortly. There were sounds of other animals in the distance. They growled and howled.

Jim fell asleep again. This time when he woke up the stranger was standing over him. He knelt beside him, rubbed a little clear oil on Jim's head and spoke. His words were like music. At first Jim didn't understand, but he began to hear in his mind the meaning. It was a voice without sound, like the voice of the serpent had been, but sweet and comforting.

"I promise that you will soon be restored to full health and vigor. You shall be at peace. The problems that trouble you now will become insignificant and you shall find happiness in your own time." His prayer ended in the name of the Messiah. Jim tingled all over. He felt very calm. He looked up into the eyes of his new friend and saw tears. He knew his eyes were wet also.

It was morning when Jim awoke again. This time Kanoki was gazing at him across the fire. He was stirring a pot of meal. It smelled delicious. Soon they were sharing the hot porridge.

"I felt your head. The fever is gone." Somehow, Kanoki's words were no mystery. Jim could understand everything he said. Kanoki read Jim's surprise.

"God told me how to talk to you. You know my words now."

"Yes, I understood your prayer last night too."

Kanoki took the hide he had skinned from the young lion the night before and began to scrape the inside surface with his knife. "I am glad."

It was clear that Kanoki was a man of few words. Perhaps living in the wilderness he had few people to practice on. One thing for sure, he chose his words carefully and spoke very slowly.

Jim wondered. "Are you a mountain man?"

"Yes, I live in the mountains. People don't like me. I kill animals for food and fur. They like the furs, but they do not like the hunters."

"You are a good hunter."

"God brings me the game."

"You look wild. Maybe that scares people."

"Maybe."

"Where do you come from?"

"I come from Cainan. It is far to the east by the sea."

"You prayed over me last night. Are you a holy man?"

Kanoki hesitated. "I visited my great great grandfather, Seth, some time ago. He took me to the holy mountain where I met Adam. Adam gave me the Holy Order."

"And you came back here?"

"Yes, this is my home. People are wicked. They worry me. They can do cruel things."

"I know."

"You know much for a boy. Someday you will do great things, if you live." Kanoki had scraped the hide inside till it was smooth and clean. He rubbed it with salt and rolled it up tightly. He took another hide which he had brought with him and began working it over the stump of a small tree he had cut while making the lean-to.

After a long silence, Jim gained the courage to ask: "What do you mean: 'if I live'?"

"I felt it last night when I anointed you with oil. Satan wants you dead. He especially wants to destroy you. You are a threat to his kingdom."

"How do you know that?"

"The Holy Spirit tells me. I know that you come from the future. Satan is afraid of all young men in your time."

Jim was astonished. Kanoki spoke once or twice more as he worked the leather back and forth over the stump. They had a lunch of roast venison. They drank an herb tea made from the leaves and stems of a wild sage and ate little cakes which Kanoki baked on the lid of his cooking pot.

The evening came and Kanoki described his visit to Adam. He mentioned the grand design that God had for his children. He pointed to the stars overhead and described the creation.

The stars were so clear in the mountain air. Jim felt he could touch them. It was cold all around, but Jim was warm inside. He fell asleep looking up into the stars.

* * *

Noni and Jaydee were contemplating one missing star in their lives. They summoned all the camp before Jack caught up with them. By the time Jack arrived, they were all ready with supplies and blankets. He directed them as they started up the canyon.

Jaydee had another idea. He found Dr. Zanhope resting in the tent of Sirock Shum, his father. He quickly explained the situation and asked Dr. Zanhope to use the mysterious ball to help find his friend.

The two of them unpacked the monitor and set it up in the partially completed sleeping quarters. Here, Dr. Zanhope would guide the little ball up the trail and explore each byway, always coming back to the main trail to check with Noni and Jaydee. "Lea" was on her way.

Noni and Jaydee saddled up fresh horses and followed the probe. Occasionally, the probe returned to them from its sweeping sealed and went on from check point to check point in this fashion until they had passed the main body of searchers.

In the evening they caught up with John camped on the trail. They shared some food with him and extra blankets they had brought with them.

The brass ball rested the night with them. The next day, Jaydee started out early leaving Noni with his grandfather. He was anxious for his friend. The little ball followed, scouting the side trails and checking back. There was no way of communicating with the little probe, but Jaydee knew by prearrangement that when it found any sign of Jim, it would lead Jaydee to him.

About noon, the ball returned and buzzed around his head. He followed as it led up a knoll and into a grove of trees.

When Jaydee found Jim, he was seated in a lean-to, wrapped in the skin of a young lion and eating a piece of venison. The lean-to was covered with the skin of deer and a fire was burning beside him. There was enough wood for one more night.

"Did you see him?" Jim asked excitedly.

"See who?"

"Kanoki."

"Who is Kanoki?"

"The guy who saved me. He just went up the trail."

"I didn't see anyone."

"He's a mountain man. He's leery of people."

"Yeah, you probably saw the original big foot."

"No, he is really nice. He stayed right here with me all this time. He told me we are all special."

"Who, you and me?"

"Yeah, all the boys in our time."

"What does he know about our time?"

"He knows a lot. He prayed for me. He is a holy man."

"I think you hit your head."

"I didn't do all this," Jim said indicating the camp with a sweep of his hand.

* * *

When the search party returned to camp, there was a lot of talk about the stranger who had nursed Jim back to health in the mountains. Who was he? Some were frightened to hear of a wild mountain man in the region.

Samyaza speculated that he was the long awaited Enoch. After all, in the language of the ante-diluvians,

Kanoki meant Enoch. John noted that he was the great great grandson of Seth and Jack reminded John that the stranger was the right age. This Enoch was spiritually minded, he was slow of speech and he thought that all men hated him. He met all the tests.

Jim was thrilled to think that he had seen the "real" Enoch. Jaydee asked him a lot of questions. "What an experience!" he said, after exhausting his friend.

Now it was time to say goodbye to such experiences and to the people of Sirock Shum. In two days, the aliens would go back to the twentieth century.

The landing field was prepared, the airplane was repacked and the passenger list decided. Jim and Jaydee would be going home after all. John was happy.

Alex was not returning. He and Rachel had announced their engagement. Unfortunately, the wedding would be delayed until all of the Klan of Sirock Shum could gather.

Now, the thoughts turned to the final day and concern for the success of the return trip. There was enough fuel in the tank for one hour of flight. Major Bailey had inspected the runway. Once in the air, Zanhope would shoot them into the future. Then, they would open the jump door and the mysterious ball would leave them forever.

Perhaps in deference to this plan, the avowed enemy of the little ball could not be found at the last minute. Somehow Tabitha had disappeared. Moke too was missing. The travelers concluded that the two were roaming together far from camp. Just as they were about to give up on Tabitha, Dr. Zanhope went to get the brass ball to put it aboard. There beside the mysterious ball, Moke and Tabitha lay curled up like three friends having a preflight snooze. Moke would miss the fluffy golden cat.

Before they left, Dr. Lystra explained that they were going forward in time to the very day the plane crashed at Jack's farm. She said they had discovered that in this manner they could erase future events which they had tampered with, but for some reason, events in the past which they had experienced didn't change.

Memories were different. She thought this action might erase the experiences of the past week from their minds. They weren't to expect more than a fleeting memory of their life with the ante-diluvians.

Noni was concerned that Jaydee and Jim would forget her. They didn't feel that it was possible to ever forget Noni. She told them both goodbye in the best sign language she knew and they both received a kiss.

Jim didn't mind being second. He would take away with him a special memory of these ancient days. He knew that the young man, who prayed for him in the wilderness of Shum, was the Enoch whom Brother Sloan had described. No one could take that away from him.

* * *

"We came out from the holy mountain in the year 502 of the ancient one. We settled among a fallen people. We brought much wisdom with us to teach them. Our men were good at first but became corrupted and began worshipping idols.

"They have built a powerful and rich city. They dominate the whole land of ancient Eden. They are great in warfare and terrible in defense.

"I have known much good in my day. I have clung to the teachings of the fathers. I have tried to rear my children in the truth, but my son has abandoned both me and the faith. He has become an assassin and does the bidding of the evil one. In our day the women and children suffer much.

"Please defend yourselves against these men who can plant themselves in your midst without the possibility of defense. They come in force. - Madame Zanhope.

Epilogue

Did the time travelers remember? Well, not at first. When they landed in Kansas City, neither the boys nor their adult partners knew why they were on board C119 907. Major Bailey, Captain King and Sergeant Thurston were questioned for hours. They remembered nothing.

The top secret cargo was rushed off to its final destination so fast that no one noticed its seal had been broken and that two missiles were missing. They were thankfully received in the foreign country where they were needed without question.

But 907 was inspected carefully. After a good night's sleep, Major Bailey did recall an attack by an unidentified interceptor. The bullet holes in the wings and fuselage confirmed this act of aggression. The bullets that were recovered proved to be of some inferior manufacture, probably handmade, which could not be traced.

The report of the incident was quickly classified Ultra-Top Secret, and, since no one has ever heard of such files, nothing more can be said about this.

As time passed, the crew and the passengers of 907 began to remember. It was as though the time required for their adventures in the time of Enoch had to go by before they could recall their exploits. When they did remember, it was like a dream or nightmare as the case may be.

Of course, Alex was missing. John and Jack explained to Freeman how that was. Freeman would miss Alex, but knew that Alex was where he wanted to be.

Sometimes the sons of thunder get a little provocative in Sunday school class, but they never do have the courage to tell Brother Sloan how advanced the people are in the times of Enoch.

Nevertheless, Jim has written a perfect description of Enoch. He is looking forward to meeting him again, and seeing the City of Holiness.

Both Jaydee and Jim have a clear understanding of what makes a true prophet. They tell their friends that one may know a prophet by his fruits.

What about Stanley? Well, since the curious ball didn't break the window, he didn't have that experience with Jaydee and the glass man. Furthermore, he didn't track down Jaydee's grandfather and for all we know he is still tracing clues or whatever he does.

About the author

Bob Little is a native of California. He is married to Carla Werner and has four daughters and one step son. He graduated from California State University in 1979 with a master's degree in art.

He retired from the State Military Department in 1993 where he was employed as an administrator and later as the graphic artist for the department. He and his wife have since served missions for his church in Puerto Rico, Brazil and Spain.

The plot for *The Enoch Probe* stems from his fascination with science fiction and references to Enoch in the Scriptures. Bob is currently working on a biography of Jesse Carter Little and is preparing other books for publication.

Other Works by Robert Leonard Little or Bob Little
(available in paperback or on Kindle Editions on
Amazon.com)
*The War Letter – Jesse Carter Little and the Creation of
The Mormon Battalion*
ISBN 9780980027914
Mother Goose in a Bathysphere ISBN 9780980027921